REWIND

CHRISTOPHER BARNARD

BLITZBEAR PRESS

1

The pharma trial was suicide. That was the word on the street. The folks I hung about with – the drug-addled junkies and alcoholics – they went in, but they never came back. No one ever saw them again.

I didn't believe this *suicide* talk because the key selling point of the program was the free scrubbing service. *Scrubbing* was the millionaire's oil change: a removal of all known pathogens and infections, a little gene editing. Why spend that money scrubbing people just to kill them?

My take was that the volunteers disappeared because the trial had cleaned them up. Then they'd hopped on the train that led to a fancy land called Bigger and Better – where they didn't have to hang around people like me.

I wanted a ticket on that train.

A simple drug trial. Easy money. Get scrubbed, try some new pill, get injected with something – and then go on my way, merry and fresh. That's what I told myself.

This was late spring, 2045 AD. I had just turned twenty-five. According to everything I kept seeing on the news, it didn't look like there would be a 2050 AD.

I had some mad idea I would spend the last few years in relative health, happiness, and sanity. Get a farm. Milk some goats. That sort of blue-sky stuff.

Then again, I was off my trolley on booze and heroin when I signed the papers, so my motivations were nebulous at best. At worst, suicidal. But since I could barely stand being myself, I figured it was worth the risk.

When I'd sobered up a little, I realised where I was and what I'd done. I freaked out. Withdrawing from alcohol and opiates was the worst idea I'd had in a long time. Forget the scrub, forget everything. The room I'd been shut in was very comfortable, but I made myself busy atop the wardrobe, trying to smash the lock on the window. A nurse came in, pushing a trolley, interrupting my escape. She talked me down with a wide selection of spirits and beers, along with a chaser in the form of pharmaceutical-grade morphine – in a shiny new syringe.

It wasn't like any drug trial I'd ever been involved with. I decided it was the best one ever. Hands down.

Sounds highly unusual, but this was Romania – where they've always played it a bit fast and loose with the bioethics. With any ethics, when you think about it.

Two years previously, when I got through the airport in Bucharest, I threw away my UK passport, my driver's license, my keys – everything. Society didn't seem to want me around, and so I gave it the middle finger. In Romania it was easy to scrape by, off-grid. I lived in haylofts, tents, cellars, orchards.

Did a job, moved. There was always plenty of cheap dope to be bought. Plenty of moonshine.

In the clinic, in my clean and comfortable room, I spent a few days drinking beer and staying heavily stoned on morphine, reading Romanian translations of Austen and realising that I could make money in this racket since the translations were bloody awful. Tobacco was illegal in Europe, but they kept me well stocked in black market smokes. I was happier than a clown winning a happy clown contest.

They finished the scrub and pronounced me clean.

Then they brought me into a large room where everything, including the floor, was shiny stainless steel. Highly amenable, with a skinful of beer and opiates inside me, I let them strap me onto a trolley.

A spindle-thin man in a grubby white coat appeared next to me. In heavily accented English, he informed me that I was to be sent back in time.

I laughed, thinking this was either a hallucination, or part of the psych evaluation.

It wasn't either of these. They wheeled the table, with me tied to it, into some pod-like structure. It turned out that this skinny scientist was a batshit-crazy evil genius. He meant what he said. He really did send me hurtling through time.

Well.

Colour me *surprised*.

2

Even before I open my eyes, I feel the insane cold. My first breath in makes my heart stutter inside my chest, like when you dunk yourself in a freezing shower. My diaphragm seizes up for a few seconds. It's an effort to breathe out. I take another breath.

The last several weeks of my existence is a blank. I don't know where I was or what I was doing. I can't remember a fucking thing.

I open my eyes. What I see doesn't make any sense. There's a glacier in front of me, a gigantic white tongue, several hundred foot high. A wall of ice, just *there*.

I push myself up. My head is ringing, and I can feel liquid cooling on the tip of my nose. My nose is bleeding but the blood is almost frozen by the time it's ready to pitter-patter on the ground. I fumble in my pocket and find my lighter. I hold it up and flick it a few times. As if I'm expecting it to banish the all-encompassing cold that a part of me knows is completely and continental-shelf *wrong*.

Slim tree stumps poke up from raw earth, as if they decided to grow here and then gave up and shrivelled. Branches, dry as bones, litter the ground. Dried-out rotted wood gives way to thick fluffy flakes as I scrunch it up. A Mexican wave of shivers goes through my body.

A thought pushes me from disorientation into near panic.

If I don't get a fire started, I'm going to die.

I grab a few sticks and snap them up. My hands are going numb. I make a rough pile of twigs and sticks over the flaky crumbly stuff. I flick the lighter. It's windy.

Shit.

I flick the lighter again. The flame licks at the tinder and makes a small glowing dot that vanishes when the wind again blows out the lighter.

Fuck.

Fluffy stuff, a bit like hair, blows in the wind, caught on some of the branches. I'm shivering, my legs are shaking, fit to buckle. The fluffy stuff looks dry – like it might burn well.

Better than ok. When I ball it up and stuff it into the centre of the broken-up sticks, and flick the lighter, it catches and *floufs* into a ball of fire. The kindling is going to catch.

I place a few larger pieces on the fire, which is burning freakishly well. It might be cold, but everything is bone-dry. I lie down, shivering convulsively, as close as I can get to the fire. The smell of the fluffy stuff comes to my nose as the wind swirls the smoke in a gasping eddy. It *is* hair. Burning hair.

Jesus Christ. *Hair?*

————

Once I stop shaking like some dementia patient, I build a second fire, so that both sides of me get warmth. Perhaps I am still a little stoned, as I fall asleep. When I wake both fires have burned low.

My memory starts to come back.

I was inside a pod-like thing, for some reason I can't fathom. Then, a big ball of light, a massive bastard of a sun, in a void of pitch black. Something grabbed me and sent me hurtling in a direction that wasn't forward or backward, up, or down. It was like gravity went spiracular, pulling me in all directions at once.

What the fuck?

———

Trees, far to the south, stretch all the way to the horizon, which is clearly visible; a blue wedge of sky clipped neatly onto the edge of the earth. I'm on a plain, a great big flat expanse of. . . pretty much nothing. Flat earth. This glacier is either in the wrong place for the 21st century, or something has seriously gotten fucked.

The pod-thing. Something about time travel.

I was in. . . Serbia? One of those Baltic states. Maybe Bulgaria. Something ending in -ia. I signed up to something. . . some program?

I *feel* I'm in Eastern Europe, near enough to sea level. That's my gut feeling. But I'm looking at a glacier.

I don't *feel* delusional.

Just mildly scorched by being too close to fire.

Am I like Moses, talking to a burning bush? Tripping his tits off or whatever it was he was up to at the summit of Mt Sinai? No. I feel sane. More than that, I *know* I'm sane. I might have heavy emotional baggage, but I've always been firmly set in the cement of reality.

I know *sane* when I smell it.

I touch my right pocket, reflexively, where my phone should be. Where my phone *always* is. Ensures I can look up important things like whether Praktiker (Romania's answer to Home Depot) has any oak panelling or self-levelling concrete in stock. Or what the capital of Mongolia is. Information that simply *cannot wait* to be grasped.

There's no phone in my pocket.

Fright pulses through me. A semi-crippling sense of loss that makes me double over slightly, like you do when you feel the first stirrings of diarrhoea. A feeling of nakedness. Having no ID and no fixed address is one thing. Having no phone is quite another.

There is no cavalry. I can't say *fuck it I want out* and just call an Uber to come take me home to. . . to. . . wherever I was.

I lick my lips. I have a sense that if I touch my left pocket and don't feel a pack of cigarettes there, I will properly lose my shit. Forget Armageddon, time-travelling, black holes, or the future of the human race.

If there are no cigarettes, I am going to fucking slaughter myself right now.

I slap my pocket.

Blessed is the holy lord oh god thank fuck!

My cigarettes are there.

Weirdly, it's not the brand I normally smoke.

Who cares? I open the pack and fumble out a ciggie. I light it with hands that are trembling again – from cold – from relief.

Jesus that's good.

I'm beginning to think that Jesus might not be around for a while yet. I laugh. The sound is hollow. I sit down, between the two fires which have died down to thick coals which give off a pleasant baking heat. I reach for my phone again, meaning to check what time it is.

Damn.

OK, where's the sun? It's over there, in the west quarter of the sky. Going by the distant trees, which seem to be denuded, it's got to be autumn or winter, which leads me to guess 3pm. Dark around 4:30pm?

I might be an unwitting time-traveller, possibly lost in the quantum foam of reality, but I know where the compass points are, I know roughly what time it is, and I have cigarettes. Things are at last going my way.

At least, things go my way for about another five minutes, then they go squarely to shit.

3

I'm concentrating on the cigarette, not thinking beyond it, because when I finish, I am going to have to get up and *do something*. I'm going to walk towards the trees in the distance. It's an instinctual response, is my guess. You move, like any rodent or avian or reptile or mammal. You move, run, scuttle for shelter. It could be through a crack in a wall, a hole in a tree, into pondweed, or in the case of humans, into a house.

Next best thing to a house are trees. I feel exposed, out here on this plain. In the trees – well, perhaps there I can find things. Water. Food. Out here I might shortly become a meal.

For the moment I focus on the soothing nicotine hit.

Contrary to my plan, I don't move. I smoke two more cigarettes. The wall of blue-white ice is at my back. I touch my right jeans pocket several times, each time meaning to search online for "ice age". It might seem that I'm jumping to conclusions, but it's probably a wiser search term than "tropical rainforest."

No phone.

I'm watching the cigarette smoulder when I become aware of a smell. It's the smell of a human being. It's not bad, like a horribly unwashed hobo. It's... earthy, somehow *leathery*...

An arm goes around my neck.

I have time for the thought: *what in fucknutting Christ?* The arm tightens. A headlock.

The forearm is across my windpipe, squeezing it shut. I'm pulled to standing, my neck feels like it's being wrenched off. I try to cry out, but I can't even inhale, far less belt out a scream. I try to push backwards against the attacker, but my feet aren't even touching the ground. I can't breathe. My arms are pinned by an arm around my torso.

Mute, I struggle. It's like shoving against a mountain.

I can't breathe.

I black out.

———

My head is throbbing. It hurts to breathe, and it hurts to swallow. I'm lying down. I keep my eyes closed, but I can see a pink play of light against the insides of my eyelids. There must be a fire. I can smell it. It crackles and spits. I hear hushed tones of human voices speaking a strange language.

It's too real to be a dream. I feel a dampness around my crotch where I must have wet myself as I passed out. Well, it was my very first headlock. I think I can forgive myself for peeing my pants.

I open my eyes. Only a blush of pink remains in a dark and star-strewn sky. It's late sundown. I'm warm – some sort of blanket has been thrown over me. There's a fire. Four figures are hunched around it in a semi-circle, watching me. Shadowy firelight-dancing faces with eyes that glimmer with reflected flame-light.

All eyes are fixed on me.

All males. All bearded. Shaggy head hair, with the odd plait in it adorned with either small shells or animal bone, I can't tell which. In the firelight, their clothes are muted shades of brown, perhaps even black. Trousers of crudely (but neat) stitched-together leather. The same stuff covers their upper body, but it's more as if they wear a puffed-up shirt than a coat. I suppose they have on undershirts or something.

If Central Casting had gotten a call to supply four hombres dressed as pre-civ mammoth hunters, in full make-up, then I'm guessing these fellas would fit the bill. But their eyes – I tell myself it's the firelight – glitter with something close to insanity.

I suppose I should be grateful that I'm not dead and currently suspended over the fire, turning medium rare. I prop myself on an elbow. The murmur of voices stops, and all of them go completely still. It's not like they *freeze*, like a game of musical chairs. They simply finish the movements that they were making, and then don't make any other. They all stare, rapt.

Miles away, a wolf howls. All four men move the same way: their bodies and faces shifting a fraction towards the sound, their heads tilting at exactly the same angle. No one says anything and no eyes leave mine. It's like when you're watching someone who's sitting down and unconsciously, they lean over slightly, raise a buttock and fart. It's such a perfect moment of puppetry that I forget everything, and I simply laugh.

Correction: I try to laugh. What comes out is a gasp, a bullfrog croak. One man raises his eyebrows and mutters something, and one man's lips twitch – in what looks like amusement. I hope it's that. I didn't hear what was said. I find myself hoping they also speak English.

But they don't. Of course not. They can't possibly speak English, looking like this. Maybe they just grunt, fart, and kill mammoths? And not just on their days off.

I see their spears – wooden poles tipped with a pointy flint blade. Flint. Like folks used in the ice age. If this is some virtual reality test to see how I do under pressure because the Romanians want to train me for a black-ops kill-squad, then it's *very* realistic.

I push back the heavy blanket that's over me (it seems to be some leather-like cloak) and pull the pack of cigarettes out. I pop one in my mouth, conscious of the four men following every movement of my hand. Well. Shit. Big deal. My last pack. I'm not offering to share. I flick the lighter and light the ciggie.

I inhale deeply, happily, ignoring my throat which feels like I've had a weak acid poured over it.

The men are standing before I can blink.

Oh shit.

The magic of *fire*.

I conjured fire from my fingers.

A fist, this time. It connects with my temple. I see stars, a shower of a sparkling *clunk* as my skull reverberates sickly. It's like colliding with a brick wall. My hands are pinned to my sides, and groggily I hear them shouting.

I want to puke; I've got that sour spit welling up in my mouth, and all I can think of is that thunking *clunk* of my skull hitting a fucking concrete fist. If I puke, I think I'll inhale it and die. I can barely see. I'm going to pass out again.

The stars lurch overhead.

mother

And wink out.

fucker

4

I wake up to stars, and thankfully they are speckled across the night sky and not whizzing around my brain. A distant part of me realises that this is what concussion must feel like. I'd quite like to know how long I was unconscious for. No point in asking. They *definitely* don't speak English.

Great. Wonderful.

It was the lighter. To them I must have looked like I was magicking flame out of my fingers, my hands. Like a wizard. It doesn't help that I'm wearing jeans and a Rolling Stones t-shirt, the one with the tongue sticking out of the fat lips. This outfit doesn't scream *fifty-thousand years ago*.

Ok. I'm out of place, strangely dressed, and I can conjure magic. My hair is cropped short and I'm clean shaven. I couldn't appear more different from them if I had tried.

But they appear to be humans, as regular as you or me. Dressed differently and pig-ignorant, but still human. The man who is closest to me is properly blonde, I can see that even in the yellow-red hue of the firelight. His blonde beard is the size of a large loaf of bread. It juts out from his face. Narrowed eyes stare at me from under the same colour eyebrows.

My hands have been tied together. Christ's sake.

If I'm going to end up being sacrificed, then it'll be to a god I'll never have heard of.

Carefully, this time, I speak. I speak my name. It hurts.

Charlie.

The men flinch. Blondebeard holds a spear diagonally across his lap, the tip almost pointing at me but not quite. He stares at me.

Charlie.

At my second attempt, Blondebeard's hand curls tighter around his spear. He brings his index finger up to his lips, which he purses; the universal signal for *shut the fuck up.*

I lick my lips. I'm thirsty. My head hurts. Concussion, I suppose.

The men share something, some food, but don't offer me anything. Afterwards, they lie down on the bare ground. Blondebeard takes the first watch. I don't try to talk.

I lie back and stare up into the sky. There must be alien life up there, stippled and smeared across intergalactic space. *Intelligent* life.

As I watch the stars, a strange sort of finality creeps over me: I don't just think I'm in the distant past, I *know* I'm in the distant past. It feels like casting off in a rowboat, into a river where I have no choice but to go with the roaring current. It feels like letting go. It's not frightening.

Maybe it takes a knock to the head to truly appreciate how fucked I might be.

This sky will never be recorded on star charts. Some of the stars I'm seeing will already have gone supernovae. Their bursts of light may well have fizzled out by the time humans invent writing and telescopes and get around to creating NASA.

Blondebeard is replaced on watch by another man. He's quite muddy, greasy. He's like a car mechanic – a *grease monkey*. I imagine him in dungarees, a bit bedraggled, with grease everywhere. There is similarity to an ape that's been messing around with engine oil. He actually does look like that. It's just the way it is.

I feel queasy again. I look back up at the stars and try to ignore my thirst.

––––––

Dawn. The men are all on their feet, moving about, shouldering what I'll come to regard as ice age man-bags: a large leather pouch hung at each end on a length of cord that hangs off a shoulder.

Blondebeard comes over. I look up at him. He could, if he wanted, just spear me straight through my chest. Instead, he hunkers down and brings a container, some sort of squishy bag, towards my face. Water. He tips it gently over my open mouth. I'm insanely thirsty. The water tastes disgusting, gritty, but I swallow as much as I can without choking. My throat hurts. A lot.

The men kick dirt over the fire and haul me to my feet. I'm giddy. My hands are still tied in front of me. One man walks ahead of me, and the rest follow behind me. We move across the flat plain. Flakes of snow, just a few, here and there, drift down. The sky now is as white and misty as the flakes themselves, so when I look upwards, I can't see any definition between anything, and I feel even more dizzy.

I've no idea where the sun is.

No idea which direction we are going. I suppose it doesn't matter. It's warmer, with the cloud cover and the stillness, and they have tied the leather blanket-thing around my upper body like a cape. My trainers get slowly soggy as the snowfall continues.

I follow the lead man across the flat and grassy prairie. Visibility is capped at about a hundred feet by the white mist. I could be on a plain the size of a continent, or a just a large clearing in a forest.

The men walk with purpose. I get the impression we are on a path, a straight and faintly foot-worn byway that skirts around strange boulders that are just lying around, like some giant has been having a rock fight.

The snow, my wet feet, the silence, the scuff of footsteps. The hunger gnawing at my insides. My bruised throat. This isn't a dream. I'm not going to wake up.

The snowfall thickens. In this perpetual whiteness, it's hard to judge how far we go and how much time passes. My palms are damp and I can feel my heart thudding, accelerated, in my chest. I'm scared. I'm craving a cigarette. I'm not scared of the concept that I am in the past. I'm scared of the future – of what is going to happen to me.

At what I guess is noon we start to hit trees. Birch, larch, pines, mostly stunted and wind burned. A frigid wind must periodically sweep down off the glacier. It was high summer where I came from. Here, the trees are leafless; it must be winter or autumn. I'm not sure which. I tell myself it doesn't matter. I'm in a time where time doesn't matter. Years, months, weeks – these things have not been invented yet. My stomach clenches, my heart throbs. A wave of giddiness makes me stagger slightly. A hand from behind clasps my shoulder, steadies me, and we keep walking.

Disorientation is an understatement.

But my animal needs anchor me to reality: I'm devilishly thirsty. I hold my tongue out to catch the odd snowflake. They taste like they always have. There's *that*.

My feet squelch and slide inside my wet trainers. I can feel blisters forming, though the pain is blunted by the cold that keeps them almost entirely numb. Moving is the only thing that will stop them from freezing solid.

As the day passes the tree cover becomes thicker, the trees more robust – healthier.

The group stops. The men hunker down and share out some sort of food – dark brown strips that I imagine is dried meat, some sort of palaeolithic jerky. I'm not offered any, though I do get some of that muddy water. I gulp it down and lean against a tree. My guts have been doing a squeezing, contracting thing, and I've been passing it off as nerves.

I foresee a potential problem. You know when you get the insane idea to fly to India and drink the tap-water? Well, ten times out of ten, you'll get the cholera-shits as a reward for that stroke of genius. Oh *god*. I wonder how to mime *your fucked up water has given me the shits so please untie my hands so I don't soil myself, epically.*

It's not urgent yet. But it's only a matter of time. I think of my cell phone, how I should google the nearest gas station or a department store. Yeah, sure.

———

Near nightfall in a shallow and lightly forested valley, the men make camp. The trees are bare, the ground slicked with dead leaves.

One of the men unfolds a stitched leather tarpaulin and they tie the four corners to the trunks of silver birch trees. A tarp-roof. Another tarp is then tied horizontally, forming a windbreak. A fire is started – not using my lighter, since that is devil stuff. It's the old twirly stick trick, which takes about ten minutes of faff with tinder and bollocks and twirling. Fallen logs are dragged up and I'm instructed to sit. My hands are untied. Blondebeard doesn't help the men who are arsing about lighting the fire. He sits on the other side of the now-smouldering pile of wood onto which a man is blowing and huffing madly. Blondebeard keeps his eyes on me and his hands on his spear.

Once the fire is properly burning, the men relax. They sit in a line on the log next to Blondebeard. I'm as cold as blue testicles. I edge as close to the fire as I can get without burning myself, and the wave of warmth that envelops me is like the welcome embrace of an old friend.

The main man, not bigger than the others but somehow more *still*, more *John Wayne* – he reaches into his shirt-thing and brings out a necklace that has animal teeth attached. Big fat molars like from a giraffe or elephant. Spiky canines from a bear or a prehistoric wolf. Really fucking cheery.

John Wayne strokes this amulet thing. He makes a deep rumbling noise. The others join in. Clearly it is evening prayer-time.

John Wayne carries the magical stuff. The religious stuff. The guy with the magic spirit stuff is the boss. Like priests used to be.

John Wayne puts his amulet away and raises his eyes to mine. In the firelight they look brown. His gaze is mild, holding no meaning that I can deduce. He looks at me the way one might look at a tree. Or a table, a sofa, or a mildly interesting artistic print. A non-committal appraisal. In the near future I will come to understand this look very well.

The last man is the one I want to avoid mentioning, the one who in the future I will find myself wishing he had never existed at all. Now, my thought about him is a single word: *weasel*. His beard is the thinnest – perhaps he's just younger – and he's compact, wiry. He was the guy who spotted all the mushrooms and grubs that the men had stopped for now and again in the last two days. A human ferret.

I don't like him. *At all.* Thinking about him, my stomach swims and my palms go damp.

For now, I see his eyes. They move too quickly. He's too quick, too slick. Like some awful used-car salesman. An image forms in my mind; an evil cartoon mouth, wide, the tongue lolling like a dog's, eyes big dollar signs, and all ten skinny spider-fingers stuck deeply into ten different little pies.

A sneaky little bastard. A weasel.

So, sitting around a campfire in this arctic paradise you've got Blondebeard the Pirate, Weasel, Grease Monkey and John Wayne. And me, Charlie, the rolling stone with wet Nikes, a sore throat, and a serious hankering for a cigarette. And, I realise, a slight touch of the DT's. For the uninitiated, that's *delirium tremens*, the wonderful side effect of alcohol withdrawal. It's beginning to hit me. My hands tremble, my stomach gnaws itself, and a monkey hammers on my back, hammers me hard to *find some fucking beer already.*

I think the earliest beers were brewed by the Egyptians, and they are, like everything useful, aeons in the future. I hope to almighty Jesus and Juju the King of Fancy Mountain, that these clowns have managed to figure out fermentation. I could murder a keg or two right about now.

But the world gives not a flying monkey about my needs or my problems. Night has fallen, and the five of us are alone in the snow.

With no booze.

I'm given some more water and a hank of rawhide to chew on. Instead, I fumble out my pack of cigarettes. The men watch me, warily now. I pick up a long twig, dip it in the fire for a moment, and bring the flame to me. I light the ciggie. My throat complains less than it did. They watch me with interest as I puff away. Their eyes follow my hand movements and the plumes of smoke that I breathe out. When I toss the butt into the fire and start on the food, they begin muttering to each other.

My feet are warm – finally – and I'm relieved that I can feel all of my toes. Frostbite would be a poor start. The strip of dried meat smells high, like those strips you buy for your dogs. This thing tastes like kangaroo ass, but I'm not going to raise this with the John Wayne posse. Best keep quiet, warm my feet, eat my kangaroo ass and check my emails. . .

Shit. Zero bars.

5

I realise that zero bars, no phone, zilch on the satellite and telecoms front – means that I'll never be tracked or called or messaged again. No need to dodge tax. No debt collectors. I can't contain a chuckle. The men look at me, only briefly, and then go back to muttering among themselves. Plotting how to exorcise the demons within me, for all I know. Discussing what ingredients to braise me with.

This gang of knuckle-draggers is probably a foraging party. Maybe a spiritual journey. Fuck knows. All I want is for it to end so I can take off these squelchy-wet trainers and warm my feet by a fire whilst hopefully getting my hands on some homebrew.

A wave of shivering passes through me like the onset of fever.

I lie down, close my eyes, and try to ignore the word *withdrawal*, which is a glittering neon sign in my head. I concentrate on my breath. Mindfulness.

The air streaming through my nostrils when I breathe in is clean. Clean like carbon dioxide filtered through a leaf, stripped of the carbon, pushed out as oxygen, mixed with air that has had no dealings with factory cyanide or city smog, only glitter-pure raindrops stirred by photons streaming through a linen-fresh atmosphere. Admittedly tinged with a spice of woodsmoke, but hardly a synthetic adulteration, more a perfume. I fill my lungs, and even though the strip of kangaroo or baboon's ass has hardly touched the sides of my ravening stomach, the air fills me with a sense of calm power. Perhaps there is something to be said for the peace of nature.

The fire is pleasant, the wind is cool on my face. The heavy bearskin rug is beautifully heavy and warm, like some sort of amniotic sac for grown-ups. I start to drift.

———

A growl, impossibly deep. Like rock splitting. Blondebeard clamps his hand across my mouth.

Growling, a crunching that seems to make my bones vibrate. My eyes feel fit to pop. Adrenaline. A naked, screaming fear surges through me. But I lie still. Rigid.

Blondebeard shifts his eyes to me, raising his eyebrows questioningly. I nod in understanding, and he removes his hand, his other moving to his own lips in the universal sign that means *keep your yapper clamped*. The other men have their hands on their spears.

A minute passes whilst the noise reverberates, stops, starts, branches snap, leaves rustle. It begins to grow fainter. Shaking silently, I wait for a cue from Blondebeard, who eventually moves, nods at me and with the tips of his fingers presses against my chest; *lie down, it's ok.*

I want to ask: *exactly what in crying fuck was that?*

I can't. I don't say a word. I lie down, my heart still yammering. I turn my head to the other men. They are going back to whatever they were doing – whittling, shaving, telling stories, cleaning fingernails. No, not all; Weasel is looking at me. Aggression – even hatred – is writ across his acne-scarred face.

What in Christ is his problem? I haven't done anything to him, other than glance in his direction a few times. Maybe it's one of those cases where people just don't take to each other? But I doubt it. He looks like a properly creepy motherfucker.

I turn my head and look up at the stars through the branches, made skinny and twisted by the unclothing of winter. Like stick-thin starved old ladies, bent and twisted, stripped naked.

But the stars are bright, even next to the clumps of cloud that are silvered by a quarter moon. It's quiet again, except for two or three human voices and the snap-crackle of the fire.

The wet roots of the trees around me clutch at their fistfuls of cold earth and hold on.

They hold on.

6

Murky light, singed with mist and a pinch of old smoke. It's a struggle to see a fucking thing. My throat is still bruised but added to it is the morning dryness that will only go away after a cup, or several, of coffee. And a litre of beer.

Blondebeard cuts the cords securing my wrists. I guess this means they've realised I'm not a threat. I stumble after the men. Apart from the odd look backwards they have stopped paying me much attention. They seem excited. I think they are nearly home.

I could die or get buggered to death by a cave bear and they wouldn't notice.

Today is warmer, and the snow from yesterday has turned to muddy slush. My hands are trembling. It's the lack of bastard booze and opiates, the reduction in nicotine, the lack of processed sugar, caffeine.

It's not beyond impossible that I might be withdrawing from smog, ozone, unburnt hydrocarbons, microplastics, synthetic oestrogen, bisphenol-a, DDT, pesticides, herbicides, nuclear waste, and God knows what else.

I stamp after the men. I want to scream. I want to holler and yell until that giant prowling beast from last night comes back and slaughters all five of us. Maybe it was a ten-foot-tall cave bear with claws the length of swords. *Start with me, O Wise One,* I'd say. *Tear my head off, but spend a lazy afternoon fucking these other clowns to death.*

I'd have appreciated something hot, like coffee, before a forced march across Pointless Fucking Ice Age Tundra. I might as well be in Siberia. I've read *One Day In the Life of Ivan Denisovich.* Let me put it like this: Ivan Denisovich's life sucked major ass.

I also recommend *The Gulag Archipelago*, since right now I seem to be starting out on the guided tour.

Fur-wearing fuckers.

There is no way to light a cigarette. I'm down to fifteen. Fifteen moments of sanity left. From somewhere to my left, away in the trees, I hear a honking and grunting sound. It sounds like a warthog. God, I hope woolly warthogs are a thing around here. All shaggy, making that adorable grunting rumble. I've always wanted to raise a warthog as a pet. Raise it alongside a dog. That'd be just awesome.

Wait.

I bet these assholes have not got around to domesticating the wolf. If they had, then these assholes would not go on a foraging mission without some hunting hounds or some heroic guard-dogs.

What complete morons. How more obvious an evolutionary leap can it be? It's staring them in the fucking face, for shit's sake.

A bone-heavy sadness pushes me against the tree trunk I've stopped at.

Dogs were about the one and only sodding thing that I found I could ever rely on not to cheat me, not to fail me. That I am fantastically unreliable and cowardly is beside the point. The point is that there are no dogs.

Weasel looks back at me, and barks some gibberish - some sort of command. Seriously, did I piss this guy off in some previous life? And anyway, he *knows* I can't understand him, so he might as well cease acting like a tool.

I'm going to get a wolf pup. A live one. A female. Somehow. I'll call her *Eve*. Or *Ninja*, or *Shadow*. I will train her to kill Weasel. If I'm not allowed to do that, I could train her to at least shit in his sleeping roll.

Nothing to smoke. No steaming beverage. And no dogs. Nothing to do but follow John Wayne and his posse. Their pace has increased, and I have to push all this shit out my mind and concentrate on keeping up if I don't want to fall behind, get lost and then turned into some cave bear's bitch.

Hours wear on. The men halt. I'm huffing and puffing, my heart rate at a fair clip, and I'm actually hot, with sweat on my forehead. They look at me like I'm a joke. First, they were afraid of me. Now they are seeing me for what I am: a human, woefully unprepared for the rigors of life in the pre-pizza-delivery era.

I'm handed another strip of kangaroo ass, this one with bits of hair attached. It feels like midday. I look at my feet and I'm dismayed, but not surprised, to see that blood seems to be oozing out of the sides of my trainers. They hurt like. . . well, I might as well be walking on raw stumps. I don't even want to take them off and look.

The men start walking again, with not so much as a ten-minute sit-down. I follow. Their pace increases again. I can't keep up; I slide and slip. I begin to lose sight of them as the trail winds through the trees, over streams and little hills.

Fuck it!

I sit down and yank the trainers off. Fucking bullshit Nike. Built for the toughest conditions my fucking ass.

The blisters have progressed to open sores, raw flesh, and they are bleeding freely. I hurl the shoes away into the forest. Fuck Nike. I'll do it Ice Age style. Siberian gulag style.

I start walking. It hurts, but I need to catch up to these bastard men. I labour up a small hill that is all silver birches and quite pretty yellow-brown leaf litter. There's a brightness beyond that looks like a big clearing or break in the forest.

It's not an unpretty place to curl up and die. Instead of doing just that, I emerge from the treeline. I've reached the edge of a small hill, and it drops away sharply in front of me.

Below me is their home. Just like that. To my left, the hill continues in a large crescent that steepens nearly to vertical, where raw rock has been exposed by timeless erosion. Entrances to caves are visible. The land levels out. No trees, just a large plain almost imperceptibly sloping down to a sizeable river that looks like it might be quite important. Not Thames or Nile important. Maybe a tributary of. . . the Danube?

Beyond it, the plain continues to the horizon, mostly flat with copses of trees scattered like you see on the African savannah. A floodplain, I suppose. Here and there tendrils of campfire-smoke drift like fat bootlaces into the white and blue sky. I can smell cooking meat. A baby cries above a smattering of raised voices that speak in a strange tongue.

John Wayne and his posse are talking to a group of women and men. They are pointing up the hill at me.

7

People gather around John Wayne's group. Some are hugging them, most are standing around, their faces turned up towards me on top of the small hill. I take a step forward, and several people in the twenty-odd group take a few steps back. Somewhere there's a scream. One person – a woman, I think – stoops down and puts her hands on the crown of her head, like she's afraid of something falling on it. The sky, maybe.

I start walking down the steep hill that leads onto the level plain. My feet are half numb, and I stumble, try to right myself and end up falling on my ass. My thighs tremble with exhaustion when I attempt to get up, so I scratch that as an idea. I sit there, propped up on one elbow. They'll come and get me. I'm like a meteorite fragment, a fancy fossil, a diamond, an alien from outer space: you don't just leave that stuff lying around. You bring it indoors, turn it this way and that, stare at it, put it on a shelf.

Kill it, even.

After what seems like a short argument – raised voices, gesticulations – John Wayne and Grease Monkey trudge back to where I'm sitting. Grease Monkey scoops a hand under my armpit and hauls me up like he's righting a fallen chair. He turns me so I face away from him. My hands are taken and put behind my back. My wrists are tied. That done, they lift me between them and start down the slope. How they don't slip, and fall is beyond me – they must have the skill of mountain goats.

They take me toward the knot of men and women. Children have appeared, though they are waved away and shouted at by both the men and women. The knot parts as I approach, and Wayne and Grease lead me towards the single man who has not moved, who stands still whilst the others step back and gape.

This man has something else about him aside from his massive body. It's his eyes. He looks at me, unblinking. His eyes aren't wide and popping out of his skull like everyone else's. His gaze is analytical, a slight frown creased on his brow like he's a museum curator peering into an old box.

But he's the furthest thing from a museum curator. I picture Indiana Jones' bumbling museum-buddy Marcus Brody, who, millennia from now, peers down at the fossilised bones of this man, and mutters *well, Indy, fuck me if these aren't massive fucking bones*.

It's *presence*. That's what this man has. Presence. I thought John Wayne had it, but this man emanates self-assurance like an Easter Island statue, which, if it could speak would say something like *shit on your civilization, I been here longer'n you, boy*. Easy brown eyes travel up and down my body and come to rest on my face. They flit slowly over my features, and he cocks his head to one side, then the other.

There is total silence from all the assembled adults. I can hear the sound of birds from the trees on the hill behind me, and nearer, the full-throated wail of a baby.

The big man, the headman, the clan boss (hell, he might even be a king) speaks a single word that I fervently hope doesn't mean *sharpen up them steak knives.*

John Wayne and Grease move around the headman and carry me towards one of the caves that I saw from the top of the hill. I twist my head around and I see Weasel, that slimy bastard, speaking to the boss. He can't be saying nice things.

Shit.

———

I guess these cave-dwelling monkeys have never heard of the Magna Carta, which, if I remember correctly, stipulated that a person accused of a crime has the right to be judged by "twelve good men and true". That's why today (sorry – a million fucking years in the future) we have a jury system with twelve jurors. *This* is not what's happening here. Wayne and Grease put me to sit next to a small fire in the shelter of a large cave. What seems like the entire rest of the tribe has assembled, facing me on the other side of the fire.

Actually, that's incorrect. There are only men in here. I heard a joke once – *what do you call a woman chained to a sink? A washing-machine.* I suppose that's where they are now. About twenty men face me. They are seated, on the ground, some cross legged, some with their knees drawn up to their chests. At the side of the cave the headman, the big cheese, talks in a whisper to John Wayne. Another man – a lot older, balding – is with them. They whisper together.

It doesn't look good for Charlie.

Putting it mildly; I'm shitting myself. Ever since Wayne and Grease hauled me up and took me to their boss and then dragged me off to what I expect will be my first, and possibly last, cave-camp-fire experience. Panic is roaring in my brain, like I've been thrown off a cliff and am watching jagged rock rushing up to meet me. My heart thuds like some spastic bullfrog trying to escape my chest via my throat. I'm sweating freely, beads of salty liquid drip into my eyes, stinging them. Wayne's posse appear composed but the men who are seeing me for the first time look *scared*.

When the natives of highland Papua New Guinea first encountered white explorers, they shot first and asked questions later. The natives were terrified, and so it was more accurately a case of throw spears first, and then run the fuck away. The white-skinned men were seen as ghosts. *Evil* ghosts from the spirit realm. Obviously, the New Guineans had to become acclimatized to white people (everyone did, bend the knee and so on, *masa*), but years later when asked by an anthropologist what First Contact was like, an old man replied that back then the white folk were "like people you see in a dream". Which sounds downright voodoo-creepy.

These cave-dwelling people are animists – like the old New Guineans. Their world is one of spirits, magic, superstition – and now it includes a pale and thin junkie-ghost in jeans and a t-shirt.

It'd be better if these people were angry. Anger is easier to defuse than fear.

They yabber and hoot. Several people are leaning to the ears of the big boss, who has sat down among them. He tilts his head this way and that, as if filtering and balancing all the words that are flooding over him. All the while, he's staring at me.

A rock is launched from the back row, and I have just enough time to squirm to the side, so it hits my shoulder, not my face. Voices rise.

And they are suddenly silenced. Boss man thunders an order – pointing at Wayne and Blondebeard. The two men get up and lumber towards me. They are both holding flint knives. The blades look sharp enough to shave with. Wayne's face is grim, Blondebeard seems apologetic.

He has told these two men to kill me. That much is crystal.

I lose all coherent thought. My panic notches up a personal best.

My mind shouts at me to *DO SOMETHING!* and somewhere, in the little disintegrating control centre deep in my brain, the *me* that gives all the orders reaches out and smacks a button – a massive, very red, and very emergency-looking button. Written on it in big letters is a two-word command: *shit yourself*.

What can be more humanising han shitting yourself? We've all done it. It's like sex. Show me an adult walking this earth who is a brown-trousered virgin. There aren't any. Unless I'm gravely mistaken, *everyone* shits themselves. From time to time.

I grit my teeth, bear down, and blow the baffles. Wayne has the front of my t-shirt bunched in his fist, his other hand has the knife held behind him, as if he's about to thrust it forward into my chest.

He's interrupted by the most godawful sound of crapping. It's like elephants dancing on a field of giant whoopee cushions.

Turns out the water I've been drinking *does* have a little loosening effect. My jeans are all hot and runny, and there arises a smell that's been brewed in hell – by head chef Satan.

Watery kangaroo ass. From hell.

John Wayne's tight fist around my t-shirt goes slack, his nose wrinkles, and he blinks hard as if he's got something in his eyes. There is silence. Even the crying infant a few caves over decides this is something worth shutting up for. The smell hits the assembled guests. Boss man only twitches, but the others are shifting, their hands covering their noses, shaking their heads.

It really is eye-wateringly bad.

And I start to laugh.

I'm about to be knifed to death by animist cavemen, so my brain decides the best course of escape is by *defecating*.

If I could get a hand up to my face to stifle the bellows of laughter I would. Instead, I double up, tears of pure joy and fear streaming from my eyes. My laughter bounces around the cave, echoing. And I don't stop. I laugh until my ribs hurt – like they are coming apart with each spasm of glee. I laugh until I topple gently over to lie on my side, in what is basically a big puddle of half-digested kangaroo ass and palaeolithic told-ya-not-to-drink-the-tap-water.

I'm wheezing, on my side. Throughout this whole episode, boss man's expression has not changed. He regards me with eyes that don't seem to blink.

He gives another order.

8

I'm picked up by Wayne and Blondebeard and shuttled out of the cave. They move quickly, in the direction of the river. It's perhaps two hundred metres away, and they cover this at a fast trot. The bank is muddy and steep. They put me down on my feet, not too gently, then Wayne gestures towards the river and then points at me. Blondebeard unties my hands and takes hold of a thick braided cable. It's attached to a wooden post that has been pounded into the ground. A lifeline.

The river smells frigid. I'm already shivering from the air. I'll die from hypothermia if I enter this; what must be meltwater from the gigantic ice shelf that covers half of Europe.

Wayne and Blondie are not going to let a man smelling this hideous skip out on the chance of a bath. Blondie loops the rope around my waist and ties it off. Screw it, I'll get in, get out, get next to a fire. I've no choice. I slip and slide down the muddy bank. The mud is frozen in places. If I so much as dip a toe in this river, I'll never get in.

The only way in is balls-out, possibly screaming.

I stand and suck a few breaths of air in. I let myself tip forward and I hit the water horizontally, face down.

Siberian gulag style.

Distantly, my heart stops.

Jesus

H

Christ

I come up for air, but I can't breathe in. My heart isn't working, it's frozen, my lungs

diaphragm

won't work

heart is offline

dying

The shock subsides as my body goes numb. I take a shuddering breath in. The river's current pulls at me. I flail at my jeans and t-shirt, I pull at them like they are on fire, though it feels like I'm doing it in icy treacle. My muscles are seizing up. I get the bastard jeans off. I tear off the *Stones* t-shirt. Scrabble and slosh water around my butt.

Forgetting the rope, I haul ass at a fast front crawl – I swim the ten feet to the bank and clamber up. Coughing and shaking and shivering like a palsied cripple, I scramble up the little slope.

I'm naked, my boxer shorts lost to the river which will take them far away. A cheap synthetic thing, which I don't think is biodegradable. It'll confuse the Christ out of some deep-sea explorer when they discover it at the bottom of the Mariana

Trench in the 21st Century and then carbon-date it to the middle of the Ice Ages.

Blondie grins at me. John Wayne's face is mildly condescending, like I'm some silly adolescent. They pick me up and carry me, quick step, back to the cluster of caves, past the open campfires that seem to be involved somehow with drying meat on wooden racks. I'm taken back into the same cave. Two women scuttle past us, carrying the ice age equivalent of wet wipes: a large wooden bowl of water, a bundle of hay and a worn-out pelt of some furry animal. The smell and colouration on these latter two items bear witness to my disgrace.

I'm plopped down next to the spot I'd originally occupied. The smell has largely gone.

I shuffle as close to the fire as I can bear, and some heavy blanket-thing is put around me. For several minutes I sit and shake, aghast at the spikes of ice that have replaced my bones, the freezing water that is my blood.

I'm young, though. Perhaps that's what shakes off incipient hypothermia. Eventually my teeth stop chattering. The bonkers thing is that I actually feel pretty *good*. Oddly good. Relaxed, even. Like I've been through some industrial body-scouring washing machine for four hours, emerged dizzy as a bastard, vomited up all the accumulated bad living and sickness in my life, and then been given a bracing cup of sweet tea and a warm pair of slippers.

I'm looking at my fingers, which are returning to a normal colour, when I realise that the cave is silent, save the crackle of the fire. Brown Bear – this name comes to me as I see the boss still sitting there, his expression unchanged. Around him, the men aren't gabbing like loons anymore. The thickened blood smell of fear has been blown away. The natives are still restless, but they're not on a knife edge.

My mother said I had a gift for what she called "smart-arse instinct". This phrase wasn't meant to cover all the copious and unending bad decisions I made consciously, but more the unconscious when-the-chips-really-are-down-and-fucked type of gut instinct.

Whatever.

Brown Bear looks at me, then turns his gaze to the men who'd found me on the frozen tundra. *On their patch*, so to speak. Brown bear talks, looking at each man in turn. John Wayne answers first. Then Grease, then the rest. Short sentences. Another question from Brown Bear. John Wayne frowns slightly and scratches his beard, then speaks at length, for about a minute, pausing here and there.

Their language sounds like Polish, with a fair bit of the stone-crushing sound of Russian thrown in. I know a bit of Polish – had a few friends at school, and I spent time in Cracow where the drugs were cheap. Whilst similar in sound, the words are completely un-Polish. Poland hasn't even been invented yet. Nor Russia, nor the Romans. Christ, even the Egyptians and their beer-making technology are currently the stuff of a madman's dream.

My execution has been postponed, probably abandoned.

I look around properly for the first time.

The cave is large, the size of a big swimming pool. There's even a skylight in the ceiling. This cave is embedded in a low hill, so it's not surprising there are holes in the ceiling where either Time or man has punched the odd hole. It would function well as a chimney of sorts. There is a scaffold made of tied-together trunks of slim trees that would allow someone to climb up to the hole and secure what looks like a covering over the inside. What for? Maybe when it gets really cold, like blizzardly cold?

The men are typical of your average ice age man depicted by movies. Though, I must say they wear less fur – it mostly seems to be leather, in different hues of brown. Though the words are not accurate, I'll call them *shirts* of leather, *trousers* of leather. No nice suede leather or the polished stuff that John Travolta wears in *Grease*. A mildly roughened pelt-like look. Their leathers *look* like they not too recently belonged on an animal. Some wear a sort of cloak which seems to be just a big pelt that is draped and wrapped about the shoulders, a half-toga. They look bundled up and sitting pretty, thank you very much, for ice age Europe.

And their beards. Massive things, for the most part. And the longish hair. Brown Bear has a beard you could hide a badger in. With his hair tied back to the nape of his neck and the badger beard, Brown Bear looks like a giant Canadian lumberjack who collided with a hippie. He speaks like a far distant thundercloud.

The shivering has stopped. I feel thawed. I watch the back-and-forth conversation. I clear my throat.

Everyone looks at me.

It's cheesy, I know, the stuff of probably a thousand movies and books. I tap my chest and say my name: *Charlie*.

They stare at me. No response for a full minute.

Then Brown Bear taps his chest and says his name.

It's a start, at least.

9

I repeat the name, trying to crunch the vowels like Brown Bear did. It seems close enough. He nods. His name seems to be Tazak.

He really does remind me of a brown bear. He's not fat, though. He's tall and built like a brick shithouse but he moves with the self-assurance of a bear – a bear that knows there are few things in this world that can fuck with it.

And his hair and beard are a gorgeous chestnut brown.

Now that I'm warmed again and not about to be killed, I have a severe hankering for a cigarette. I nod at Blondebeard, and make the universal sign for "gimmie a ciggie" that tramps and hoboes do – tapping forked index and forefingers against my lips. I feel a bit like a tramp. I did crap myself.

Blondebeard obviously understands this universal sign language. He holds up the packet of smokes and shows them to Tazak. They speak back and forth. Just give me the goddamn things, *now*.

Tazak assents with a shrug of his shoulders. Blondie passes me the pack. I light a cigarette in the fire, and puff away happily whilst they all stare at me.

Happily? Well, to be honest, I didn't like the life I was living, or even the person I was. No one *choses* to be an incessant boozer, a smoker, and a bit of a junkie. These habits are like a pack of wild animals that have dogged me everywhere, crapping over everything I tried to achieve. Snarling and snapping and scaring away anyone who might have actually ended up liking me for who I really was.

I guess I lack self-discipline or moral fibre or the right genes to *just say no.*

Even though I can still feel an aching thirst (and a physical tremor) for alcohol, and a weird internal sweating sensation that signals a lack of opiates, I realise I am free.

Tabula rasa: a blank slate. I'm starting from here, from *go.* All the pieces are lined up and everyone's got their $200. It's time to throw the dice in the first round of Ice Age Cold-Turkey Monopoly.

There was no one I cared for, in that past life. I had a dog, but it died of liver cancer, nearly fifteen years old. I think I spent as much money on pills and booze as I did on that dog.

I didn't care for anyone, and no one cared much for me. Not my landlord, no one. My two brothers had moved away. They avoided contact with me. My parents were alive, but I avoided contact with them.

There was a girl. Her name was Tulip. How sweet is that? She died too. Heart seizure in the bath. Congenital defect, apparently. I probably could have helped her, had I not been stoned, fast asleep in the bedroom.

Out of nowhere, the urge to drink is so strong that it drags me upwards to standing in a single movement. I wobble but find my feet. As if I'm preparing to trot off to the nearest bar or pub. Everyone just stares.

The happiness I was feeling has vanished, replaced by a disgusted soul-crushing guilt, a hatred of myself. Everything comes back in a nightmare rush. Twenty-five-year-old Tulip, in a bath of cool water, staring at me sightlessly.

I start walking, not feeling the stones and pebbles – the ground – underneath my feet. Not feeling the wind on my bare legs, on my nether regions. I pull the cloak around my shoulders.

I walk out of the cave, aimlessly, and then head for the river, which carries no sense of time, no sense of loss, nor decay. The water arrives, passes you, and is gone, indistinguishable from the water that came before or after. There *are* markers, yes; a duck, a branch, a plastic bag, a dead animal – but these are like thoughts that will shortly be gone and forever forgotten.

I'm crying. Everything – my whole life – feels like it's been squeezed into some malignant and evil ball and shoved through my sternum where it *aches* – it aches like my heart is on fire.

I cry freely, walking across the plain beneath the forest we came through, leaving the caves at my back, the river ahead of me.

There are people. Cave men and women and children. No one is attending to any of the chores that lie around, half done: a half-skinned animal, a rack of half-scraped hides, something on a fire, unattended. Everyone gawps at me. I ignore them. I just want to get to the river. Thoughts swirl madly, like Tulip when she danced, her dress whirling, her smile a sun.

The salty tears that I can taste in my mouth mix with the coppery blood-taste of raw panic.

I'm running now. Maybe into the river. I need a knife, something sharp, a sharp rock. If I hold something sharp to my neck, then they might give me some booze. They *must* have some.

A voice behind me says a word. I ignore it. Then the word is shouted. I stumble to a halt. I turn around.

Ladies and gentlemen, give a warm hand for the breaker of Charlie's heart. My panic drops away. I can do nothing but stare at her, my breathing ragged, slowing.

The girl standing ten feet behind me is pointing at my bare feet.

Universal language for *what the fuck?*

She has a point. It's only a few degrees above freezing. And my feet are bare. And bleeding. I'm standing there, my mouth hanging open; a fuckwitted knucklehead wandering off into the tundra without boots.

The girl is unusually pretty. Otherworldly pretty.

I wonder briefly if she's like me, a time traveller. If she is, she's from a future where people have perfected the human female sex-vixen.

A *rough* guess says she's nineteen years old. Pretty is wrong. She is beautiful. Beautiful beyond the root of the word *beautiful* and the bud of the bud.

She is elemental; a star gone supernova.

I'm bowled over. My hands drop to my sides. The cigarette I had forgotten about between my fingers – I stub this into the side of my naked thigh.

I emit a thin scream, and, inside my soul, something snaps. I don't *fall* to the ground in front of the girl I will soon fall in love with. It's more as if I half-fold up, half-melt onto the ground. I begin crying, again. I pull the cloak over to cover my head. I'm aware that my bare ass is saying hello to the sky above, but I find I don't care.

Smooth.

10

I'm going to skate over the next few months. Give you the broad strokes.

In the hillside there are seven caves, and the people of the tribe spread their numbers throughout all seven.

The short version is that for near on two weeks I lie on a scattering of dried grass and suffer through substance withdrawal. I'm sick, as if with some mind-and-body-shattering flu. I shed almost unending tears of regret, guilt, self-loathing. I'm anxious. I shake and I have panic attacks. I clutch the blanket thing: the one that I tried to crawl under after collapsing naked in front of the super-hot girl.

Men and women come and go, and build a frame around the spot I lie on, a bit like when you're in hospital and the nurses pull the curtain around your bed and then do something unspeakable to you. The older bald guy feeds me some sort of meaty broth. He doesn't say anything other than his name. He taps his chest and says, very slowly and clearly, *Yaneck.*

Two weeks pass. The poisons depart from my system. Physically, I recover, but I'm *exhausted*. I'm beginning to piece together my shattered psyche when someone new appears in the cave: Jesus.

Jesus is perhaps fifty years old, thin and tall, with long grey hair down to her butt. She passes me and waltzes out of the cave. She reminds me of a child's storybook picture of Jesus of Nazareth. All that long hippie-hair. The name sticks.

I find out later that she has been in a nook in the back of our cave, fasting, and ruminating on the weather. And in my estimation, going a little crazy.

She comes back into the cave and rants on for a bit, her voice croaky – from lack of use, I suppose. I'm looking at her, not even attempting to understand, when she catches my gaze. Unlike the others, she stares at me. She mimes what can only be *falling snowflakes.*

This mad old lady reckons she's the weather forecast. My curiosity is piqued – for the first time since I collapsed in front of the hot girl. I'm clearly better because I have the energy to get up and wobble outside. It is cold, and the sky is bright blue. No clouds anywhere.

Jesus obviously commands some clout, because the men immediately set to work. They fit beams (lengths of tree trucks about the thickness of Tazak's thigh) six feet inside the mouths of the caves, up nearly to their apex, leaving perhaps a three-foot space that one would have to crawl and wriggle over to get in and out of the cave. Rough hides are pinned to this barrier.

The next day, I'm instructed (by Blondebeard pointing and miming) to put on the heavy winter clothes that the tribe has given to me. Then I wriggle over the barrier and join the residents who gather in the mouth of the cave. I have not thought about anything so mundane as the weather for the last two weeks, and it only occurs to me now that I must have arrived here in late autumn. Winter is just getting started.

I and the eight other residents of our particular cave sit, around a fire, in the mouth of the cave. A boy, about eight, and a girl a few years younger help their mother roast what look like enormous chestnuts. I have no idea what is going on, except it's obvious these folks are battening down the hatches and expecting either rampaging mammoths, or – more likely – just *very* cold weather. As predicted by Jesus.

We sit and wait. The breeze gradually weakens, and the skies thicken to dark putty. I feel a growing buzz of toasty warmth in my thick furry coat, despite the slightly undercooked smell of flesh that seems to hang on it. The six other caves are doing the same as us. I can hear their voices, their murmurs, babies crying.

This must be their version of Thanksgiving. Or Christmas.

We wait. Wood is added now and then to the fire, which burns down to a thick hill of lava-coloured coals. The older man, Yaneck, says a few gruff words, and everyone quietens. The kids are hushed to silence.

In an instant the silence grows, covers the world, and seems to infiltrate my own body. We all sit in silence and stare out at the unmoving, iron grey sky that hangs above the plain outside. Sharp intakes of breath, and it is suddenly *here*: snow – *the* snow that has come to stay, to change everything. It falls in flakes the size of a fist, with not a breath of breeze, each flake barely even turns; a great and silent carpet bombing.

I watch it fall. I hear Nature grant, in its silence, the reverence this snowfall deserves. I see brutal power. It's like watching a man have a heart attack in slow motion. Vital, moving – then frozen, unmoving.

Yaneck begins a low hum. Like a Buddhist monk. The sound slowly shifts, his voice high and low at the same time, lilting into a melody that raises hairs on my skin and makes me blink back tears. I hear six other voices join with his, six other men from their caves, joining in.

Chanting in unison.

A swansong for a departing sun, an appeasement offered to whichever force deigns the length and the fury of an ice age winter.

Sounds kind of gay when I say it like this. But that's what it is. We watch the world turn white. Turn into some *other* place.

A higher place.

A harsher place.

———

You know those nature documentaries of penguins in the Antarctic, when you see the poor bastards spend three months huddled in a big circle whilst Christ-knows-what sort of hurricane-blizzard rages? Well, one of those kicks off the winter season. I won't sugar-coat it: I am petrified. I listen to the wind howl. It doesn't seem possible, structurally, *or* biologically, that *anything*, plant or animal, can survive *this*. Everything outside is just going to die, get blown away, freeze well below -900 Celsius. That must be like -30,000 in Fahrenheit. The locals aren't particularly concerned. They shrug their shoulders at my obvious anxiety, and they exchange wry smiles – clearly at my expense. It is warmish in the cave, probably about 15 degrees Celsius. That's about 60 degrees Fahrenheit.

There's a snow-patrol guy who is stationed at the mouth of the cave. It's his job to watch through the cracks in the hide coverings of the wooden buttresses and make sure snow isn't blowing in – to the extent it covers the mouth of the cave. The hole we had crawled back through after the ceremony has been plugged with dried grass bundled up in cords of leather. When the snow needs shifting, the guy pulls in the plug of grass, and pokes his twenty-foot birch pole through the gap and jiggles it around to loosen the snow. I guess if you leave it too long it will freeze over. Ventilation is always a good idea. Oxygen is good.

The storm lasts several days. People from the other six caves come and go. Either the seven caves naturally formed with interlinking passages at the rear, or some clever ancestors of these people have chipped and hacked their way through, as the passages themselves are at most only a few feet long. The girl who had admonished me (or at least pointed out that I was crazy) when I was running off into the wilderness barefoot, is not one of the residents in my cave. She doesn't visit. I don't ever see her.

This is a good thing, I think. It would drive me crazy. I think about her. A *lot*.

The days pass. I don't know what anyone is saying to me. There is lots of pointing, lots of (mostly embarrassed) smiles, and clearly a lot of bad manners on my part: faces go red when I drink first, breathe first, fart first, or touch something I shouldn't. I guess it is December.

Tazak comes to visit every few days. He sits by the fire and talks with our cave members. It appears entirely genial, but there are many times when they discuss me; the two kids shift a glance to me when the word that sounds '*Kharlie*' is uttered. Tazak keeps a beady eye on me.

In our cave are two couples (and they make sure you know it, I think, with the unabashed noise levels of their screwing, almost every night). The two kids – the boy and girl – belong to the older couple. I say *older*, but these two have nothing to distinguish them as actually old. The woman looks to be about twenty-one. Her name is a word that, to me, sounds like *Salad*. The guy is probably the same age. Hard to be exact with the beard.

The other "man" and "woman" are essentially hormonal children. Perhaps fourteen years old. The guy, Teenage Dirtbag, has bad teenage acne. Him and the girl, Yala, go like hammer and tongs, sometimes all night long. The older couple holler at them to keep it down, but only after they finish their own rutting. After all, they have their kids to think of.

Life is more organised, more civilised than I expect it to be. Every living area is partitioned by frames made from the slim trunks of birch or some other type of tree, lashed together with leather and something that looks like glue (I later find out it *is* glue – made from boiling down hooves of animals). From the frames hang a kind of curtain made from a woven plant material, though on some are hung wide sheets of animal skins, stitched together to cover the frame.

As far as I can tell, Yaneck has some sort of love-hate relationship with Jesus. They each have their own separate living section, like I do. They generally avoid talking to each other, but every few weeks she summons him to her bed.

In the morning, without fail, both of them are in a mood sour enough to curdle yoghurt. Which is difficult because it's already been curdled. You get what I mean.

———

It takes me a while to get used to the smell. Christ Choking Jesus! It is *bad*. There is a screened-off section which is the lavatory. Comprising of two big buckets. At least they don't leak, lined as they are with the stomachs of some large herbivore. There are regular clean-out details, which involve taking the buckets outside, tramping through about twenty feet of snow, and then just chucking the contents of the buckets into a deep trench that had been dug out before the snows came. It is cold enough to freeze your eyelids together. You come back into the cave freezing your ass off.

I suppose that one *could* go out for a wander between blizzards, but I'm not sure there would be much point. Nothing seems to be out there. It looks like the planet Hoth – the frozen planet that the Rebel Alliance hides out on in *The Empire Strikes Back*. But the Rebels had lightsabers, spaceships, and possibly hyper-warm space clothing. Not to mention fantastic central heating.

During the blizzards, there is no way of getting out there. And the buckets get full and are then set aside, and two more appear. They stack up, until they can be taken out. Jesus, it is horrible. Han Solo would have a thing or two to say about *that*.

But by January I am half-used to the smell.

By February it is like TV: it really doesn't bother me, and I don't bother with it.

I play silly games with the two kids. They aren't as reserved as their adult/teenage compatriots. I play catch with a ball of leather sewn around a pebble.

I ask them the names of *everything*. They teach me the words.

They look curiously on while I do push-ups, bicep curls (with rocks), and sit-ups. I am woefully weak compared to the men (and even many of the women) and I suspect life will be a lot easier if I can actually join in with stuff – as far as I can see this means lending physical strength.

By March I can ask for water, volunteer to do the bucket-run (especially if they aren't *too* full). I can say, *no thank you, I cannot eat anymore.*

My head is sore/painful/hurts. Do you have some medicine?

Snow is white.

My name is Charlie. Lose the harsh C for fuck's sake.

This food tastes good.

Your name is Yaneck.

Kangaroo ass tastes like the number-two lavatory bucket.

I can probably ask the way to the beach. It isn't hard to learn. It just takes time. And there is plenty of that.

It is clear that I am an outsider, an alien. Even dressed like a cave man, the adults do not interact with me unless necessary – like to prod me awake when I am manning the snow-pole during a storm, or to ask me to help cut up what looks like dried flax for basket weaving. Or to catch my attention when they are holding out a bowl of food. Stuff like this. It is clear that no one has made up their minds about me. And I don't blame them.

There is a managed, slow quality to this cave life, as if each individual day is irrelevant, as if the whole of winter is just one long stretch of time. I watch people sit by the fire for six hours or more, turning poles of wood into spears with fire-hardened tips. They mend clothes. Nothing is done in a hurry. It appears to me, with my small but growing comprehension of the language, that sometimes a question only merits a response the next day.

It is a balmy, hallucinatory passage of time where life is lengthened, as if smoothed out by long fingers. I have no watch, no timepiece, but I swear that we are sleeping ten hours a day. Well – they are. I do lunges until my thighs spasm in cramps. Push-ups. I shadow box until I can karate-punch the air for twenty minutes at a stretch, sweat streaming off me. I become fit (like Iron Man fit), and I am always the last one asleep and the first one to wake.

Boy Wonder, the eight-year-old, tries to join in these cardio sessions. His father, Deakel, always calls him brusquely away.

I am worried that will expel me once the snow melts. I am not going out into this world as a quivering baby lamb.

With a sharp sliver of flint, I mark the passage of each day – on the post that forms one of the vertical supports of my little bedroom. On what I think is the 15th of March, Teenage Dirtbag (who by now I understand is called something like *Grab* or *Grape*) gets into a godawful row with his missus Yala. They properly *get down*. There is screeching and stamping. She throws something. And then, bold as brass, in front of everyone, he socks her in the face. She stumbles backwards and half-sprawls on their sleeping roll.

I freeze. None of the other cave members move. No one goes to help. I haven't seen any violence so far, but it appears that this, whilst an aberration, is not exactly an unknown event.

I'm on their patch. Their rules. I look at my feet, at the fire, and sneak some glances at the others who are watching. To their credit, their faces are twisted in disapproval. I look up, and I see the little pipsqueak-fuck advance on Yala and slap her across the face as she tries to rise. The sound is louder than the punch.

All I think of is my mother. My mother, being slapped and kicked by my stepfather whilst I cower in the corner.

A fuse shorts in my brain. A circuit pops. I stand up and take a few strides over, and as he rocks back his arm for another home-run hit, I grab his wrist. I hear voices rise, all around me.

He whirls around, sees that it is me. His face is all pimpled and I know in some sad part of myself that I am only able to intervene because this was a *boy* that I am looking at. I have at least six inches and a good many pounds on him. But he twists his arm away easily and shoves me, and Jesus he is *strong*.

I go backwards, and trip on some bollocks fucknuttery that is lying on the ground. I nearly end up cartwheeling into the fire I had been sitting next to and staring into space, about ten seconds previously. I was minding my own business.

Acne-riddled fuckface.

Yaneck steps heavily in front of the kid who is now advancing on *me*. Yaneck speaks harshly, coldly. He's a big man and he can snap this teenage twat like a twig. It strikes me that amongst these primates, dudes hitting girls is kosher, but dudes hitting dudes is off the menu.

My breath has been knocked out of me, and I sip at the air. I gag and huff. Tazak materialises, almost magically.

I pick myself up and I leave them to it. I go and sit by the snow-pole.

———

Two days later, I awake to the sound of dripping water. Yaneck unplugs the crawl-hole. I catch a glimpse of the outside world.

The sun is just peeking into view, and the sky is a rich blue. The cluster of four-foot icicles that hang down over the mouth of the cave are melting.

Everyone goes batshit with excitement. Can't say I blame them.

A breeze that isn't frigid wafts in.

11

All of us except Jesus crawl over the cave barrier. We clear the snow away from the cave entrance and Yaneck, who seems to be this cave's senior partner, builds a fire. The sombre atmosphere of the ceremony that marked the coming of the first snow, a few months ago, is absent. Joy pervades us. Even Teenage Dirtbag (who I now understand is called Grebel) hugs me. Everyone hugs each other, about ten times. The children are delirious with glee.

I'm feeling the same sort of exuberance. But at the same time, I'm still a little shell-shocked. Living in a cave for four months where people shit in buckets will have that effect on you.

It's still cold – maybe a few degrees above freezing – but the light wind feels strangely balmy after the icy hellscape of winter. We all sit near the fire, and Yaneck takes his spot, in front of us, and for several minutes he silently contemplates life. Or he meditates. I'm not sure which. Jesus calls from the other side of the barrier. I go with Yala (Grebel's partner, still sporting a cut lip), and Jesus passes us some steaming concoction in small wooden bowls. We distribute these to the rest of the group. Jesus crawls out to join us. I sit back down. We blow on the liquid and take small sips, grinning like mental patients.

The taste of the brew is acquired, like everything else around here. I would hazard a guess and say that it contains some herbs or leaves, but that's like saying that coffee tastes like coffee.

Yaneck starts his humming, and this builds into a chant. But this is different to the Hello Winter song a few months ago. Back then, the tone was one of mournful wonder. This time the song is longer, higher, his voice going from a rumbling glacier to a lark, ascending, up into a bright spring day. This is a different grace. The singers from the other caves join in, from the literal doorsteps of their homes.

They are giving thanks, gratitude, for the return of the sun.

I sit, my shoulders touching Jesus on one side and the older mother, Salanda, on the other. Her kid, Boy Wonder, sits half in her lap and half in mine. The fire is warm on my face and hands. Someone tightens a hand on my shoulder, roughing it happily.

The touch warms me deeper than the fire.

We stare out at the dripping icicles and the sun in the blue sky, and we are all alone in the world, all alone but for the people around us tucked like squirrels in our little caves, watching a change from frozen earth, from cold statis, into a renewal of life, food, water, birth, sunlight.

My body seems to expand and melt into the others who sit around me, and distantly I wonder if I've been drugged, but it's not that. What's happening is that I am *bonding* with these people.

My eyes are wet when Yaneck finishes his song with a sudden blast, like the sound of an overexcited foghorn. The sound rolls away to the river. In the silence someone behind me speaks, a sentence or two. There is a pause, and Salanda, next to me, says something, different, longer. When she is finished, Jesus speaks, her voice pleasantly low. Then she nudges me.

I realise that this is like a birthday – when everyone gets to make a wish. Perhaps they regard this as the Earth's birthday. Or their own. It's clear that we all get to say our piece. To pray. To ask for something.

Without thinking, I mumble a bible verse, something that stuck in me as a child, a phrase that I kept hidden away, that I never said out loud, yet it remained – a single sentence, turning slow cartwheels amongst my waking thoughts, all the days of my life. I never said it because it was something I was never prepared to do: ask for help. Looking back, I realise that I was only able to say it because no one here would understand it.

"I will lift up mine eyes to the hills, from whence cometh my strength."

The others make their own wishes, give their own thanks. I sit, thinking. Now, as I remember that moment, I see that the epiphany those words conjured only hung in the air for the briefest moment before being swept away – away from my consciousness.

I failed to notice what it offered.

I had opened my mouth and said the words. I had *talked the talk*. It was a shame that I didn't realise the enormous benefit that could come from *walking the walk*. I guess I needed a bigger reason than just joy, burgeoning comradeship, and a deep communion with the natural world to actually *change*.

I can hear my mother's voice: *some people never learn.*

———

Any ice age person, no matter how optimistic, will tell you that a thaw does not guarantee that winter will not go balls-out into one last mind-bending blizzard before it fucks off for another year. Winter's version of a farewell party.

We spend three days sitting around in the mouth of the cave, eating, talking, sleeping, watching the icicles recede, fall and shatter. It is a panacea for the inhabitants. The pressure the social bonds have been under is extreme. A sneaky-bad part of myself can admit to you that if I had to put up with a close companion for four months in a cave, I might *consider* violence.

On that note, Tazak makes me and Grebel apologise to each other. Tazak speaks in his low and grinding *I-shit-continents-for-breakfast* voice to Grebel, who trembles visibly and can barely stand to look at Tazak's feet, far less his face.

The big man speaks to me very briefly, quietly, saying the words for "bad", "anger", "sorry", and "friends". I hold his gaze. Very hard to do, but I do it because I don't want him to think I am scared, which I am.

Eyes to eyes. Giant to man. I say some of the words I know, and then Tazak makes Grebel and me embrace each other. It is weird, but it seems to solve the animosity that has been hanging around like the smell from the buckets.

Then on the fourth day everything stops melting. The temperature drops – off a cliff. We close up the cave again and the wind howls for the next three days, but the mood around the hearth-fire is elevated – even jovial.

I'm sitting, staring at the branches in the fire, drinking some sort of tea. Yaneck sits down next to me. So far, he has not directly spoken to me – other than telling me his name while I was going through withdrawal. But now, he gestures above his head, to indicate the blizzard, and he speaks to me.

'How many winters have you seen?'

I understand the question. But like many languages, the speaking of it lags far behind understanding it.

I can count up to fifteen in their language. Boy Wonder has been tutoring me. But I don't know how to say twenty-five. I take a smouldering twig out of the fire and draw little lines on the ground. I get to ten and almost draw a 'x 2' next to it. I continue until I get to twenty-five. I'm not even sure that Yaneck can count that far, but his eyes show no hint of confusion, only wonder.

'Old!' He exclaims.

I grin and nod. Yaneck rapid fires this information to the others. They look up from their tasks and frown, and some shake their head. I shrug my shoulders as if to say *what's the big deal?*

Yaneck pulls back his lips in a rictus grin and points at me, nodding. I copy his facial expression and then I feel his finger tapping along my incisors and canines. My teeth are white, and they are all present, all aligned perfectly. I'm lucky that way. Never even needed braces. Boy Wonder and his little sister Sela often make me lie down and open my mouth so they can have a good look.

Yaneck runs a finger over my face, which is beginning to sport a beard, but the skin still evident is the smooth skin that hasn't had to put up with growing up and dying in an Arctic wasteland.

He's indicating that I look a lot younger than I am. That I have amazing teeth for my age, and I have skin that hasn't been flayed raw or turned to leather.

'How much. . . winter?' I ask this and point at Yaneck. He speaks, then takes the twig from me and adds seventeen more marks. He's forty-two.

'Charlie.' He says my name for the first time, pronouncing it perfectly. I smile, genuinely happy. He nods and his face becomes serious.

'Charlie,' he repeats. He gestures around him, mimes 'sleeping', then 'waking up', then he points to the marks on the ground. His finger touches them, each in turn until he reaches ten, then he shrugs, and counts five more. He points towards the mouth of the cave, and with the tips of his index and forefinger placed on the ground, he mimes 'walking.'

I understand. *In ten or fifteen days, we will be outside.* My guts contract. Is this the part where I get told that my services are no longer required?

'Tazak wants me to –'

I don't understand the rest. He's telling me that Tazak, wants Yaneck to – to what?

Yaneck puts his hand to his mouth and mimes what can only be someone engaged in the act of speech. I understand: Tazak wants Yaneck to teach me to speak their language.

A tension I didn't know I had uncoils from my body. I'm sitting, but my knees are weak. I grin and nod. Like a lunatic.

'Yes.' I nod some more. 'I would like,' I say.

When Yaneck said he was going to teach me, it turns out that he really meant it. The old bastard drills me for an hour, gives me an hour off, then does another hour – every waking moment until winter finally loosens its grip. Which according to my calendar is eleven days later.

My progress surprises me. Hearing the language consistently for several months meant I was pretty well primed for the harder stuff. Eleven days later I am beginning to properly communicate, to properly understand fifty percent of what is being said.

I wake from a sleep that was. . . well. . . it's like sleeping on a transatlantic night-flight. Turbulent dreams, unremembered.

I lie on my back. I've gotten used to a bed of dried grass with a furry pelt over it for an under-sheet. I'm comfortable, warm, and well-rested. For the first time in over a decade, my body is at peace. I listen to the deep and slow throb of a healthy heartbeat. I keep my eyes closed because if Yaneck sees me awake he'll grab me and start up with the lessons. I can smell food being cooked. Snow is regularly brought in and melted for water, and sometimes a broth is made from dried meat and dried vegetables (the only thing I recognise is what I think are wild carrots). At first, the broth was as bland as water, but it was my habituation to salt and sugar that was at fault. In a few months, my senses of smell and taste have been dialled up to 11.

I'm thinking about bees, about willow trees, about flowers. And clay. I've thought a lot about clay, these past few weeks. My thoughts about clay come from the limitations of current technology, particularly that which pertains to the act of making liquid boil.

How do you boil water? You can't just put a saucepan over a fire. Metal is not a thing, here in the Stone Age. The Stone Age does what it says on the tin: which is to say there *are* no tins. No nails, screws, zippers, blades. And definitely no saucepans or kettles.

First you chuck a few smooth round stones into the fire. You wait a good half hour. Then using a set of tongs made from wood or bone, you pick these stones out of the fire. They are covered in soot, obviously, but you can get most of that off with a soft scrap of off-cut leather – a bit like drying a super-hot potato with oven mitts. You brush and blow away the soot and the crap and then you drop the stone into your receptacle of liquid. The stone fizzes and snarls like a mad bastard as it transfers its heat to the liquid.

You keep putting the stones in and soon the liquid comes to the boil. Small, hand-held bowls are made from wood – the hollowed-out gnarls of tree roots are the best quality – but the bigger cooking vessels are hollowed-out stone.

There are two in each cave, and they sit permanently next to the fire. They are *big* lumpy squares of rock, either quarried from somewhere or found lying around. It appears that the centres perhaps had a natural bowl-like depression that has clearly been chipped at to make a deeper hole.

Heating rocks can cause them to split – even explode like a grenade if there is sufficient moisture within it. But these people seem to know what they are doing, and no one seems to be stumbling around, blind from flying shards of a rock-bomb.

This technology is too primitive, as far as my needs go. Forget this hot-stone bullshit. When the weather warms, I'm going to make some earthenware pottery.

I'll be able to make a proper broth without all the little bits of ash and crap and bollocks floating around in it.

I'll be able to ferment vegetables, which'll mean I can eat cabbage or whatever passes for leafy and crunchy vegetables around here during these rather constipated winter months.

Thirdly, whilst I'm making clay pots, I'm going to start a clay-brick production line. Even if it takes me five years to build a double-walled straw-insulated clay brick house complete with a chimney, hearth, and a composting toilet attached, it will be five years well spent. I'll be buggered if I'm going to spend half of each year in a cave, with a horde of other humans defecating all around me.

Fourthly, with the addition of some sort of bung (wood, I guess), a clay vessel will provide a way of storing fruit juices and yeast in an oxygen-poor environment. This last feat is probably the most important since it will allow me to produce *booze*.

The truth of it is that I need to make clay pottery if I am to realise my dream: whittling away the winter months by drinking myself insensible.

And hopefully the summer months as well.

I'm not stupid. Logically I'm aware that this is a *terrible* idea. The worst. But emotionally, this idea has the gravitational force of a supermassive black hole. Inescapable. Irresistible.

I met a guy once, who said that whenever he faced a choice, he always chose the harder option, since (he claimed) it was invariably the wisest. I remember nodding along as he laid out this pearl of wisdom. I waited for him to fall asleep (he was next to me on a train) and then I stole his wallet.

I open my eyes. Yaneck is not paying me any attention. No one is. They are gathering at the mouth of the cave and are removing the wooden buttresses and the heavy bear hide from the mouth of the cave.

I get up, walk over, and help them move the last few obstacles and set them aside. A fever trembles through the group. It spreads to me – a jittery and rising excitement.

We go outside. Patches of bare earth the size of half a tennis court are dotted amongst the remains of the melting snow. Must be about five degrees Celsius. The adults tramp outside, the kids run. Our little cave mingles with the others. There are about thirty people milling around. Hugging, smiling, clapping each other on the back. Jabbering happily. I catch snatches.

It's done – so hungry – cook – sick of dark – you have grown – how is your leg – fresh meat – start a fire – blood – but I never – walking – fresh – I need to – I lost a tooth – Tazak will tell us when – grass and seeds – strawberries – not yet – spear – give it time.

They are a motley crew. Men and women, their faces pasty with winter pallor, grimed over with soot and God-knows-what that accumulates on human skin from cave life. The kids are whizzing around, twelve of them, having a running snowball fight.

I stare at the river in the distance. I remember the face-first bellyflop I performed on my first day, and it makes me shiver.

'You are well?'

I hear the question from a few paces behind me, and I recognize the voice. My stomach flips over. The voice belongs to the person who'd admonished me for being such a dickhead when I ran off, shoeless, just before winter set in. She only spoke to me that one time, but I remember the voice.

I remember her face. Next to that face, the night sky strewn with diamond stars is a pasty pigsty.

But Charlie the Smooth Operator seems to be taking a vacation when it comes to this lady. I turn and try to smile. Not sure if I succeed. She's still looks nineteen years old, if anything a bit younger. She stands next to a lady who looks like she's some sort of healer – just the weathered, knowing face suggests this to me; the stereotypical image of a witch or crone messing with herbs and casting spells.

I swallow hard, trying to hide the motion by rubbing my throat. I tap my chest. *Charlie.*

She taps the spot below the hollow of her throat - the spot just above her breasts, which are small and high in some sort of deerskin jerkin.

Look, I may have been flung back in time but that doesn't stop me being young and having a pair of testicles which are *continually* leaching primo-grade bull-strength testosterone into my bloodstream. Like some sort of unstoppable intravenous sex-drip.

It seems her name is Sara.

The crone next to her makes a sour face and pushes Sara on the shoulder, making her stumble. She pushes Sara again, in the direction of a group of women who are standing near Tazak. As for the boss, he notices everything, and I catch him glance over to take in our little scene; the crone prodding Sara over towards him, me staring after them. No expression on his face as he shifts his gaze from them to me, back and forth.

It's all too cryptic. There will be time to figure this out. I turn away and amble towards the river which is perhaps a hundred feet away. I skirt the remaining snowdrifts. A few of the kids run ahead, crazy as bedbugs in a laundry fire. Snowballs whizz by me like I'm in some crazy carnival crossfire. These kids have lived through a solid three months of what for them is like a non-stop school detention. So, I don't blame them – and I don't feel the need to react when a snowball catches me on the side of my head.

Ice crusts the edges of the river, and little ice floes drift by. Did the river freeze? It's wide, maybe thirty feet, so perhaps not. The water level is ten foot down a gentle slope. When the spring meltwater arrives from the north, this river will fill up to the top of the bank. If there are storms, or an excessive melt, it'll break its banks and flood.

The gradient of the plain is mild, but the distance means that there is another ten foot to play with. Unless the entire goddamn world melts, the caves will be fine. There is evidence of previous floods: the soil is granular, and when I put my fingers to the unfrozen spots of soil, it's loamy, fluffy, a rich dark that speaks of minerals and juicy goodness. Perfect for growing stuff.

The sun is only a few inches above the hills to the east. Not long past dawn. The obscuring clouds drift, and the sudden warmth on my face is a flood of energy and relief after a dim, flame-lit hibernation. Months of shadow.

In the play of that spring sun, my blood thin from a sparse diet of nuts, dried fish and venison, roots, and lichens, I feel a vitality that I last felt as a new-born baby, my organs fresh and my body flooded with stem cells, all growing *up,* forwards.

Towards *life.*

12

L ight the blue touchpaper and stand well back. The tribe spills out into the world. The last of the stores are dug up, the stored nuts and dried berries and the last bits of meat: all of it is divided up into rations.

In the confinement of the caves for the last three months, the chip-tap sound of stonework and flint knapping has been ever present. Men have made flint-tipped spears. Staffs of wood with flint blades embedded in the sides which function as axes. Knives – which are flint blades glued and sinew-bound into handles of carved ivory, deer antler or bone.

No one, as far as I know, has invented the bow and arrow. But they have managed spear-throwers, which are arm-length flats of wood with a groove and cup at the end where the spear base fits into. Practice targets are set up, and by the afternoon of the first day men are hurling their spears incredible distances, grinning like madmen, bubbling with excitement.

John Wayne, whose real name is Culeg, is laughing and nattering with Tazak, who can throw his spear much further than anyone. He demonstrates this, though only on the urging of the other men, and even then, with an *aw-shucks if you really wanna see it* bashfulness. Tazak hurls his spear about three lengths of an Olympic swimming pool and hits the target – a grass-stuffed old hide – nearly bang in the centre.

Gold medal in the Spear-Skewering Olympics, for real.

Blondebeard waves. Weasel glowers at me.

The women seem to have their own sport, which initially involves sitting around a fire, making tea and all of them in turn rubbing the swollen bellies of two pregnant women. They rub the bellies with some sort of grease. Probably yak-fat or something weird.

You'd think only the women would have spent the winter sewing, and the men only making weapons. But there's a lot of overlap. Women make flint knives for their own use, though the larger pinprick-sharp ones for hunting spears – these are all made by men. Men and women seem equally inclined to make their own clothes. I watched the two couples in our cave sitting side by side, night after night, stitching and sewing their own leathers and furs and whatnot. And even the men seem to have some competition going on as to who is making the best clothes. You'd figure them for a bunch of foppish dandies. Then they ruin the image by shitting in a bucket.

Yaneck appears at my side (he can creep up on you quite easily).

He says: *the men will. . .* (he mimes setting a snare with an elaborate puppetry of a man scrabbling on the ground, going away, an animal coming along and getting a leg stuck). . . *this afternoon.*

I briefly copy the mime, and then point to my mouth. He repeats the word. I copy it, several times, getting the intonation right. I now know the word for "snare".

'Spring – too early to hunt?' I ask.

Yaneck makes a see-sawing motion with his hand.

———

I eat a few of my semi-rancid hazelnuts and dried blackberries. I catch Sara looking at me. I look away. I don't want to get caught in the middle of some social taboo that'll see me ostracised, sacrificed, or cursed with death and expelled, or whatever these people do for entertainment. The tribe has only half-accepted me, and the jury is clearly suspicious of my guilt and still deliberating, if the cold shoulder from many of the women and some of the men is anything to judge by.

I can't join in with the spear Olympics, so I go for a walk. It seems that several miles in the distance, in all directions, the land rises up in a series of hills, some tall and showy, some low and brooding. The land inside this elevation is forested, the higher portions of the hills bare – covered still with snow – but any first-grade student of the ice age would guess that underneath that will be grass and rock. What amounts to the typical ice age steppe, which is kind of the same as saying it's like the typical 20th century American prairie. The tribe live in a bowl-shaped depression several miles in diameter, that contains a good amount of forest and has a river. All good so far.

I stand looking at the entrance to the seven caves. I veer to the left, the west, to where the caves end, and where the hill is solid, I trudge up to where it flattens out. There's a small stream that emerges from the forest and gurgles downhill towards the river.

I walk above the caves. The ground is flat and where the snow has melted it seems only grass grows. A one-minute walk north will take me to where the deciduous woods begin.

The woods I came out of four months ago, my feet raw and bleeding.

Turning right, to the east, I walk across what is the roof of the caves to the other side, avoiding the several little chimney holes. Around each hole, small flat rocks have been piled up to create a basic chimney stack, and the opening has some sort of woven material pinned over it. I suppose to stop all sorts of things falling in. What those things are, I don't know. Small animals. Leaves, maybe. Children?

Spruce and pine trees are green against the brown grey of the leafless deciduous trees, which seem to be mainly alder, larch, birch, beech, and oak.

I'm thinking this is the perfect spot for my little house on the prairie: the flat grassy area, next to the stream, and a long javelin-throw from the woods.

All I need to do is build it.

A knife would come in handy.

I walk back down to the throng of people.

The men are now huddled around a small fire. They scratch in the dirt with sticks, point here and there, and talk fast. It's obvious that they are planning a hunt. I hear words for animals that I've learned, animals that are painted in frescos on some of the cave walls. The pictures are exotic, and the recognizable ones are bison, mammoths, horses, deer, wolves, lions, aurochs (the as yet undomesticated cow). There are smaller animals, little more than sketches in charcoal, that I know the tribe's words for but don't know what the animals actually are. I suppose those pictures represent things like pine martens, otters, beavers, wolverines. On one of the cave walls there is something that looks like the Energizer Bunny but I'm pretty sure it's a giant hare.

Christ, there's probably a bunch of stuff out there in the wild that no one in the 21st century has even seen or found fossils for. While I'm on the subject, I can confirm that I do *not* see *any* evidence of aliens coming down to earth and kick-starting *anything*. And I'm talking straight at Erich Von Daniken. His seminal book *Chariots of The Gods?* in 1968 cemented Daniken's reputation as Germany's leading nutjob of the later 20th Century. He's more than partly responsible for the popularity of the *aliens built it and were worshipped as gods* hypothesis of human prehistory. So tiresome. I can resoundingly crap all over that theory. All the deities these people worship are definitely in realm of human imagination.

Mind you, you have to hand it to Daniken. He was pretty ballsy: imagine having the nerve to write a book in which you suggested that the Nazca lines were runways for extra-terrestrials, and the Egyptian pyramids were actually take-off ramps for interstellar freighters.

Meanwhile, here on Earth, the women have already separated into groups of twos and threes. They are heading away from the caves, in all directions. Some carry spears, all of them carry leather satchels of varying sizes and shapes. I guess they are looking for grubs, roots, tubers. To be honest, I'm so hungry I'll eat a bunch of grubs. Especially so, when compared to dried kangaroo ass, the name of which I'm thinking of changing to *camel ass*. I reckon camels smell worse than kangaroos.

Sara is walking west with two other women. She glances back at me. Some small part of me catches fire.

Yaneck, and two older men, Brekel and Zander, stay seated around the fire. The two men look to be in their sixties. The rest of the men tramp off to the west. A hunting party.

They are going to hunt deer, Yaneck says.

I nod. 'What shall I do?' I ask him.

The men raise their eyebrows. Yaneck looks at me for a long while, then speaks quickly to the other men. He asks them to leave us. They get up and walk up to the caves.

'Tell me who you are,' says Yaneck.

I've expected this question for some time. Everyone has let me alone, on this subject, and I've had time to think about my response.

I've entertained a slew of options, most of them variations on the theme of me being a god who either fell to earth or decided to take on human form. But as tempting as that is, I'd be just setting myself up to fail. Plus, my arrival in this tribe was a little less than spectacular. Very un-godlike.

I stick to the decided story. It goes a bit like this:

'I come from far far far east *(pointing)*. Land much different. People much different. Different clothes. The air is hot, always. There is no winter, for all moons. One day, the sun come too close to world. It burns our homes *(mime flames, mime being on fire, mime screaming panic)*. We travel west *(pointing)*, many many many many moons. We are cold. We don't know how to hunt here. All my people die in big river. I live. Very cold here *(mime shivering)*.'

I finish. Yaneck's expression has not changed. His gaze is so placid, so thoughtful, it might be that he's not even listening.

Yet his eyes don't leave my face. He is a human paper towel; absorbing every word I've said.

He comes out of this trance and tilts his head slightly. Then he uses a word I learned from Boy Wonder, and from experimenting with it I've come to understand that it has all the same implications in English.

'Horseshit.'

Universal language for complete bullshit.

Damn.

I'm so taken aback, so *thrown*, that all I can do is flap my mouth at him.

'Culeg told Tazak and me that you ...'

I shake my head, and repeat the sentence without the last words, which I don't understand. Yaneck puts his curled fist to his mouth, and springs his fingers open, making a puffing sound.

Universal language for *appeared out of fucking nowhere.*

It sounds as if out of the four men, only Culeg *saw* me arrive. And the sneaky bastard *told on me.* I suppose I should be grateful that he kept that detail for Yaneck and Tazak's ears only.

All I can do is shrug, my face a caricature of a chastised child. One who has been caught lying his ass off. Telling porky pies.

Yaneck leans forward, motioning me to do the same.

'I told Tazak that Culeg was wrong. Tazak trusts me.'

'Why?'

He ignores this question.

'Tell me the truth.'

There is no way to spin it.

Yaneck has stuck his neck out for me. He obviously told Tazak that Culeg was mistaken, and then privately told Culeg to change his story, to erase the bit where I *appeared*.

I sigh and pick up a stick. I draw a bunch of small lines in a row. I make the line in the middle longer than the rest. I point to it with the stick. *Today*, I say. I point to the line immediately to the left of it. *Yesterday*, I say. Then I point to the one to the right of the larger *today* line. *Tomorrow*, I say.

Yaneck nods his understanding, impassive. I start adding more lines to the right – beyond tomorrow. I stand up, adding more and more. I walk away, now just tapping the stick as I walk to indicate more lines. I reach the stream that threads across the plain. I step over it and keep walking, still tapping the ground, to where the ground begins to rise. I point my stick in that direction and make a circling motion with my other hand, miming *more, more, more*.

I walk back to the fire. I look at Yaneck.

'That is *when* I come from.' I sit down across from him.

Any detectable colour from his winter-paled face has now drained away to something worse than pure white. His face has gone a dead-like grey.

Yaneck is the opposite of stupid. He has understood me. Somehow, he's grasped it: I come from *far far far tomorrow, from a time that has not yet come.*

In 21st century language, I come from the *fucking future*.

He closes his eyes, sitting ramrod straight on his rock by the fire. Minutes pass. Slowly colour returns to his face. Meanwhile

I'm thinking this is my best chance to run to the cave, steal a spear, and strike out on a very lonely walkabout. But I don't move. The sun is warm on my back, the air cool.

Women are calling to each other, whistling to each other, the few kids are playing noisily under the watchful eyes of Brekel and Zander who have seated themselves outside the caves. These sounds are peaceful. I can hear the river in the distance. A soothing rush that mixes with the gurgle of the nearby stream. It's lovely.

I want to stay here.

Yaneck opens his eyes. The impassive soul-stare has returned.

'Are you a ghost?' He makes a sign as he does this, not a mime, but something I've seen him (and others) do. I suspect it's a sign to ward off evil. I know the word for *ghost*. Boy Wonder taught me.

I look on the ground. There are chips and flakes of flint scattered around. I swipe up a sharp little sliver. I hate pain, but this will be just like a needle jab, I tell myself.

It's worse than a needle jab. A lot worse, but I grit my teeth and I manage to make a deep enough slice so that blood emerges. Not a scratch or something weedy, but a proper slicing puncture, so that from my forearm, red blood gushes in a very convincing manner on the ground.

'Not a ghost,' I say. 'Human. Like you.' I point west, in the direction of the future. 'Accident make me come here.'

He nods, and shrugs. He says the word for what must be *future*. I nod.

'But,' he says. He looks around, circling his finger, 'I will tell all people that you come from far far far east.'

He grins. 'Truth?' And he makes a slicing gesture across his neck.

Universal sign for *they would hang you up by your balls and let the birds pick the flesh from your bones.*

Shit.

'I will sit here. You – go and walk, explore.' He makes a fluttering motion with his hand. Clearly, he needs more time to fully process the mind-fuck that I've just laid on him.

He needs space to grapple with the mechanics of time-travel. Quantum theory and all that.

I leave him, feeling like I've just crawled out of a pressure cooker. My heart is beating fast. I realise I'm sweating. I take a steadying breath.

He knows, but he'll keep my secret and will spin my horseshit to the tribe.

What he'll want in return is something I guess I will discover later. I learned long ago that there is an unyielding truth in the saying *there's no such thing as a free lunch.* Doesn't matter what time, which planet, which solar system or galaxy, lunches are *never* free. It's a fundamental law, like gravity. It applies – permanently.

But what is not a constant is *when* you pay.

And *what with.*

13

Yaneck is the head shaman. The head religious intercessor between the tribe and their spirit world. I think Jesus is somewhere on his level.

I don't know enough about the relationships or who does what. But I do know Jesus' real name: Urla. She's the witch to his warlock, sort of.

For the moment, Yaneck will keep the truth of my origins to himself. He seems to have enough clout to tell them the horseshit story about me and have it become fact.

So, the pressure is off. Looks like I'm part of the tribe now. Which is a good thing, as it's not exactly like I can just wander off, find a motorway, and thumb a ride to the nearest motel.

This valley is now my home, presumably until I die. You'd think I would find this horrifying. But it's the opposite. Sure, I'll miss internet porn and sexbots and so on. And I'll miss the morphine and the cigarettes. But not so much now that I think about it. I stand where I was before, at the spot I've picked out to build my house. I look down on Yaneck, who is still sitting by the fire. Meditating on time travel, I imagine. You have to hand it to the guy. I basically showed him that Dorothy and The Wizard of Oz story is *real*. He didn't run around screaming. I take my hat off to him.

Oh yes – morphine, fags, and booze. The previous two have lost the physical and desperate hold over me. My mind itches for them, but not my body, and that is something I can deal with just fine. But booze? Jeez, I would *really* like a drink. And since I've beaten the physical dependence, then the odd sharpener now and then would be just fine.

But first things first.

To make booze easily, I need to make earthenware pottery. All you need is clay. A bit of water. And fire. That's the theory, anyway. My speciality that kept me gainfully, if fitfully employed, was the restoration of historic homes that mad old English and American people seemed keen on buying. The Baltic States were littered with all this stuff and the owners insisted the repairs be done using the same methods, which largely involved lime mortar. I learned the skill from a very old, very mad Russian guy. He taught me to burn limestone rocks in pit kilns to make lime mortar, which is the stuff the world used before the invention of cement. You could just go and buy the raw material off the shelf, but doing that wasn't classed as authentic.

For some nebulous reason, "authenticity" meant the properties were more valuable. I look down on Yaneck and I think of this. I laugh out loud.

I go down to the river. There are two women there, hauling water in wooden buckets to a trough made out of a large tree trunk. I slide down the bank to the muddy edges of the water. The footwear I'm wearing seems to be waterproof as I feel the cold but not the wet. Good so far. Using a stout switch of ash wood that I levered and snapped off a tree above the caves, I poke around on the bank. Loose crumbly soil falls in clods.

I strike gold: a big seam of clay. And this is pretty high-grade clay, without too much of the little rocks and soil bits that you usually get in it. I claw out a big fist-sized lump. I prise and squeeze it into two smaller lumps. I bend and submerge them in the water. Freezing cold! But when I remove them and squish them up even more, I'm very pleased. This is *great* clay. Normally I hate the stuff. It's hard to grow things in. But this is perfect.

I go back to the cave, passing Yaneck, who is still meditating or – for all I know – communing with the giant spirit-monkey who birthed the world. In my cave I find a shallow bucket that seems to be made out of birch-bark. OK. No one is using it. I borrow it.

I make several trips to the river, eventually collecting a wheelbarrow-worth of clay which sits in a gooey mound near to the fire. Finding a nice flat rock takes a bit more work, but the day is young, and I find one in the shallows of the river. There are now four women, having what seems like a washing-party in the wooden trough. I ignore them. They pretend to ignore me, but I can feel their eyes on me, feel their brains buzzing with questions, gossip, things like *what the fuck is this dude up to?*

I've got my clean and flat rock set next to my mound of clay and my birch bucket filled with water. On the rock I squash a load of clay flat, and pick out small pebbles, bits of roots, specks of soil. Then I gather up this cleaned clay and put it aside. I repeat the process, ending up with a big ball of clean (or as clean as I can make it) clay. I start to mould it, recalling the weekends on the south coast of England, me at Boy Wonder's age, at the equivalent of hippie camp. Trouble is, I remember stuff very well. My brain works a little too well. A little too hard. I suppose that's what the morphine and the booze helps with. Blunts memory. For a while, you forget things.

Can't ruminate, or I'll probably start crying. I focus on my task.

Slap, mould, slap, slap, pat, mould, pat, add, smooth, mould, mould, pat, add. For an hour.

The bastard thing is too thin, it falls apart.

I squish it up and start again.

After what seems to be two hours (of more careful slapping and moulding) I have a hollow, container-shaped mass of wet clay. About the size of a football. It's ugly, clearly the work of an amateur. But it has a flat base, and an outward flaring opening at the top. It's a big jug-bowl with a two-inch high ridge around the mouth. If it works as intended, once it is fired it should be usable as a cooking vessel. The sort you can hang over a fire. Boil water in. Cook soup. Make glue from hooves. That sort of stuff. Without all the faffing about with hot and ashy rocks.

As to the firing of this earthenware thing, I'm less sure.

I think hard. What was it? Smithing? No.

Sintering – that's it. A thousand degrees C. Then *vitrification* at about 1,300 degrees – that's where the silica in the clay basically melts and you get a fully waterproof vessel. For the moment, I'm just going to do a basic pot without all that faff.

You need to put the moulded pot a foot or two away from the fire. For a few hours at least. Then you build the fire up a little and put the pot in the fire itself, keeping the fire going for a few hours. Then let it cool, obviously, before using it.

I put a few branches on the fire, and then set my flat stone (with the pot on it) one and a half feet from the fire. Hot, but not searing-hot.

Then I'm not sure what to do with myself, so I slap out and mould a brick, the size of the traditional red-stone clay brick that houses will be built out of, many millennia from now. Then I realise that it would be easier and a lot quicker to create moulds into which I could cram all the clay. Then put them in stacks next to a bigger fire. Set up something of a prehistoric production line.

I suppose I'll just nip down to the hardware store and pick up some two by four boards.

Dammit. OK. I need to ask someone around here how to get boards. I look up and realise that I've been so absorbed in my task that I've forgotten that Yaneck is still sitting there. His eyes are open, and he's staring at the pot. He shifts his gaze to me. The ghost of a smile touches his lips. The guy is like a ghost himself. He's not made a peep and nor has he moved in several hours. I suppose that he must be important around here if he can sit on his ass all day whilst everyone else goes hunting and digging up roots.

I'll take a leaf out of his book. I place the clay brick next to the pot and I go around the fire and sit on a rock next to Yaneck. I point to the clay and say *clay.*

He smiles and forms the word perfectly. I nod. He grins.

'I made this when I was a child,' I say, to account for what I regard as pretty shoddy workmanship. Also, as insurance in case the bastard thing explodes or just plain fails.

Yaneck says nothing. He picks up a twig and holds it out. He says the word for it.

And like that we are off on another linguistic marathon. One that doesn't pause when after two hours (I'm working via the sun so it's rough) the fire has burned low, and the pot appears to have dried out and gone rigid. Yaneck only stops when I wander off to gather some deadfall from the forest above the caves. He resumes when I return.

I scrape out the glowing coals so there is an ember-free centre a bit wider than the pot is. I place the pot here and build a thick tepee of wood around it. We watch it catch. I learn what I think is the word for *a small tepee of wood on a fire.* Whether it describes the structure in general terms – I don't dare ask.

———

The fire has burned low again. The shadows are longer. I think my counting of the days got screwed whilst I spent two weeks withdrawing, then several weeks weeping on my bedroll. I think we must be in April. I should work out a way to tell the time. Then I realise it doesn't matter what the time is. Yaneck doesn't seem to pay it any heed.

Many of the women are returning to camp, some with smug expressions and bulging sacks, others looking more careworn and empty-handed. None of them want to look at me, and they don't pay any heed to the ash-covered lump that sits amongst the coals. That's fine. Fuck off already.

None of the men are back. I go and get some of the damn heating rocks from the cave, along with a litre-sized birch-bark container. I take a big pinch of some dried mint (or its pre-hybridized palaeolithic equivalent) that Urla keeps on her shelves at the side of the cave. I place the rocks in the fire and go across to the stream to fill the container. Then I seat myself next to Yaneck and wait.

He keeps up with the language lessons, asking me inane questions. He asks me if I'm hungry. He asks me how old I am, again. He asks me about how I made my trousers so very blue. He means my jeans. Now that I think about it, I realise that I have no idea what happened to them. I say that someone else made them and I don't know how they did it, though I don't put it as fluently as that.

He begins to hum, then to sing. I don't know what to make of *that*, so I start on the tea. I use two sticks to prod the stones from the fire. Holding them with the makeshift tongs I blow on them to get rid of as much ash as possible. Bastard ash. Then I pop them in the birch-bark container. They sizzle and the water spits and froths, coming to the boil inside of a minute. I add the mint leaves and lever out the stones. Wait ten minutes and the liquid has cooled enough. I tip some of the mint tea (ashy, of course, but still recognizably and palatably mint tea) into two wooden bowls and hand one to Yaneck. He stops singing and nods a thank-you.

I wave at Brekel and Zander, who have been knapping flint by the cave, and I point at the tea, and not wanting to attract too much attention by shouting, I hold up my cup. They come over.

It's cosy. The air has cooled. The sun is going down, and it'll be setting inside of another two hours. The two men exchange pleasantries, thank me, and sip their tea. They talk with Yaneck. Something about hunting. Something about hazelnuts, skins, and fat. Lots about fat. Fat is a big thing around here. They store it in skin bags for winter. Fat is the most energy-dense food available, and they clearly know it. The last stores ran out about seven days ago, and everyone's hungry. *Really* hungry. A few old nuts and a palmful of dried berries each day does not fill the stomach – or the soul.

Yaneck says that the hunt will be successful. I trust Yaneck, but I'm not sure he can see the future. I'm wondering if I should take the pot out of the fire when we hear a whistle. Distant. The three men stand up like they've been stung on their asses. I copy them. We all listen. Women, wandering here and there and bent over their various tasks – they all freeze.

We listen. Another whistle-blast, coming from the east. The tone warbles. They are communicating. And it must be a pretty welcome sound, as everyone starts smiling and slapping each other on the back. The four of us and the women and the kids nearby – we all run to the brow of the little hill on the eastern side of the plain.

The men are heading our way in single file. Most of them are hefting large loads over their shoulders. Unless they came across a particularly well-stocked supermarket freezer section, I'd say they've had a successful hunt.

I salivate like a hungry dog. Or a wolf. On that note I remember my plan to domesticate the species, but I file it away for consideration once I've mastered pottery and the art of getting wasted for the entirety of winter.

The women hurry back to the large stack of deadfall that many of them have been building throughout the day. They bring this over to the fire which has almost burned out apart from a few glowing embers. They chuck branches on it. My pot!

Without any social niceties, I elbow my way through them and grab the upper rim, which I'm praying is not so hot that it welds my skin to its surface. It isn't, and I manage to get it out in one piece. The women hiss at me and suck their teeth, smacking their lips to express their displeasure. Screw them. I spent all day on that pot. They don't pay it, or me, any more attention.

I find I *have* burned my fingers. A little.

The meat came disassembled. Which is to say, the men butchered the two deer where they had killed them. They gutted and skinned the carcasses, then cut them up into sections for carrying. I only know they were deer because the men brought the heads with them. I worried – perhaps they were going to do something weird with them. Make hats? Honestly, it's hard to keep up sometimes.

It turns out that the heads were for eating as well.

Of course they were. Why not? It's the fucking head of an animal. Why *not* eat it?

The brains, the eyes, the flesh of the cheeks, the lips and the tongue. They probably even ate the ears, toasted them like crispy bacon, though I didn't stick around to see that. I turned away when they thwacked open the first skull with a hand-axe. I retreated to the quieter end of the fire. The women had built it slim and long, so it could be used to roast several spits of meat laid crossways across the fire.

It's dark. Early evening, though without the sun I've lost track of the time. Yaneck says he will teach me to study the stars and the moon. The air is colder, and I'm grateful for the large fire and the bellyful of roasted venison and the side of liver. I feel stronger, less light-headed, and quite comfortable. Once everyone has stuffed themselves, Tazak stands up and makes a speech. I don't try to listen. I'm exhausted. He talks all about the hunt, though I lose most of the details. Then he calls on Weasel, who he hands most of the credit to, and sits down.

Weasel stands up and begins what must be special night-time entertainment: a re-enactment of this hunt. He's the one who picked up the trail of the deer, and his spear struck home first.

So somehow this makes him king of the castle. To be fair, he's part of the reason we are all eating so well. I suppose I am grateful, but it's annoying to watch him prance and mince around, miming *looking, following, running, throwing a fucking spear.*

Talk about edge-of-your-seat-stuff.

He makes a comment just before he sits down. I'm not listening much at this point, or at least I'm trying not to listen, but I hear my name and something about *useful.* It's obviously a well-crafted joke, to judge by the roar of laughter from the enraptured crowd. He has the gift of the gab, that's sure enough.

I say nothing. To my shocked surprise, the barb cuts me *deep*, in a manner I haven't felt for years. Why? Well, I suppose that we are here in a wildness that is not just the *countryside* outside of a city teeming with humans, but an entire *planet* of pure wilderness. And being the butt of a joke suddenly feels desperately scary. If people joke about you, and you have no perceived use, then logically you must be expendable.

Tribal ostracism is a well-known killer: the person cursed and cast out for some unpardonable crime was recorded by anthropologists as lapsing into madness, then delirium, and then physical death. The assumption was that the psychological injury of ostracism was so shattering that it compromised the physical functioning of the body. Their brains shut down their bodies, and they died.

I get it. Sitting here, being laughed at, feeling well and truly expendable, *is* truly terrifying. Soul-destroying. I feel like I am one joke away from being shown the exit onto the lonely Eurasian steppe, where my only company will be antelopes, trees, and the odd coterie of cave lions.

I get up, grab my pot, and stalk off towards the cave. I glance at Sara, who I've avoided looking at for the whole of the evening. She's laughing. Sudden tears sting my eyes. I put my back to their entire stupid bastard feast and fuck off to the cave.

In the cave, a small fire sputters in the hearth. I hide the pot in my (meagre) pile of donated furs. I lie down, tuck myself into my bedroll and turn on my side, facing the cave wall, thinking again for the thousandth time that I've got the worst spot in the cave.

I decide that come the morning I will smash the pot to smithereens, borrow some spears, and bugger off into the great beyond. If I have to go, I'll do it on my own terms.

I *hate* being laughed at. But I am bone tired, and the wave of fright and adrenaline has wiped me out: while I'm laying my plans for world domination, I fall fast asleep, and I don't wake until the dawn.

14

I'm awake before anyone else. Even the children are still asleep. I feel happy for a few moments, then I remember the previous night's humiliation. A winter darkness smothers my thinking.

Fucking *primates*.

I remember my decision to strike out on my own, Lewis and Clark style. They were the first European explorers to cross North America.

But Lewis had Clark, and vice versa. And they planned ahead. A lot. And they had guns. Rifles and so on. A shit-ton of ammo for fending off the pesky North American Indians who had been living there for millennia. Probably the Indians thought that since they were there first, it meant white people shouldn't come along and steal all their shit, kill them, and generally destroy their way of life.

I don't even know how to start a fire.

Well. OK. I decide to put off having the *I'm-running-away* tantrum.

Think logically.

A hide drape is across the entrance to the cave. I slip past it and stand looking south, towards the river. The turbulence in my head smooths out a little.

The sun has not risen yet, but the sky has lightened to the blue of pale blue eyes, a violet scudded by white-grey puffball clouds edged in purple and pink. The brightest stars still glitter from their sentinels, their younger light reaching me in an older world. A *younger* world, I correct myself, but now as I stand here watching it, I feel that this world *is* older and wiser – beyond imagining – than the gouged, raped and hobbled one that I travelled away from not so long ago.

Not wisdom, perhaps. How can a planet or an ecological system be *wise*? It is just a *thing* and a *system*, after all. There is no intelligence, either wise or stupid.

But this beauty I'm seeing. . . The river flows, the sun rises, the stars shine, the clouds drift and snow hares bounce between the drifts of snow, and the birds – their sound absent to my ears for months now – have started their songs, their spring and summer lives. Sap will be rising in the trees behind me, gathering in their buds, building the leaves and flowers that will be visited by bees untroubled by the synthetic perfumes of weedkillers and acid rain.

It will all *unfold*, unconscious of itself, and what can be a purer consciousness than that which lacks a sense of itself – an ego?

The same feeling as that which I felt hearing Yaneck's swansong to winter creeps over me – a melting of myself into the earth around me, into the air and into the sky, an indivisible stretching. Becoming mixed. Like water is, in water.

This growing wonder is rudely interrupted by a sound behind me. One of the children, it sounds like. I realise I am clutching my pot loosely in one hand. OK. I didn't notice picking it up, but there you go.

In the stream I wash my pot, treating it as delicately as the ivory keys of an antique grand piano. With a handful of river sand and grit, I don't scrub it – it's more of a caress. The pot is heavy in my hands, the walls thick and hard, but I've no idea how brittle it is. When it's clean I fill it with water. I drink from it. The water is clean, fresh, a slight earthy taste, but so what? I sit the pot on the ground. It sits there. It holds the water and doesn't explode or leak. It doesn't melt. Good so far.

I stir up the ashes at one end of the long fire from last night's feast. Last night's Charlie slagging-off session. A few glowing coals. I take the Y-shaped branches that had served as spit holders and place them either side of the coals. I find an unused stem of birch as the crossbar. Then I realise that I've been a dummy – there are no handles on the bastard pot, so how in Christ am I going to hang it off the crossbar?

No worries. I go back into the cave and *borrow* a length of cord that is some sort of braided sinew or root. Urla is asleep, so she won't mind.

'Charlie?'

It's Boy Wonder. His actual name in their language is Willow, which I think is an awesome name since it actually is the same name that they have for a willow tree. All of the other names seem just made-up horseshit. Like Tazak. Tazak is a bit of legend, but still, there is no such thing as a *Tazak*. Why not call everyone Tiger, Lion, Spear, Flint, Rock, Gazelle, Toad? You get

the idea. Much cooler. Tazak should be called *Grizzly Fuckin'
Bear* or something similarly badass.

I'm excited by my experiment with the pot.

I look at Willow and put my finger to my lips. I wink at him. He
giggles and winks back. I motion for him to follow quietly, and
he does. If I leave him in the cave, he will wake everyone up,
and I'd rather conduct this matter with as few people around as
possible.

I get the cord around the outward flare of the mouth of the pot,
and I string it up so it hangs from the crossbar. Slightly
lopsided, but screw it: it is a water-filled earthenware pot,
hanging a foot above a fire. I add a few small twigs to the fire.
Willow watches, his gaze only mildly curious.

When the flames have caught, I add a few more twigs, nothing
thicker than a fat thumb, keeping the flames wide and low.

I sit next to Willow. I practice my words.

'How did you sleep?' I ask.

'Like a bear!'

'Very good,' I reply.

'What are you doing with that?' He points at the pot dangling
over the fire.

'I am boiling water.'

His eyes go wide. Then they narrow. He gets up and peers
inside the pot. The rude little bastard sticks his hand in.

'It is cold.'

'Give it a hundred breaths.'

He's not really a rude little bastard. He's a sweet kid. He taught me words when everyone avoided me. He's brought me little things – trinkets and little gifts of food. He's a sweet and generous child. He picks up a small hand axe and whittles the end of a straight small pole. He tires of this fast.

'I'm hungry,' he announces.

'Willow,' I say, pointing towards the cave. 'Bring me a hand of your mother's morning herbs. Do not wake her.'

I wink at him. He grins, returns the wink, and scoots off, leaving me rather smug at my command of the language. I'm not quite at university level, but I reckon that's not far off. I just need to work on the more esoteric vocabulary. Smooth out the use of tenses. The pluperfect, the past, the future, the way the verbs adjust. When people speak slowly, I reckon I get eighty per cent.

Willow runs back to me. Willow is always running. Yaneck says he's eight seasons old, but he already has defined abs, and his body has the sinewy grace of a karate champion. I suppose that's what a lack of TV and crisps does for you.

I think that for my next trick I'm going to show Willow how to make willow bark tea. The bark contains the chemical salicin, which when ingested, is metabolised eventually into salicylic acid, commonly translated as aspirin. This tribe use willow a lot – they split the long slim branches and weave baskets, among other things, but I've seen no-one making willow bark tea. And I've seen Urla treating people with headaches, fevers, toothaches. Whatever she uses, willow bark is not among them. Willow will be credited with the discovery, and I'll have a solid ally. I hope. I sorely need them.

On a side note, you can also get your aspirin from beaver's asses. I mean it. They have a gland in their asses, or at least their tails, that produces a yellow goo that has something to do with scent-marking their territory. Beavers chew up and eat a lot of willow, and metabolise it into salicylic acid, which accumulates in their ass scent-glands. People used to use the contents as a painkiller. This is a major digression. But useful knowledge. Out here in butt-balls nowhere.

Willow hands me the herbs. I don't know exactly what they are. The odour is a typical leaf smell, a bit like fresh meadow grass. But they *are* used to make tea. I put them in the water, which I can see is warming. Willow goes back to his whittling. I wait, watching the sky above the hills to the east. The rim of that distant rise, still capped in snow, is glowing bright pink.

Steam begins to rise from the pot. My heart is thudding, my pulse doing a merry hop. I strip off the bark from a switch of birch and I stir. More steam rises, then a few bubbles appear. Less than a minute later the crazy bastard pot is boiling – actually boiling! I'm trembling with excitement (and fear that it will all just disintegrate) and I leave it for another full minute, counting Mississippi's all the way to sixty.

I kick the twigs and embers from beneath it, and when I realize I've singed my leather footwear I get a larger stick and properly scrape away all the coals and embers until the ground is bare baked earth. I want to leave the pot hanging, untroubled. Just in case.

Steam rises!

'Willow, would you like tea?'

Of course, the answer is *yes*.

'Please bring us two cups.'

In a jiffy he's up to the cave and back, but he must have woken his mother because by the time we have scooped out a wooden cup of the tea and are sitting blowing on it, she appears at the mouth of the cave. Salanda is one of the women who is most comfortable around me – which is to say that she's not outwardly hostile and rude to me. She's a slim and wiry lady with dark hair and angular good looks. All she needs is a pair of spectacles and she'd be hot – in a sexy librarian sort of way.

She walks over.

'Willow, what are you *doing*?' She emphasises the last word like she might do if she caught him defecating on the table during a five-course meal.

Willow looks unhappy, but he is part of something unusual – special – even if he doesn't know it consciously. He whines an appeal: 'We are having tea, watching the sun come.'

I watch her eyes wander over us, the bowls in our hands, the fire, the pot hanging from the crossbar. Steam, as visible as smoke in the cold morning air, froths from the round clay vessel.

Fuck you all to hell. I made me some goddamn *pottery*.

'Willow!' she says, her face tight. 'Come here!'

He gets up and goes to her. Salanda takes the cup from his hands, sniffs it, then upends the contents onto the ground. She grabs his arm and marches him back to the cave. I hear screeching. Within a minute people begin streaming out.

I become scared. Memories of lighting my cigarette come to mind. I've been a damn fool, again. Clearly, they will say that I magicked this shit from the air and I'm an evil ne'er-do-well.

Oh *shit*.

I *was* so excited. Now I'm going to get the shit kicked out of me. Or speared to death, burnt at the stake, or drowned in the river.

Take your pick. Suddenly, in my stomach, anger squirts like flame-hot vinegar and curdles the fear. I feel sick. And now I'm *angry*. This shit isn't magic, I want to scream. Suddenly I want to stamp and shout and tell these dumbfuck pricks that there is no such thing as *fucking magic*. Of course, I don't. That would be an own goal.

They gather in a wide semi-circle in front of me. I remain sitting, which is as unthreatening a move as any evil warlock or wizard can make. Willow's half-sharpened kid's spear lies near my right foot. I suppose if they try and grab me. . .

Salanda is speaking, her voice loud and high. She is scared. She says something about poison, about making stuff, trying to brainwash her child (*brainwash* is my translation).

Perhaps there's even a charge of child molestation thrown in. Who knows? She speaks so rapidly I miss a lot. Other voices join hers, but no one moves towards me. They are waiting for Tazak, who ambles towards us.

Taking his sweet goddamn time if you ask me.

Meanwhile I notice something heartening: Blondebeard and Grease Monkey have picked their way through the crowd and have come to the edge of it at my far right. They step ever so slightly away from the crowd. I hope this means *we are on your side*. That trek after they found me meant something to them. They saw me as human, and a scared one at that, and even though I have seen little of them over the winter, they always nodded at me with a smile. They have been friendly, at the very least.

'What is THIS?' Tazak booms out the last word to silence the nattering, accusing crowd. He points at Salanda. 'Well?'

She unleashes another torrent, pointing at me, the pot, Willow.

When she has finished, Tazak looks at me and repeats the question.

'Well?'

I don't know what to say. I'm in the process of shrugging when all our heads turn at the sound of a whistle. It comes from the level ground above the caves. I see nothing for a moment, and then a shape moves. Yaneck unfolds himself from the ground, along with John Wayne – Culeg. No one speaks whilst these two folks walk to where the caves end, and the slope of the hill is even enough to walk down. Tazak goes back to staring at the pot. Everyone else watches Yaneck and Culeg approach.

'I saw it all,' says Yaneck, his voice light and idle. He speaks slowly and carefully – I suppose for my benefit, but it serves to add gravity to his words.

'I sat and watched Charlie *make* this yesterday.' He points at the pot.

'He made it from sticky mud. He made it using only his two hands, carefully, the way a man makes a flint blade. Culeg and I watched Charlie this morning, finishing off his work.'

Muttering breaks out but Tazak raises his hand sharply, cutting the sound off. Yaneck carries on.

'We work flint into blades. Is there life in the flint? We believe there is. Perhaps there is life, a little magic, in this. . . mud. Charlie's people discovered it, and released it, the same way our fathers and mothers did in the flint and the trees and the animals.'

There is silence as Yaneck, followed by Culeg (who I think must be Yaneck's shamanic disciple) moves through the crowd to the hanging pot. Yaneck touches it with no hesitation and runs his finger around the rim.

'It is a vessel, fashioned from mud and water. Shaped carefully by human hands and hardened in fire. It is all of these things, and it is nothing more.'

He motions for my empty cup. I hand it to him. He dips it into the pot, draws it out, steaming slightly. He blows on it, then takes a sip.

'Tea,' he announces, shrugging his shoulders as if reaching the punchline of a deadpan joke. Then he smiles. 'Without ash,' he adds. He tilts his head at me.

'Charlie, how long can you keep this bowl on the fire?'

'I am a novice. I learned from my people. I am very bad at making. If I practice... properly... it can stay on the fire for...' I make the motion that means *for a full turn of a day and a night.*

'And it holds water without losing any?'

'Yes, it will.'

'So, you can cook meat in it. Stew.' This doesn't seem to be a question, but I reply in the affirmative.

There is a long silence. People look at each other, at me, at the object hanging beneath the spit-bar.

Yaneck breaks into a chant, a singsong. I catch some of the words. Something along the lines of a blessing for a showing by mother nature of a gift to humans. That's a very loose translation. It lasts several minutes. No one interrupts.

Yaneck finishes. Everyone looks at Tazak. He smiles.

15

They say that life can turn on a dime. In this case my dime is Yaneck. For the second time (that I know of) my execution as a heretical heathen dumbfuck has been averted. The first time I had the presence of mind to shit my pants. This second time I owe clearly to Yaneck, the sneaky dawn-meditating bastard. Thank God for Yaneck.

The dime does a complete one-eighty-degree spin. The women crowd around the pot, basically cooing like lovesick doves. They might be savages, but they are as clever as modern humans, and I can practically see the thoughts in their heads. They are all yammering questions at me.

Because all of a sudden, all sorts of technological hurdles have been jumped. No more faffing about with hot rocks, no more endless making of birch-bark containers and wooden cooking bowls. All of these have a finite lifespan – you can only heat stuff in a birch-bark container about five times before it gets all flaky and starts to disintegrate. Now, cooking vessels can be large or small, portable, and last for years. You can cook stuff for as long as you want. You could boil a bird or a badger for an entire week if you really felt that was necessary. Now food can be stored, the mouths of the pottery stopped up with wooden corks or whatever these people can rustle up that serves well.

This is basically like inventing a washing machine. One with a ten-kilo capacity and a built-in dryer. No wonder this gang of bunny-boilers are doing backflips.

They crowd around and gabble at me. Tazak pushes his way through them.

'One at a time,' he says.

The questions go on and on. Yaneck moderates. He's like a president taking questions at a podium. He points to one woman, and she gushes a question. I try and answer. Then he points to another.

How big can you make it? What shapes? How long will it last? How hot can you cook a stew? Where can I get the clay? (I teach them my word for it) *Make another one! Make two! Show me!*

An hour passes. Eventually Yaneck, Culeg and Tazak usher them away. The men stand around talking about sizes and storage and practical stuff. The women stand at a distance screeching like loons. In a good way.

After months on the bench, all of a sudden I am the golden boy. All the women smiled warmly at me, touched me on the shoulder and arm, rubbed my cheek with the backs of their hands (a gesture of affection for a friend, nothing sexual - apparently).

Now that I've done something useful, I'm suddenly human to them. They think I'm the best thing that ever happened to them.

Women. Deceitful wenches. Two-faced harpies.

But it's better than the way it was before. Light years ahead. I'm numbed by the affection. Tazak sits next to me. He takes my hands in his.

'Thank you for this gift.' His big brown eyes are as unblinking as ever. A sincere man, through and through. A *stand-up guy*, I think the phrase was – will be.

'It is beginning,' I say. 'I do not know much about. . .' I point at the pot, which is hanging there with Culeg standing guard next to it. I want to say *we all must experiment,* but I don't know the word.

'We must. . . play with it. Everyone plays. . .' I mime handling, chucking, shaping, scratching my head, furrowing my eyebrows, more handling, shaping.

Tazak says the word. Yaneck nods. *Experiment.*

'Yes, we all make big experiment.' I say it like this and Tazak smiles, wide and sunny. *Yes*, he says. *We will.*

I walk towards the cave. Everyone stares at me – the women particularly. They are all smiles and nods. Sara is among them, smiling at me, but I can't scrub the image of her laughing at me last night.

Wait, she wasn't exactly laughing at *me* – she was laughing at the joke. That seems like I'm giving her the benefit of the doubt, and I know I'm only doing this because of how insanely hot she is. I look at my feet and continue walking. She's as pretty as a prayer book, sweet as an apple on Christmas day, she's as –

I look up. Weasel is sitting outside his cave, staring at me as I approach. His eyes are slits, and his mouth is twisted in a bizarre and evil upside-down grin, showing his gritted teeth. The kind of face you'd have if you just got bitten by a big and hairy spider and then fell over, screamed, stood up, and then stomped on the horrible little bastard.

A look of savage disgust and hatred.

That sort of face does not scream *best buds forever*.

Tazak seems to have a soft spot for the guy. God knows why. I suppose it might be that being a weasel, he's very cunning – a talent that is sorely needed to survive in this hard, hard paradise.

Being cunning probably means he's handy at manipulation.

This is a problem I didn't foresee.

I don't stare back. I just look at my feet and go into the cave, where I lie down on my bedroll. It's probably only 8am, and I felt fresh as a daisy when I woke up before dawn. Now I feel like I've spent several hours being dragged through a hedge, backwards.

I close my eyes, meaning to get an hour's kip or so. As I do this, all the jigsaw pieces of the last twenty-four hours fall neatly into place, and I see the full picture: Weasel is sore because I've stolen his big moment. I've swooped down and whipped away his thunder. That big performance, his dancing and mincing last night; with his success at the hunt he was going to be the star for the foreseeable future, for at least several weeks. He'd broken the long and hard fast of early spring when food was critically low. And now all the meat-drying racks have strips of venison spread out on them and he should be basking in the spotlight, strutting amongst the glory of his achievement. The spotlight has left him and now he's sitting alone, in the shadow of the cave, all but forgotten.

The focus has shifted from him to a far distant universe where all anyone can talk and think about is the magic of earthenware pottery, and how it's all thanks to Charlie.

Shit. I think we all know someone like Weasel. Or we have at least had a brief encounter with them, shuddered, and turned away. In small doses he might have his uses, but in larger doses he's a toxin, causing disease and illness in everything that surrounds him. The Greeks prescribed one leaf of hemlock for fevers but advised that five leaves could kill a grown man.

This kind of person never forgets or forgives a slight. And I think Weasel is like this. I hope I am proved to be wrong.

Granted, *I've* been quite toxic for most of my adult life. I've stolen stuff, lied and cheated. I lost all my friends, all my family. It's easy to blame the booze and the drugs. I do have principles, but these always dissolved when they stood between me and feeding a habit, a craving I couldn't control – one I didn't even try to control.

Here, without the booze and drugs, I feel non-toxic, in a social sense. I *like* being kind. I *enjoy* being helpful and seeing the smiles of thanks on people's faces, the small joy that you see fill someone's soul when you do something just plain *kind*.

If it's *easy* to blame my past behaviour on the booze and the drugs, then what is it that is *hard* to blame my past behaviour on? I have no answer to this.

Fuck it, I say to myself as I stare up at the cave ceiling, *I'm an ok person and I blame the booze and the drugs*. I banish Weasel's evil bastard face from my thoughts and fill it with Sara's smile. Prettier than the dawn I just watched. By a million miles.

I fall asleep.

16

Spring is a stormy month. The gusty days bring with them hail and rain. The buds on the trees grow fat from the rain and the freshening sunlight that follows the showers, and in the warming air they unfold into acid-green leaves. The food from the hunt is rationed. In the first moon of spring the animals are apparently scarce. It's not like they are hiding – I get the impression that there are migratory patterns.

Caribou are apparently a thing, here in ice age Europe. It makes sense – as the centuries pass and the ice retreats into the future, the caribou will move north into Siberia and Scandinavia. They obviously get off on the cold. They dig the big chill.

If I ever get a tattoo, I think I will get *dig the big chill* tattooed across my butt cheeks.

I'm also led to understand that this tribe goes off on a few hunting expeditions every summer, mainly to hunt caribou. Not sure if I want to go. I want to build a clay-brick house and start an apiary. Make some pottery and start up a mead factory.

Get hammered. Experiment. Maybe I'll try and dredge up a hidden memory of how to smelt iron.

While I'm on a roll, what about gunpowder? It is a mix of sulphur, carbon, and potassium nitrate, but even if I can source some sulphur, I think the potassium nitrate will be too tricky. Think it can be derived from guano – bird poo – but you might need a chemistry set to figure it out.

Copper is perhaps not beyond the realm of possibility: you need to dig up/mine copper carbonate (known commonly as malachite), and really just heat it to melting point, whereupon the carbon and oxygen separate, leaving you with lovely pure copper to smack into cauldrons, frying pans, shields, and spear points.

In the meantime, I'd really like to have sex with someone. After a winter of sit-ups, press-ups, lunges, and shadowboxing, then a spring fast to tighten everything up, I feel pretty awesome. With that comes a desperate need to get laid. Masturbating is ok, but even twice a day is not depressing my sex drive. The needle remains firmly in the red, nudging the mark that says *basically a sex pest*.

The problem is that there are no available women. The adult females of this tribe are all paired with men. The non-adult contingent are all pre-pubescent or pubescent girls. I'd rather stick to masturbating.

Except for Sara. She must be eighteen or nineteen. Very much a woman. But she's not with a man. She is permanently surrounded by the older women. Like they are protecting her from something. Or are they protecting everyone else? Impossible to tell. Maybe she's clinically insane. Maybe she killed her last husband. Mistook him for a bear and stabbed him to death in a psychotic frenzy.

I've seen nothing to suggest that this tribe has much conception of free love. The women have been unerringly kind since the pottery business, but after nearly being executed twice for the high-crimes of wizard-fire and pottery magic, I'm going to avoid the less cosmically dangerous but probably more insulting crime of diddling another dude's dame.

I'm not going to rub another man's rhubarb.

Now that I think about it, Urla seems to have no one, except for Yaneck about once every few weeks. But she appears to like it like this. And she shows absolutely no interest in me anyway. Yaneck is a monk, except for when Urla gives it up. Everyone is getting it on. Except for me.

Perhaps Sara is a witch. Perhaps she's promised to some fella in another tribe. I have no idea. Whenever I ask Yaneck about her, he sniffs and mutters, saying only *women's business.*

Indeed.

In the warming days, the women and men go down to the river and wash in the still-freezing water. There is a lack of any rules surrounding nudity. They also don't seem to mind me sitting on a rock, chewing a stem of grass and perving like some public park masturbator. I sit cross legged because most of the time I have an erection.

Can you blame me? Really?

Sara's skin is a cream white, her eyes a sparkling verdigris green beneath smoothly arching eyebrows. A cute nose that I want to kiss all day long. Lips that are crying-plump and stained with a wine of pure sexiness. Her hair is ripe-hay blonde and when unfastened from the pretty tresses she wears, it falls in waves to the middle of her back. A slim waist below which swells an ass and legs that would halt motorway traffic.

Her breasts are *Grecian goddess*, full, untroubled by gravity, the small nipples pointing forty-five degrees upwards, as if straight to Venus which hangs in the sky at sunset only because it has this divine creature here on Earth as a protectorate.

Her pubic mound is neatly furred in blonde (I'm honestly *not* making this up). I could think about it all day long.

Her right arm has a pattern of defined scars from her lower shoulder across her bicep to her elbow. Whatever injury it was, it must have hurt. A lot. She wears the scars like a pro: it looks like a badass tattoo a sexy warrior-woman might have.

She probably is one.

I want to rest my head on her tummy the way you sometimes do with a girl after making love – you flop down between their legs so you can put your chin on their tummy and kiss it for hours whilst saying *I love you*. I want to care for her and make babies with her. I want her to hold *me* like a baby.

It's clear that I am in love. Or in lust. Either. Both.

I tell myself it's an honest and noble love. One that soars above mere mortal trifles.

I tell myself it cannot be love because I don't actually *know* her. I repeatedly and feverishly tell myself that she might be a complete bitch.

To be fair, many of the adult men in the tribe lust after her. I see the looks. I'm not alone. I sit on the rock today, having washed earlier. I tried it once at the same time as them and I got an erection for my trouble. Since then, I don't wash at the same time. I turn away and decide to go up into the forest to masturbate. It's almost tedious.

Where was I? Oh yes: spring. That time of year when stuff blossoms.

I'd kiss my way up her thighs, higher and higher to kiss her. . .

Jesus!

Slightly doubled up, I walk away from the river towards the slope to the left of the caves. As I pass them, Yaneck emerges and flags me down. Something is on his mind. He motions towards the flat rocks that are seats next to a fire that has burned low. My morning jerk-off session will have to wait.

'What other things do you know?' he asks.

He's asked me this question several times and every time I've just shrugged my shoulders and said 'nothing.' But he keeps asking me. In truth, I know stuff like fermentation and copper and bees and crops. None of which has caught on in these parts. But I know I will stumble through them, and it'll be an experiment, a bit like the pottery. It will be easier to show him things, rather than explain. Now, I line up the words in a row, and I speak slowly, trying to get the grammar correct. I think I manage ok.

'I will show you new things,' I say. 'But I will not get them right at first. Other people did them. I only watched. I will have to experiment.' I still think their word for *experiment* means roughly the same in English. Without all the scientific connotations of course. I add a riding clause. Small print.

'But I would like you to show me things.'

'Like what?'

'Healing herbs, plants, tracking, animals, the stars.' I gesture around me. 'I want you to show me your life.'

He nods happily. 'Culeg is learning all this. You can join him in his lessons.' I *love* the idea of hanging out with Culeg and Yaneck, but I'm not finished bargaining.

'But I want to know two other things, now.'

Yaneck looks at me, the happy grin fading away. He sighs.

'What two things?'

'Raka.'

Raka is Weasel's name. I have learned their word for weasel. Sadly, it sounds nothing like *Raka*.

'What about Raka?' Yaneck is a master of the poker-face, but a sliver of something like a shiver slips over him.

'Everything,' I say.

'It is not wise to talk about people. Their stories are their own to tell.'

I sit in silence – a trick I'm picking up from him. Eventually Yaneck sighs again and begins speaking.

'Raka is the best tracker in our people. He is the best knapper of flint. He finds things easily. People say he was born with more luck than is usual. He took some else's luck. It does not matter. He is important to us.'

And that's it. Yaneck shuts his trap. He says no more, despite me pressing. What I actually want to know is why Raka is such a slimy little bastard. I want to dig into his background. Why doesn't he have a woman? Why does he seem to have so much *hate* inside him? Mainly I want to know why I'm so worried that he'll fuck me over at the first opportunity. I'm not stupid.

Yaneck isn't playing ball.

'He hates me,' I say.

Yaneck nods and prompts me.

'The other thing?'

'Sara.'

Yaneck sniffs.

I lay down my ace: 'If you want me to show you more things, then tell me something about her.'

I hear myself stepping over a boundary that I only just realise is there. He's the shaman, and I'm bargaining with him as if I'm his equal. He looks at me, distaste rising in spots of colour on his cheeks. I see my mistake, and I start to mumble, to backtrack, but he cuts me off, his words more of a hiss than speech.

'Sara's birth mother died delivering her. *That* is not uncommon. But the father, one of our best hunters; his mind was taken by the Earth. He became as immobile as stone. He sat for two seasons, staring into space. At the end of Sara's second season, he walked out of the cave in the middle of the night. We found him the next day. Dead. He cut his wrists with a blade.'

'Jesus.' I say this in English, shaking my head.

'It is the worst death. An insult to the Earth. It brings bad, bad luck. The worst luck. It was agreed that Sara be sent out to join her father, to placate his spirit. She was brought up into the forest and left where we found his body. She could not yet walk. It was near winter. Cold. She would die from cold or be taken by an animal.'

'Fuck's sake.' I realise I've spoken again in English. Yaneck ignores me.

'We stayed in the cave, waiting for the Earth to take her. But on the second day a she-wolf brought her back, holding her arm in her jaws.'

'A wolf... *brought her back*?'

'It was nearby, passing. Tazak, then a young boy and ignorant of this business, saw the wolf near the front of the cave and pelted rocks at it. It dropped Sara and fled.'

Yaneck holds up his index finger.

'The first night, Sara *should* have died of cold.'

He ticks off a second finger.

'The second day a wolf got her. She *should* have been taken away, eaten.'

He flips a third finger alongside the two.

'The bites in her arm were deep and she bled very much. You see the scars she carries. She *should* have died from that by the third day - that and fever from the poison in the wolf's teeth.'

Yaneck runs a hand over his nearly bald head, and lets out a long breath.

'But the Earth wanted Sara to stay with us. Mother Earth gave her back to us. For his part, and without any prompting from anyone else, Tazak took to mothering the girl, and her older brother, Raka.'

I look at my fingers. There is mud and clay under the nails. I pick at them. My thoughts are jumbled. Raka – her *brother*? I try and gather my thoughts. Eventually I speak.

'But Raka wants to. . .' I search for the right word. There is no vulgar word for sexual intercourse in their language. There's *forced sexual intercourse* of course, but that's not it. Nor is the term for mutually desired sex. I find the word. It equates to the English word for *join*, but expressed in a sexual context.

'But Raka wants to join with her.'

Yaneck shakes his head.

'It is allowed. You see, Raka was not the birth child of Sara's parents. Raka was an orphan, the birth child of a man and woman who joined us, who trekked far from the south, away from their own tribe. They never explained why. They were sick. Our shaman at the time cared for them. They were starving. Raka, a mere babe, was near death. The parents died. Raka survived and was adopted by Sara's parents, who were childless, and who had given up all hope of having a child. Shortly after the adoption, Sara's mother became pregnant.'

Yaneck's expression shifts. He moves from controlled anger into something approaching curiosity, or even philosophy.

'From that time, Sara has lived a life of two sides. She is both unlucky and lucky. She *is* free to leave – if that is her wish. But the women will not risk the anger of the Earth by prompting her to leave, and certainly they would never attempt to expel her again. But as long as she is here, they keep her close. They will not see her join with a man and have children, for fear that it will express the bad, rather than the good. I think they want her to either just leave, or to grow old and die.'

'What does Sara think of Raka?' I ask.

Yaneck looks at me. He knows where I'm trying to get to, but he evades it.

'It is said that Raka took his adopted parent's luck, and none was left for Sara. But the Earth does not want her, yet. As for their relationship. . . it is complicated.'

'And you?'

'Me what?'

'What do *you* think?'

'I believe that humans will live and die. That we will pass through Earth like all animals do. We were like animals once, before the sun burned off most of our fur. Luck is important, yes. Whether bad or good, it exists as a spirit that surrounds a man or woman. It ebbs and flows, moving from one to another as the Earth wills it. But what do I think? Well, I think that we meddle too much. Luck will come and go, and we will be born, and we will die. All anyone can do is live. That's all we are good for.'

He points a finger at me.

'We make bad decisions, all of us. And we make good decisions. Without menfolk, women would be lost. Without womenfolk, men would be lost. But not all decisions are sane. Women can be crazy. Tell anyone this last part and I will cut your balls off.'

For the first time, I see Yaneck not as the magic-man, the shaman, the guy singing songs of thanks and praise and performing rain dances; I see him as a living, breathing, shitting, grinning, walking, talking, get-laid-once-a-month human being. A man. A dude who points at you and says *I will cut your balls off.*

I stare into his eyes, ogling him like a crazy person. Then I chuckle.

Cut your balls off.

I start laughing, aware I wouldn't be able to stop even if he *did* cut my balls off. Yaneck watches me. Tears begin to run down my cheeks. He stares, smiling, and begins to chuckle, shaking his head. At me.

I remember something and laugh harder.

'This... is... like... remember... when... I shit myself?'

Yaneck roars with joy and slaps me on the back so hard I slip off the stone I'm sitting on. My ass thuds onto the ground. I smack him back.

Holding his sides, Yaneck slides slowly down the rock to the ground, shaking with laughter, his own tears running across his cheeks. His body shakes as he topples to lie on his side, still shrieking with glee.

People are gathering nearby to watch. Tazak, a big smile on his bear-face, comes over and with his foot he prods Yaneck in the ribs. Yaneck just laughs harder. Tazak puts his hand on my shoulder and shakes me slightly. I wipe away tears.

'We were just talking,' I say.

Tazak prods Yaneck again in the ribs. Yaneck looks up, still giggling like a loon.

'Yes, Charlie made a joke.'

———

Right. Where was I? OK. After sharing these titbits of information, Yaneck went off, probably to do his morning check-in with the universe. I had a lot to think about. I didn't want to masturbate anymore. I was kind of turned off by the whole *leave the baby on the frozen hillside* routine. Fuck's sake.

Tazak was the kid that saved Sara's life. Yaneck said that he took her and Raka under his wing. I can imagine Tazak, maybe the same age as Willow, just *taking charge*. He would have already been something of the massive brick-shithouse that he has become. And Tazak is kind. He would have become like a father to them. His soft spot for Raka begins to make sense. It's the blind spot that parents have for the foibles of their children.

Obviously, I hadn't spotted Sara and Raka were stepsiblings. All I had seen was him perving after Sara, and I figured he had some sort of magic ticket since he was the only young guy who seemed to have freedom of movement as far as she was concerned. Tazak's missus, Vala, is the leader in the group of witches that chaperone Sara. Vala doesn't shoo Raka away because she sees them both as her kids, sort of.

Sara is like a big sister to Vala and Tazak's twin girls. They are angelic little cherubs, five years old, with the same big brown eyes and chestnut hair as their dad.

Raka ignores the twins but to Sara he brings gifts, trinkets, choice cuts of meat. I don't know what she makes of it. She smiles at him and seems to talk easily with him.

Shitballs.

———

I've managed to get Grease to help me make moulds for clay brick. He's a helpful fella who showed me how to chop down small trees and then split them to make slim boards. One mould will make thirty bricks. I have two moulds, but it's a struggle to find enough firewood to keep firing the bricks properly. I have a stack of nearly a hundred fired bricks.

I fill the mould with clay. A set of bricks are being fired. In the waiting periods, I work on my hive, using the same type of planks I've used for the brick mould. It's rough workmanship, and it all has to be held together with cords: some type of braided root that Urla kindly gave me. Long switches of willow also work: I twist them around the house-like structure I'm creating, using them to patch gaps between the boards. The important part is the home for the queen, and the racks on which the bees will build their honeycomb.

I'm gambling that no one around here is allergic to bee stings.

'A toy,' I say to anyone (everyone) who stops to ask me what the hell I'm up to.

When I'm happy with it I take it to Tazak.

The days are getting longer.

17

I 'm in the forest, looking for bees. I've tried to divide up the area into search grids, but I'm not sure that I'm getting it right. Which translates as me wandering about, so far fruitlessly. Bees should be out now, swarming, looking for new homes. I pad around the forest, stopping every ten steps, listening for any buzzing. All I can hear is my own breathing and the wind rustling. I'd make a terrible hunter. First, I sing *Sugar* by The Archies. Then I belt out *Honey Pie* by The Beatles.

It's late afternoon and I'm humming *Just Like Honey* by The Jesus and Mary Chain, thinking that by *plastic toy* they are referring to a dildo. I blunder into a clearing and find Sara.

Alone, she is on her knees, a digging stick in her hand, a small mound of earth in front of her. She turns her head and sees me.

Oh Christ.

I hold up my hands and start to retreat. Any moment now one of the women who follow her about will launch herself from some bush like a deranged harpy. Away from the safety of the caves, I'll be hunted down in the forest and slaughtered like a dirty pig.

'No, no,' she says. She beckons me forward.

I step forward carefully, scanning the undergrowth. When I reach her, she motions for me to lower myself. I kneel down next to her and sit on my heels. She speaks in a low voice, but hurried, like she's on a time limit.

'I'm sorry I laughed at you,' she says.

'When?'

'After the first hunt. Raka.'

'It was funny,' I say.

'It was not fair,' she says, almost admonishing me. 'I'm sorry.'

I'd rather move on to other things. 'What are you looking for?'

She says a word I don't know. I shrug. She reaches into a small leather bag and pulls out what looks like a gnarled lump of wood. Even without bringing it to my nose, the smell is unmistakable. It's a truffle. A black truffle. Which would retail for about forty grand.

'Where I come from, these are hard to find. Rare. My people will. . . will trade this for much things.'

'*Many* things,' she says, slowly, correcting me.

'Many things,' I say. She smiles at me. Wisps of her blonde hair, lose from her Grecian tresses, touch the pink skin of her lips.

All of the million things I've imagined asking her – I can't remember a single one.

'Where are the other women?' I ask.

'Around,' she says simply. 'But I'm safe.' Her right hand flicks upwards. In it is a small flint knife, produced in the blink of an eye.

I jump. She laughs.

'If they see you, they will curse and scream.' She rolls her eyes. 'So be quiet.'

I mime zipping my lips shut. She looks at me and shakes her head.

'Forget it,' I say.

'You nearly died,' she says. 'When you first arrived. You were so sick. I was worried.'

'About me?' I'm genuinely surprised.

'Of course. You, running around without boots, like the Earth had taken your mind. Then, you fell down, all naked.'

'You remember?' It seems to me like this happened years ago. So long ago, almost in a previous life.

'Of course. I'm not stupid.' She slaps her forehead. All that is missing is the 'duh.'

'I am very ashamed.'

'Silly. You were sick. Yaneck said you nearly died. He took care of you.'

I don't want to dwell on my unhappy first few weeks. I look around, just to check we are not being observed.

'Tell me about yourself,' I say, immediately cringing inwardly at how corny this sounds.

'There is nothing to say about the past.'

'Why not?'

'The past is gone.' She shakes the stray locks of hair off her face, tucks them behind her ears. She lifts her chin and looks into my eyes.

'The past is gone,' she repeats. 'I am here, now.'

And she is. Oh god, she really *is*. Something subsurface passes between us, and I see that she is offering herself to me. The forest opens outwards. The earth stutters and ceases to turn. I catch a bird-quick flutter of true peace, true completion. The event horizon of human purpose.

I kneel before her. She looks me in the eyes.

Lust, I tell myself, this is just *lust*.

Lust! You idiot!

But she sits on her heels, her back straight, her green eyes locked on mine, inviting. In the hollow of her throat, I can see her heartbeat thudding soundlessly, quickening. She puts the digging stick down and rests her hands on her thighs.

The air is heavy, thick. In the tangled furrows behind the skin of my nose, my cheeks, I breathe her in. I can taste her skin. Honeyed salt. An image forms, bright, a honey-dripping beehive.

Her hand extends and with her forefinger she traces the line of my jaw from beneath my ear to my chin. I almost grab her hand and pull her to me.

I shake my head and shuffle backwards. I shut my eyes. The *things* I could do to this girl...

'Have you not been with women before?' I can taste her breath on the breeze, sweet with mint and mellow leaf.

'I have.'

'Many?'

Under some jedi mind-trick she has cast, I whisper: 'Yes.'

She's about to say something but I get in first: 'Slow down,' I say.

'Why?' she asks, apparently baffled.

'I need. . . I need time to. . .' I can't think of how to say *get to know you*. 'I need time to be friends.'

'But I have watched you for many moons. I see you looking at me – sometimes – especially when I bathe.'

In truth, in any other time, with any other girl, I would have kissed her minutes ago, lain her on the ground and made long and sweet love. But this is different. *Utterly* different in some way that I can't get my head around.

'You are very brave. You stopped Grebel from hitting Yala. You are kind. You are very handsome.'

'Thank you,' I mutter tightly. 'I'm very old though,' I add, as if I fell out the stupid tree and hit every branch on the way down.

'You know many things, it seems.'

'I –'

'So,' she says, her perfect brows creasing, 'if you know so much, then tell me: when I think of you, why does my heart feel. . . so bad?'

She touches two fingers to a spot between her breasts. 'It hurts, here,' she says.

My throat is a pinhole. I try to change the subject.

'The others, the women.' I gesture around us. 'They don't want you to be near me.'

'They don't,' she says. 'But they are not here now.'

'No, they are not, but I cannot just. . .' I lose the word. And apparently all rational thought, because in a brainfreeze-moment of *utter dumbfuckery*, my hand extends, and I point at her crotch.

Jesus H Christ.

What did I just *do?*

Her brows furrow, but her lips widen into a half-smile, showing those white teeth.

'Why me?' I ask.

'Oh,' she says. 'I don't know.'

It's not a cryptic response. She looks at me, and it is clear that she doesn't care to know the *why*. But her body and mind feel the *why*. It's coming off her in waves like a baking heat. *Turned on* doesn't even begin to describe what this girl is. She's *on fire*.

'But you don't know me,' I say. 'So how –'

'At the beginning all I heard was the women complaining about you, some of the men too. Then all of a sudden with the *pottery*, many are in love with you. They never saw the sparkle in here –' she reaches out and taps my chest, above my heart.

'I see it,' she continues, 'because I have spent many years being a half-person, wondering whether I am to be killed or sent away. I have had plenty of time to look into the hearts of men and women. I know what their hearts look like.'

I've no idea what to say to this. As far as I'm concerned, I'm about as exciting as a bucket of water.

'My sparkle,' I mumble, eventually. 'What sparkle?'

She holds up her hand, lightening quick. We hear voices. Female voices.

'Go,' she whispers. I scoot backwards and get to my feet. She picks up her digging stick and stabs it into the ground at the base of the tree.

'Go!' She says.

She doesn't look back as I scuttle away.

18

I returned several times to the spot where I had met Sara, but she was never there. I traversed the woods in my spare time (lots of that). I saw her around the caves, of course, but all I could hope for was her catching my eyes when none of the women were watching.

My time will come.

My time will come. Like some sex-mad monastic mantra, I repeat this to myself, as I lie on my back, night after night, and listen to the sounds of couples screwing.

It is May. The average daily temperature is about fourteen degrees. I'm so hungry I could eat the balls off of a shrew. The meat from the hunt is gone. Snares bring in the odd rabbit or small mammal, but that doesn't go far. Nets cast into the river trap the odd minnow. The trees are bursting into life, but it'll be summer and autumn by the time they are pushing out their berries and nuts. If it were not for the handfuls of leaves that we eat each day, I think our digestive systems would just stop altogether.

Strange, to think that in a land un-buggered by civilisation, a person would go hungry. But I guess that is winter for you. Here and there you find the occasional dead animal – a wolf, a deer, a lynx – that the tribe say has died of starvation. But there is nothing left but the bones, picked clean by birds, bacteria, and fungi. Winter means the same to both humans and animals. Every animal, plant or bug will take whatever it can get.

With spring come the flowers. Above the caves, on the plain between the caves and the river, beyond the river, everywhere that is not tree or rock – all of this is carpeted in inch-high flowers. The tribe pay this no heed. None of it appears edible. It's like some gene-edited Alpine meadow that escaped from a lab, mutated, and has now run riot over all Creation. Colours, beggaring all description. Like Monet got drunk. The oranges and red burn gold on the ground, the whites are silver, which tilt their shining faces to the tune of the sun. Purple and blue drifts, so scented that the breeze, bemused, can only circle in eddies.

I stand on the shelf above the caves. I am bathed in the yellow god-rays of dawn. Blondebeard, Grease and Yaneck are with me. I look at the colour of Nature's glory, laid out before me, and all I can think of is the bone-crunching hunger that seems to chew at the very air in my lungs. I take a deep breath and bellow:

Broken windows and empty hallwaaaays

A pale dead moon in a sky streaked with greeeey

Humaaan kindness is oveeeerflowing

And I think it's gonna rain todaaaaay

My voice breaks on the trees, on the ground, and rolls away to the river. There are answering shouts of alarm and confusion from the caves beneath me.

Yaneck whistles, and I suppose he's saying something like *it's Charlie.*

We tramp off eastwards, towards the line of hills about two miles away – atop which the desolation of the steppes begins. We cross the eastern stream and enter the trees. We are not hunting for game, though if we come across a track or spoor, we will deviate from our mission: bee hunting. Although I do want to find the source of the bees that visit the spring flowers, I would happily follow the guys and chase after a horse or a deer. I've practiced with their spears – a little. At twenty yards I can hit something about the size of a barn door. This means I'm next to useless. But one extra throw is better than nothing.

There don't seem to be any bees, none that I can see, but Yaneck says he has been studying them for a few days. As far as I could see he just sat by a fire, staring into space. Maybe he *was* investigating. Maybe he was also cheekily snorting the prehistoric equivalent of angel dust. I can never be sure *what* Yaneck is up to.

Urla seems to have the keys to the company supply closet, because mostly everything I ask her for she is able to provide me with. This time it was long lengths of what appeared to be very thin leather (*skin* – that's the word she uses, and I don't ask what of). I've sewn this, very crudely, into a onesie, with a cape that I can draw over my head. I'm carrying this in my satchel.

We trek through the woods in single file, without speaking. The guys are able to move without much sound. I try to copy them, step where they step, but compared to them I make more noise than a woolly rhinoceros crashing into a piano factory. About every twenty paces we come to a halt. They just want a moment's silence without my noise, so they can get the lie of the land. They sniff the air and examine the ground. Then off we go again.

Two items blanket my thinking. Honey. Meat. And that's not in descending or ascending order. I'll eat anything: badger and kangaroo asses. Beaver balls. Marmot tits. Don't care. I just want something juicy to plough my teeth through, all dripping and greasy. Hunger is a phenomenal motivator. We nibble on the odd grub and mushroom as we scuttle through the woods, but it doesn't touch the sides.

And the honey. If we find a hive, it'll be an effort not to just smash it to bits and scoff the entire thing, wax, honey, pollen, bees, larvae – the entire thing. I've been stern with the guys, and they have solemnly promised that the hive needs to be *collected, not scoffed.*

It can't be messed with or used for wax candles or ceremonies or shoved up a zebra's ass. It can't be worshipped, or tinkered with, or used to start a war. It must be *collected.*

It must *not* be eaten by four hunger-crazed spear-wielding primates. The destroyers of the earth. The ruination of all. A virus with shoes. If I were God, I wouldn't even have waited until Eve ate the apple. I would have taken one look at my creation, and they'd have been out on their butts – pronto. *Go mess with someone else's shit*, I would have shouted after them as the garden gate hit them on the ass.

After a half hour of this wandering, I'm even more crusty. I'm getting the feeling that Yaneck really has been at whatever passes for the local nose candy and in fact has no idea about bees and is on a wild goose chase. But Grease stops short, halting our column. I listen to my own breathing and the whispering of the leaves. Grease touches his ear. I strain mine (if that's possible), and I *do* hear it. A throat-deep buzz, on a different tonal level to everything else, as if it is embedded in the air around us. I don't want to tempt fate, but I can feel a sick excitement building where my stomach used to be – before it packed up and left. We move forward. Twenty yards further and there it is.

A hive. Lodged into the trunk of an old birch tree. About seven feet up.

I yank out the onesie skin suit. I'm going to dress myself in the skins of animals, steal some insects, bring them home and make them my unwitting pets so I can eat the exudate from their ass glands. I cackle as I think of this.

The suit is far from perfect. I've made it too big. It's floppy, all over, and I think I must look like some weirdo. A comic version of the dude in *The Silence of the Lambs*.

Actually, there really is *no* comic version of that guy.

Grease is making a small fire, using a glowing coal that he has kept in a small leather-wrapped ibex horn. I have my own little invention: a foot-long cone of thin leather stuffed with the things you usually use to make a fire with: dried out and half-rotten wood, fluff, moss, dander, dry leaves, lichens, hair. All mixed up in proportions that I think will make an adequate smoker.

Blondebeard goes onto one knee. I scramble up and sit on his shoulders. He stands up.

The honeybee is the insect that literally makes the world work. The housekeeper that polishes the world of flowers, that helps flowers and trees make love, producing new plants, new flowers, new life, sweetness to nourish generation upon generation of busy bees all bustling about, the lifeblood of countless millions of creatures on the sacred Earth and the blue yonder of the sky, from now until the end of time.

It is a creature of grace and perfection.

And today it arrives at a date with destiny.

First Contact with the human race. The beginning of relationship that will define both species and elevate each to greater heights of glory.

In this case, it is an ape dressed in a skin onesie, coughing and spluttering in the self-inflicted and acrid fumes of burning moss and hair, sitting on the shoulders of another ape who looks like a big blonde pirate king.

An historic moment.

I dull their insect wits with a good cloud of smoke and lever the hive out of the cavity in the tree. I stuff it into my satchel.

Granted, the moment has a lot less pomp and ceremony than I'd imagined, but it'll have to do.

First was pottery. This is *paydirt.*

On the walk back, I keep thinking of the colour of honey. Golden. Which keeps turning my thoughts towards Cortez, the Spanish explorer who made first contact with the Aztecs, and who coveted their gold. It's not a pleasant story, for either side. I actually consider putting the damn hive back where I found it.

Gold. Sparkling things. Sweet things. Man always covets such things. They infect him with madness. A madness that leads him to work evil. Should I really be domesticating bees? Harnessing honey?

By making pottery, and by this act, I am bringing progress down upon the heads of these people.

Solzhenitsyn said that oceans of blood are spilt, *always*, whenever humans see "progress" as the means to reach social and technological utopia.

Fuck it, I tell myself, I'm sure others have already figured out beekeeping. It's hardly like splitting the atom.

I just need some honey. I banish the thoughts. I'm starving. I want sugar.

I just want some honey. I want to ferment it into mead and get drunk.

And anyway, there's not enough of these people to make an ocean of blood.

Twenty adults equates to about one hundred litres of blood. Fifteen kids – call it forty-five litres. That's only one hundred and forty-five litres of blood.

That sounds a lot, but it is barely enough to fill an average bathtub.

I just need the honey.

19

With hives, you really just leave the bees to get on with it. Bees get their own water; they get their own nectar. It'll be mid or late summer by the time there will be an appreciable amount of honey to extract.

In the meantime, I make clay bricks and brood on Sara. There's not much else to do. Now not only does Yaneck pester me for new inventions: everyone else does. Salanda, who was the lady who first accused me of doing evil pottery-magic with her boy Willow, has the makings of an excellent potter. She has made a big clay bowl, and this sits near her hearth, full of water, and she smacks and moulds the clay on a flat rock, experimenting with different shapes and sizes.

Once I explained to her the mechanics of heat and silica and showed her how to dig and operate a pit-kiln, she was off to the races.

Pottery-fever swept over everyone after Yaneck blessed it, and after two days Tazak had to intervene. He pointed out – politely but firmly – that the entire tribe couldn't just sit around slapping at clay. We'd starve. Pottery had to be put aside, a fancy only once regular chores were done. Mostly this involved foraging.

The moon has fattened by about ten days before the food really starts to come in. Migration is obviously a big thing, particularly amongst the bird community. And they've started arriving. Ducks and geese in particular. The women and men use slings to knock them senseless. The hunters come back with more deer, with beavers, even with the odd wolf. They don't eat the meat of carnivores – there seems to be some prohibition or taboo against it – but they have no compunction about using them for fur and leather.

I'm sitting by my fire on the flat plain, a stone's throw away from the caves. Tazak and Yaneck have allowed me to co-opt Blondebeard for a few hours a day. His real name is Zavik, but I have trouble thinking of him any other way than Blondebeard the Pirate. He doesn't speak much, and he rarely smiles. He always looks to be in a brooding fury, but that's just his *look*. He's actually quite a happy camper. Zavik is tall and built like a Greek god. His partner seems to adore him. I don't blame her. I suspect he could match Tazak in strength. He doesn't talk much and communicates largely with looks and acts of gentle kindness, his large and blue eyes expressive, liquid, alive. If I were a dame, I might just be totally enamoured. His missus, Greta, is a slightly plump, jolly, and very pretty brunette with killer brown eyes, who stops by a lot to stroke my cheek with the back of her hand, and to stroke his with the inside of her palm, and to pass to us a few extra berries and edible roots before she brings her haul into the cave.

Zavik drags great piles of wood on a travois down from the woods to feed my clay brick factory. A travois is two or more long poles which you put loads on and drag behind you – the basic way of moving heavy loads if you have not yet invented the wheel. The wheel is something I've been wondering about, but I want people to concentrate on perfecting one thing before moving on to another stage of technological evolution.

Today, whilst we fire the bricks, Zavik is training me with a spear thrower. I'm beginning to get it, and my throws sometimes hit the target – a grass stuffed hide lashed to a post.

'Better!'

We both turn around. Greta is standing a few feet away. She is with Sara. This is perhaps the closest I have physically come to her since the time in the forest clearing. Three very dead ducks hang from a cord around Greta's waist.

I've noticed two things over the last several days. The first is that Tazak, Yaneck, Urla and others have had several conversations with the three women who form the core group that protects Sara. They sat in huddles and spoke in low tones, sometimes for hours.

The second thing is that I then realised that the knot around Sara suddenly relaxed. The women didn't abandon their vigil entirely – they just retreated a little. They relaxed. Sara had more physical space. The women also have stopped giving me such cold shoulders. Vala, Tazak's partner, the ringleader, is suddenly warm towards me.

Vala isn't a bad person. She's actually very funny, smart, and kind.

These women aren't bad. They've just been shitting bricks with worry over Sara. Scared about her bad luck. I really wish I could explain to them that there is no such thing as luck. And no such thing as magic. But of course, that wouldn't work. It'd be futile, and it might well be criminal.

But something seems to have changed.

I suspect a set-up.

I'm just about on excellent terms with everyone.

Except Raka. He seems to hate me more with each passing day. I keep expecting to lie down in my furs at night and find he's pissed all over them or laid a massive dump on the headrest. But I know that when it comes, it will probably be worse than that. A knife in the ribs in some desolate forest.

Why the taboo around Sara is being lifted, I'm not sure, but I can't help but figure that it has a lot to do with me. Perhaps they regard me as having a lot of good luck. Enough luck to counterbalance Sara?

That would make sense. I begin to kindle a small flame of hope.

'Hi Greta,' I say, then I add 'Hi Sara.'

Sara looks at me quickly, then down at the spear in my hands, then at Greta.

'Ducks,' says Greta. 'Lunch.' Like her husband/partner dude, she is a woman of few words. She nods towards the fire where my bricks are.

———

'I took your advice.'

I say this to Sara, who hasn't looked at me so far. We've plucked the ducks and roasted them. Zavik and Greta explain more about migration. I half-listen, frankly dazzled by finally being allowed to be so close to her. Tiny freckles have appeared on her nose and on her cheeks, but the early summer sun isn't responsible for the blush of colour that turns her pale cheeks a rosy red. She seems obscenely uncomfortable, and every time I speak the colour seemed to rise, as if she were a kettle about to pop.

Sara looks at Greta, instead of me.

'What advice?'

'About shoes,' I say, tapping my foot on the ground.

'Oh.'

Greta stares hard at her, as if pushing her to say something else. Sara remains silent, and Greta looks at me and shrugs.

I desperately want to remain near Sara, to soak her into me somehow, but this tension makes me angry. *Wrong* vibrates in the air like the low-pressure preamble to a vicious summer storm. I'm angry. And scared.

I tear off a leg of the nearest duck and stand up.

'I have to check my snares,' I say, realising that everyone knows I don't have any snares. I glance at Sara, and finally she is looking at me. She holds my gaze, her green eyes glistening, shining. I almost take a step forward towards her, but then my somersaulting brain takes over and spins me around and marches me away towards the western stream. In a fit of pique I fling the duck leg away, in full view of everyone. I keep going, across the stream, up the small hill in the direction of the valley above the caves. Everyone is watching me, but I don't care. Fuck them all. I make it to the trees and disappear into the forest. As soon as I'm out of sight I sit down and lean my back against a tree.

A few minutes pass and I'm not any closer to getting my swirling thoughts lined up. A rustle in the undergrowth announces a human.

It's Raka. He's followed me here.

I groan: 'For fuck's sake.'

He mimics the English phrase, a touch of glee in his voice.

'Hello Charlie.'

'Hi wea-, I mean Raka.'

He puts his hands on his hips and looks around.

I kick the ground with my heel, and I ask: 'What do you want?'

'Oh, nothing. I was just coming through here, to *check my snares*.'

'Oh yeah?' I speak in English, my anger rising. 'In that case you can fuck off then.'

He ignores what I'm sure he knows is an insult. He scans the forest then looks at me.

'Did you catch anything?'

'You know I don't have snares. I came here because I wanted to be alone.'

He sits down opposite me, resting against the trunk of a coppiced hazelnut. 'It's not good to be alone.' His voice is silk, but a rotten silk. It seems to touch my skin and set it crawling.

'A man needs to have a woman. A man without a woman is still only a boy.'

I don't want to indulge him, but I can't help myself. 'You don't have a woman,' I say, unease crawling into my stomach.

He makes a flapping motion with his hand. 'Of course. My life has been... different. But I think it will change.'

I stare at him.

'Soon,' he adds, stretching the word out.

He jumps to his feet. 'It has been a nice talk, Charlie. Enjoy your alone-time.'

And just like that, he saunters off. I sit for a further few minutes, then I get up and start walking further into the woods. The ground begins to gently rise as I start up the side of the valley. I follow the stream upwards.

After an hour I scramble up onto the plain northwest of the camp. Here is the Eurasian steppe: vast grasslands that extend across the continent, broken only by deep valleys such as the one below me which sustains the tribe. I'm hot, sweaty, and the exercise has not straightened out my thoughts. My skin still crawls. I sit on a rock and look southeast. Beyond the forested valley, I can see the wide river that we bathe in.

Something very bad happened just now. I don't know what.

Something about this situation is seriously fucked.

Later, it gets a lot worse than *fucked*.

20

I'm embarrassed that I had such a public tantrum; storming off and chucking duck legs all over the place. I don't want to see anyone. I don't want to go back to the caves, but late afternoon is giving way to twilight. And there are bears and wolves knocking around these parts. And I'm desperate to know why Sara was so upset. I have a horrible feeling that it is somehow to do with Raka's little speech.

But she doesn't want him, I tell myself. *It won't happen.*

When I reach the plain outside the caves, the whole tribe is gathered around a large central fire and a handful of smaller ones. There's a surfeit of food. Haunches of meat are roasting. On three smaller fires, earthenware pots are steaming with bubbling stews. It looks like some sort of occasion. I wonder whether I have my dates all screwy: perhaps it is the summer solstice? I thought people were supposed to go on summer treks: hunt caribou or mammoth or meet other tribes. Perhaps this the send-off ceremony. But no one has been packing, not that I've seen. No one has talked about anything imminent.

Greta nudges Salanda and they scoot towards me. They take me by either arm and guide me to a large log, where they were sitting with Deakel and Zavik. Even when he's in a good mood, which is mostly always, Zavik looks like he's about to lose his shit and spray up a schoolyard with a full-auto AR-15. It's not like Zavik ever says much to make himself interesting. He just *is* interesting. He looks like a crazy pirate king who is angry all the time. The fact that he is not, I find seriously funny. But now, Zavik doesn't look angry. He looks, well, dejected. Off kilter.

The two women sit me next to Zavik, and Greta sits down on my other side. Salanda is making a stew with what looks like a complete duck. The head and bill float on the surface, still attached to the carcass. For some creepy reason, I get the impression that if I try and get up, Zavik will stop me.

'What is happening?' I ask.

Willow and his sister Sela scamper up.

'Hi Charlie!' sings Willow, climbing onto my lap.

Zavik looks at me sideways. He holds my arm, my upper arm. 'It's a joining,' he says.

I blurt: 'Joining who?' I turn my head about.

Oh Christ on a woolly mammoth. Raka, it's Raka. And he's going to frigging marry Sara. The slimy little motherf–

'You,' says Greta.

For a moment I have no idea what they are talking about.

'What do you mean "you"?' I ask.

Zavik tightens his grip on my arm, inclines his head towards mine. He speaks low.

'It's a great honour, so do not insult Tazak or anyone else. Do as you are told. You are being adopted by our tribe. It was decided yesterday.' Zavik looks at Greta with a slight shake of his head.

Oh, thank God. I was about to start a stampede. I breathe out shakily.

'You scared me,' I say to Greta. I bump my shoulder against Zavik. 'I'm very honoured.'

He doesn't say anything, but that's normal for Zavik. I breathe in the smell of all the cooking. My heart rate slows. I'm going to be *joined* with the tribe. Thank *God*.

Salanda takes Willow's hand and tugs him gently. 'Come, Willow,' she says. 'Leave Charlie alone now.' Willow gets off my lap and stands next to his mother.

A strained silence descends. Deakel, Salanda's fella, makes a fuss of helping Greta stir the duck-broth. Deakel hates cooking.

The only person who seems happy is Raka, who looks over the tops of the heads of the women tending to the food, straight at me, a smirk plastered all over his face.

What an absolute dickhead.

In fact, as I stare back at him, I realise that he's happier than *happy*. The little cock-nosher looks jubilant. He's finely dressed too – tarted up. What's all this about?

I see motion at the mouth of the second cave. Yaneck is holding up a flaming torch – a stick with fat-soaked bulrushes wrapped around the end.

Zavik nudges me, and hands me a medium-sized bladder. It's heavy.

'It'll help,' he says. 'Have some.'

'No – no thank you. I –' I catch the smell and stop talking. I stop trying to see what Yaneck is up to, I stop everything when the aroma from the bladder hits me. Whatever is in there, it's alcoholic.

'What's this?' Even as I say the words, I sense my mind losing touch with my mouth and the words that emerge. I guess you'd call it an *un-mooring*.

He says something that sounds like a combination of *birch* and *tea*. *You'll relax*, he says.

Still trying to see what Yaneck is up to, I tilt the bladder and sip the liquid. I almost choke – this is about 9 per cent alcohol. I splutter. Some kind of drink made from fermented birch-sap. Birch-sap wine. I take a *big* swallow.

'*How* did you make this?' I ask. Yaneck is moving ahead of a small group of people who are coming towards us. Zavik is answering my question but I'm not listening.

'Sorry?' I ask. He talks, again. Again, I don't listen.

There's a girl, standing with Yaneck and some other people. She's dressed in some sort of bikini, some kind of leather bikini like Raquel Welch in the film *50,000 BC*. But the similarity ends there. Raquel Welch was smoking hot - a grown, busty woman.

This girl is a child. Her name is Freda. She's thirteen years old, I think. I don't really know her. She bathes in the river, often near Sara. She is a year into puberty, at a very rough guess. I don't rightly know. Small breasts, a little hair on her crotch, her still-skinny hips and ass only beginning to fatten up. Freda is still a child. *She still plays with the other children.*

Everything comes queasily together. Raka's happy. That can only mean that Charlie is about to be made crushingly unhappy. I'm about to be adopted. But I'm older than most people here, so adoption must mean I'm marrying into the family.

To Freda.

I take a huge draught from the bladder.

'I didn't even propose,' I say to Greta. But I'm speaking English. She understands me though, and she shrugs her shoulders, a little sadly.

I tilt the bag back and drain it.

'More,' I say to Zavik.

'Later,' he says. 'After.'

Yaneck is talking to the bridal party. I stand up and pass by a few of the smaller fires, where pots and bags have been placed. I blunder over to Grease where he sits with his woman, Cela.

'Birch-tea?' I inquire, trying not to appear manic. Which I am. Grease, smiling, holds up an even larger bladder. It probably belonged to a horse. I take it from him and wander away from the light of the fires, towards the river. I drink as fast as I can.

My mission is to get immediately shitfaced, since I'm now convinced that this will solve all my problems.

This star-bound venture, I christen thee *Mission Birchtea*.

(t minus seven minutes, flight controls are go for launch)

If they realise what I'm up to, they'll put a quick stop to it. So, I stay in the darkness, tripping over stones and spilling some of the booze over my face. I drink the stuff in swallow after swallow. A delicious, religious warmth begins to overtake me.

At *fucking last!* A drink. *Finally!*

I finish the bladder and drop it on the ground. I circle wide, like a wolf, a tingle-toed *darkwolf*, in the darkness, away from Zavik and Grease, towards another cooking fire where Brekel and Zander are sitting. Towards my prey.

I pounce.

'Birch-tea,' I say. It's not a question, but I am handed another bulging sack. And I'm off again, like a sloshy twinkle-toed elf-wolf, into the darkness, towards the river. It takes a few minutes of struggling, but I manage to get the contents inside me. I've drunk so much, so quickly, that my stomach is distended, and taut as a drum, and when I move, I feel a liquid heaving, like rough seas, a storm brewing in my belly.

Zavik, Greta, Deakel and Salanda are standing, peering into the darkness, looking for me. I move back towards the firelight. Zavik sees me, and he hustles over and grabs my arm. I let him. I let out a gut-wrenching belch that lasts about four seconds. Zavik shakes his head. He shoves me down to sit, and he barks something at Grease, who comes over. They talk, quick-fire. Grease sits on my other side. His face is grim. They lean against me. I'm pinned.

'Pinned like a prickly pear!' I sing.

Zavik *growl*s at me.

Shit. Maybe I'm mistaken about Operation Birchtea. Or was it Mission Birchtree? Whatever. I'm not sure, but I think it might have been a bad idea.

(t minus five minutes)

Raka saunters back and forth. He's dressed like some raccoon, with white and black stripes of fur hanging off him. It's smart, I *suppose*.

What a twat.

Wouldn't you know it, ladies and gentlemen – *another* bridal party is on the way. From the cave where Sara lives. Yes, you all guessed correct: Sara is dressed in the same crazy bikini catwalk bullshit as Freda.

'Oh for shit's sake.' English, again. Neither Grease nor Zavik say a word. Greta is looking at me strangely, her brows furrowing, tilting her head as if I'm a problem she's trying to solve. She turns and walks quickly to Tazak, speaks in his ear. He waves her away.

She thumps him on the shoulder, but turns and says something severe. Greta walks back towards us, her face red, throwing a worried look at Zavik.

A wave of nausea sweeps over me and a sour spittle forms in the back of my mouth.

A moment later Tazak calls my name in that booming mountain voice.

'CHARLIE. COME TO ME.'

Everyone goes quiet. The head of state has called for me, by name.

The guys release me. I stand up, sure that I had a plan that I was about to cunningly execute. I can't remember what it was though. It *was* smart. I tilt myself forward and walk quickly over – it's an effective method of walking in a straight line.

I'm sure if I keep this all very light, very low key, chilled, super-tranquillo, then everything will be right as rain. Nothing bad will happen. Nothing bad is happening, anyway. Nothing to worry about. Tazak will wipe away all my tears and send me off to bed with a big mug of cocoa. That's all.

'Hi Tazak,' I say nonchalantly.

The crowd titters. Tazak frowns at me. Then he motions to Freda. She is led, her father, Hukel, on her right and her mother, Dera, on her left. A child.

She joins us, stands facing me, across Tazak's width. Tazak takes a few steps backwards, and is replaced by Yaneck. There's no sound save the soft snap of the burning fires.

I put a hand on Yaneck's shoulder.

Everyone flinches. Yaneck jumps a little and stares at me like I'm about to knife him. I speak in English.

'Seriously dude, I dunno, Yaneck man, I'm not sure this is –'

Yaneck shrugs my hand off, tilts his head back, holds up his arms and bursts into song.

Shit.

It lasts about a minute. In the meantime, there is this girl opposite me. She looks at the ground, clearly afraid. My focus is beginning to go a bit funny, and in a drunken letch that today makes me cringe, I examine her. She's a pretty girl, and will be a good-looking woman, and tonight she looks somewhat Japanese anime, but that's due to the charcoal make-up around her eyes. That, and the fact that she appears to be in grade school.

She's available, I think stupidly. And I can hear the thoughts in Tazak's head, in the heads of the people of this tribe: *she's old enough*.

Yaneck finishes his song of praise and moves over to the other group. He starts another song, facing Sara and Raka. Her face is. . . devoid. Empty of animation. She looks at Raka, but she looks through him. Raka is so excited he's practically slobbering. My stomach takes a sickening turn. I see them – together, Raka's hands all over those delicate features. All over her breasts, reaching between her legs. . .

'GUUUUUUYSSSS!'

I shout this, sticking my hand high in the air like a pupil with a super-bright idea. Yaneck stops his warbling and lowers his hands. I keep my hand up in case anyone is unsure who has just interrupted. They all stare at me.

(t minus two minutes)

I glance at Sara, and she locks eyes with me. Her eyes shine wet in the flickering firelight. I lower my arm.

'Listen,' I say softly to Freda. Then I realise I'm speaking English. So, I gather my thoughts, line them all up. I'm getting drunker by the second. The searing flame of sanity that the booze initially lit is dwindling fast.

'Freda,' I say, and my heart almost breaks as I take in her beseeching look, both afraid of me, and afraid of the very public rejection I'm about to scar her with. 'You do not want to be joined with me. You are beautiful and sweet. I am honoured. You honour me. Your father and mother honour me. But you must join with someone your own age. I am too old.'

Shocked gasps from mum and dad. I look at them. Fuck *them*.

(t minus one minute)

'Raka only made this happen because he wants to join with Sara.' I look over at him. He exaggeratedly rolls his eyes. No one laughs. No one seems to care, either. Why should they care what I think?

(t minus forty seconds)

'Sara doesn't want Raka,' I say my voice rising. A hand comes down on my right shoulder. It shakes me, jarring my brain. Culeg hisses in my ear.

'Shut up! Quiet!'

Zavik and Grease take hold of my left arm. Zavik shakes me, his voice a hoarse whisper. 'For your own sake, shut up! You are making a fool of yourself!'

Raka smiles at me, shrugs his shoulders.

My stomach contracts in a sharp pulse. I feel a burning in my throat. I swallow hard.

I shake free of the three men holding me. I've remembered my genius plan.

It was a speech!

(t minus thirty seconds go flight go flight)

Everything will be hunky-dory once I explain, coherently and politely, that there's no way on God's green earth that I'm going to shack up with a *child*, far less *have sex* with her, so they can all fuck off if that's on the menu. And on the other more pressing topic of making Sara marry that weasel-faced fuck-tarted asshat? Well, that'll happen over my dead body, since by carrying on this way this whole tribe is going straight to hell, where they can all fuck off to and suck dicks. In hell.

Once they grasp all this, everything will be put right.

(t minus twenty seconds good luck Birchtea and God speed)

'Fool?' I shout at them. I pause for a moment, getting all my words right. But the words are sliding all over the place, leaking out my brain as my brain begins to tilt and roll.

(t minus ten seconds)

'Me fool?' I shout. 'You are all a. . . flock of buffalo. . . vaginas. You are all. . . stupid. And when you die. . . when you are in the spirit world. . . or place. . . in there you will. . . eat the cocks. . . of. . . other. . . dead people!'

(lift off)

It's not really what I wanted to say, I tell myself, as Mission Birchtea reaches t-minus zero seconds, and the soupy brew shoots up from my stomach with the force of a NASA rocket out of Cape Canaveral. *I should try saying all that again*, I think, as I projectile vomit over Freda's legs and feet, and I think, *if only they understood English*. I could explain it all properly, with clear references, so they could honest-to-God truly *get where I'm coming from.*

Once they catch my drift, everything will be peachy.

I'll get that cup of cocoa.

I'm dragged away from the firelight. Everything goes dark.

Ah. . . Houston. . . this is Birchtea.

Go ahead Birchtea.

Birchtea?

Birchtea?

Shit.

21

I'm never going to drink that hell-water *ever* again.

Ever.

I can barely put the words down, now that I look back and remember myself, covered in dried sticky birch-sap vomit, with a headache so *clanging*, so *alarm siren* shattering. Just thinking about it now makes my stomach swim. I'll give you the details from the start of this day, though the mission report from this period could actually be confined to a single word: *clusterfuck*.

I struggle to open my eyes, and for a moment I am certain that I have gone blind. Then I realise the birch-sap stuff has dried in a crackly sheen over my face and it's gummed my eyelids together. I pull them open, wince, then turn on my side and retch. My ribs ache. Dimly, I remember puking and puking and puking.

'Drink', says a voice. I twist my head and I see Yaneck, standing next to Culeg. Culeg holds out a bowl. Water. I down it. Then I puke it up. I close my eyes. The recent past is a blank wedge of time. I remember Sara, kneeling in front of me, inviting, in that small forest clearing, her eyes sparkling. This image swirls and forms a weasel-thing stalking me in the forest. Raka seeing me, talking, smug, saying something horrible. . .

'Pitiful.' Tazak's voice.

I feel fingers on my wrist. Someone is taking my pulse. Then fingers on my eyelids, peeling them open.

'Fuck off,' I say.

Culeg ignores this. 'Show me your tongue.'

I open my mouth, and he peers into it. He lets me go and I close my eyes against the bastard bright day. My headache is off the scale.

He speaks to Tazak.

'He will be well again. The drink won't harm him.'

I hear this and feel frightened. Yes, I was drinking that birch-sap poison. I stifle a dry heave. My mouth is dry as a rat's ass. Unlubricated, my tongue feels like a dehydrated toad. I can barely swallow. My head bangs like the Devil's dinner-gong in Hell.

'Thank you Culeg,' says Tazak. 'Leave us now.'

I was drinking that stuff – downing it in great swallows, because. . . because Raka was there. . . making me. . . marry. . . Freda. And Raka. . . was marrying. . . Sara?

Oh. No. Dear God, please.

The rest comes back in a rush. Sara was crying. Raka was smiling. I refused to marry Freda, and then I told everyone to go and suck dicks in hell. Or something very similar. And then I puked over the poor, probably terrified girl. In front of her parents. In front of the entire goddamn tribe.

I close my eyes, but they are already closed, so I shut them even harder, squeezing them against the daylight reality of what I've done. It's not enough, it's never enough, so I cover my face with my hands. I realise that Tazak and Yaneck must be still there, so I roll onto my front, and press my face, my hands covering my eyes, against the earth and away from real life.

It's not enough. It never is, and despite the sickness I feel, I actually want *more* of the birch tea. Anything. Anything to block off the awfulness of what I've done. That supply will have gone cold. They'll never let me near another drop of it.

Sara, married. Probably Raka is ploughing that sweet girl right now as I lie here: the biggest loser this side of prehistory. Probably he's fucking her for about the sixth time.

But he doesn't care about her!

If he did, he wouldn't marry the bitch in the first fucking place.

I sit up. Time to take control of this situation. The earth sways. I cough. My head splits.

Fuck it. I have a damsel to rescue. Yaneck will help me. He always helps.

'Yaneck,' I say. 'Tazak. It's wrong, Raka should not have –'

Yaneck darts forward and kicks me hard in the ribs. The bastard winds me. Tazak grabs him, shoves him backwards so hard that Yaneck pitches over backwards, landing on his back. Tazak rounds on me. His large brown eyes are narrowed, like a predator. I struggle to get air in. My headache launches into an as-yet-unexplored realm of agony.

'You shithead,' snarls Tazak, 'I *knew* you were bad luck. I *knew* that we should have gotten rid of you!'

Tazak begins pacing in a tight little circle, smacking his fist into his palm. Like some cage-fighter waiting to be unchained.

Shit.

'You messed around with things! You messed around with our minds!'

He stops and points a finger at Yaneck, who has pushed himself up on his elbows. 'Yaneck is reason you are here! Thank Yaneck! But we cannot always be right. Even the spirits trick the smartest of men.'

I look at Tazak as he shouts and paces, smacking his fist harder.

'You come here with lies about your tribe from over the hills and far away! You come to us with *lies!*'

Tazak pulls out a long blade of flint. It catches the light. He comes towards me. 'I'll end all of this now!' Behind him, Yaneck is scrambling to his feet, but he will be too late to stop Tazak, who now grabs me by my puke-stained shirt.

I grab Tazak's wrist, but it's like a cord of iron, immovable. He raises the knife.

I hold up my hand against the fall of the blade and shriek my zero gambit: 'Yaneck knows!'

'What'd you say?' Tazak shakes me like a rag doll, my neck snapping back and forth. I feel his fingers bunching around my shirt, tightening. The flint knife is still raised. It hangs. Waiting. Like Isaac and Abraham. Cain and Abel.

'Yaneck knows the truth,' I say. 'And he didn't tell you.'

'The truth about what?' shouts Tazak, shaking me harder.

'About where I came from!'

Yaneck *lied* to Tazak. The shaman lied to the headman.

Tazak is smart as hell. He takes all this in, but he doesn't move or let me go. His breathing is heavy. In amongst my pain, I feel a surge of guilt for what I've now set in motion. But it's the only choice I had.

I just hope it distracts him enough to let him calm down, to let Yaneck stop him from cutting my throat.

Tazak sees all this. I can see the calculation in his eyes. He's being manipulated, and he knows it. He doesn't like it at all. He proves this by lifting me, bodily, off the ground, and hurling me several feet into what is soft grass; a hollow mercy.

I roll over. Tazak stares wordlessly at Yaneck, who accepts the glare calmy.

'I had to keep this secret, or risk a crisis,' Yaneck says, his voice soft, but firm. 'My only mistake was not telling you. It was too much to understand. I am sorry. I will explain it to you, but –'

'Enough!' Tazak shouts. He whirls around, moving insanely fast for such a big hunk of a man. He storms off in the direction of – where? I realise I don't even know where I am. It seems to be a meadow. Above me, puffball clouds sail gently across the blue sky. I put my arm across my eyes.

Great.

The sun's warmth leaves my skin as a shadow falls across me. I know Yaneck's there; I can hear his breathing, slightly elevated. Angry. His voice is a growl.

'Thank you for dipping me face down in shit.'

I don't say anything. In truth, I don't even know how to begin the mountainous task of apologising. It's so massive. I've betrayed him. Stabbed him in the back. After everything he's done for me.

'I know what you will say,' he says, taking the half-formed thoughts from my mind as if he's reading it. 'You will say you had no choice. But tell me this, Charlie: have you never had a choice?'

'What?' I ask. I'm confused.

'You had many choices that led you to this moment.'

'That doesn't make it right that Raka –'

'This is about me and you as much as them.'

'Why did you suggest I join with Freda? She's a child.'

'I didn't want Freda to join with you. I argued against it. I didn't want Raka to join with Sara. I argued against that. But Charlie, you are a stranger to our ways, our customs.'

I don't say anything. I want Yaneck to say his bit, and then sod off.

'Even the shaman can be overruled by the headman. There are other people the headman has to listen to.'

'What will happen to me now?'

'Now? Nothing will happen. When I tell him, Tazak will keep our secret. The only thing that has changed is that today you have far fewer friends than you did yesterday.'

With that, the shadow over me departs as Yaneck stamps off. I listen to him go. I lie with my arm across my eyes. I raise my voice slightly, even though it hurts my own ears.

'Yaneck, I'm sorry.'

The footfalls pause. The reply comes.

'Not enough. And Charlie?'

'Yes?'

'Now I think about it, I don't think you have any friends left, at all.'

———

The rest of the day passes like any other atrocious car-crash of a hangover. The I-just-pissed-my-life-up-a-wall guilt lies heavier than the physical discomfort, though even I have to say that as hangovers go, it was pretty darn rough. That birch-sap wine is worse than port or sherry, which are pretty much the granddaddies of substances you *don't* want to get wrecked on. Seems these people already knew the secret of fermentation. Obviously, they keep the stuff stashed away for special occasions. I can't see why – if you can make alcohol, you might as well spend your life half-cut.

The rest of the day was standard. There was a pitcher of water next to me, and eventually I managed to get some of it down and keep it down. I was near the riverbank, a hundred yards or so west of the caves. Eventually I hauled myself down to the river and drank more water. I stripped the bark off slim willow stems and chewed on them. I think it helped.

I stayed there until late afternoon when hunger forced me back to the cave. I did the walk of shame past the few people who were outside, looking only at my feet, feeling their stares burning. Someone had put a platter of food next to my bedroll, someone who obviously knew what hungover people needed – big fatty legs of duck, starchy tubers that I hadn't bothered to learn about. They'd left me another pitcher of water. I cried (silently) at this kindness. I forced myself to eat, eat like a machine, robotically chewing and swallowing every scrap whilst the mental image of Sara and Raka grew like a thundercloud over me, over the cave, over everything.

I lay down and closed my eyes.

I shed more tears.

22

Eight days later, Yaneck is still not speaking to me. No one except Zavik and Greta have spoken to me. I spent the first night in the cave recovering, but then I moved my bedroll outside, to a spot near the western stream. I couldn't bear people looking at me. Their gazes felt like hot shame.

Zavik came along on the afternoon of the second day, carrying four long wooden stakes which he hammered into the ground in the formation of a square. Without a word. He strung up a leather tarpaulin over the top, forming a very basic tent. Then he gestured at it, and said: 'In case of rain.' Then he left.

Greta came by every day to give me food. I ignored everyone who passed by on their way foraging or hunting, since they were ignoring me. Greta never said much, but she looked sad.

I made a pile of deadfall the size of a small mammoth, then I made a pile of clay the size of a buffalo. It took me two days. Then I made some more moulds for bricks.

I made and fired bricks. When the moulds were packed with wet clay and my pit kiln was full and burning, I took the completed and cooled bricks and stacked them neatly in a spot near the treeline, where the stream emerged from the forest.

I worked like a mad bastard. When I had nothing to do, I gathered more wood. Even though I fired bricks by the several score, the woodpile got bigger and bigger. The only thing I had to give back to Greta, when she brought me food, was firewood. I made sure her arms were full when she left. The pile still grew.

At night, I continued making bricks.

I found two additional hives of honeybees, and so I made two more hive boxes, putting them near the first one. I went out myself with my bee-suit and manage to retrieve both hives. Turns out I'm still not allergic to bee stings.

I continued working out. Push-ups, shadowboxing, running for miles in wide loops, swimming in the river. In the eight months I've been here, I've morphed into Captain America. I have washboard abs, shoulders like mountains and a chest like two rocks. And biceps the size of Brazil.

And little else.

I go to bed late at night, exhausted, and I wake up early. I work like this so I don't have the time or energy to think about Sara, or booze, or anything else. It doesn't work perfectly, but it at least blunts most of those splinters which, if I sit still for too long, start to sting and burn in my mind.

I experiment with clay, making some of the bricks with dry grass mixed in. They seem tougher, and I suppose it might make the bricks better thermal insulators.

I have nearly three-quarters of the bricks I need when I realise that I will need mortar. The sides of the valley that stretch up to the steppes have areas of exposed rock, and there are several sites to choose limestone from. I fire the limestone in a pit kiln (a hole the ground) to calcinate it, turning it into highly caustic unslaked lime. Nasty, smelly, pretty horrible stuff. If I feed it to Weasel it'd burn a hole in his face. Water added to this stuff produces a less caustic slaked lime. This stuff needs to sit for a bit, minimum a month, to mature. Then I will mix in sand and more water and I'll have lime mortar, which will act as cement for the clay bricks.

I find all sorts of fossils in the rocks. Ammonites, and things I don't recognise. It's a bit pointless, but I collect the nicest ones. They sit in a corner under the tarpaulin. I suppose they are just for decoration. Like I've been to a home décor store and come back with some nice prints to hang on the wall. Tart the place up a bit.

Several times, I wander off, quite far afield. An hour's walk west, in a wide curve of the river, I find a shallow section where the water is crystal clear and runs shin-deep over pebbles. I make a strainer out of strips of bark around a circle of two sections of deer antler. I look for gold and silver, but I only find only the odd diamond, which if you ask me are near useless, since I've no idea how to cut them. Hit them the right way and they will only shatter into smithereens. Even if I did manage to cut them into gems, they'd be functionally useless.

I suppose the sensible thing to do would be to collect as many as possible and bury them in a cache under a spot that will eventually become my home. Millennia from now. I suppose I could try and find a cave that I know will be discovered around the period preceding my lifetime, like the Lascaux caves in France, and paint in a cryptic message that only my future self will be able to untangle. Maybe write something like *Charlie the bookworm, father of the dog Goldie and the cat Fruity, maker of cheese-wine, when you are nineteen, dig deep, deep in your backyard to find your lucky stars.* Trust me, if this weirdness was discovered at Lascaux, then you can bet your bottom dollar that I would have understood it was a personal message, and I would have dug *deep deep.* The only problem is that I'd first have to try and find the Lascaux caves. If that were even possible, I would then have to figure out the precise geographic coordinates for where my house will eventually be built in Cornwall. Further, I'd need to remember which way it faced so I don't end up burying them in what will become my bitch neighbour's garden, as opposed to mine.

A task that will bear no fruit. Also, almost impossible.

Gold and silver: I figure if I get enough of it, I can smelt it into big lumps. For what? I suppose I have reverted to the spurned lover. In the back of my mind, I entertain grand notions of winning Sara with gifts made from shining metals. Fucking pointless, I realise.

Eight days after the spectacular balls-up that was Mission Birchtree, I'm digging a large circular trench at my spot on the level ground near the forest. The stream will pass by, only ten feet from the front door. A rectangular house, whilst awesome and nostalgic, will mean I have to worry about *forces* and *loads* and whether the roof will be too heavy for the sides and so on.

Screw that.

A circular house – an igloo – means I don't have to worry about all that rubbish. It's also the most hurricane-proof structure that one can realistically build, outside of drilling a hole in a mountain. Or living in a cave, I suppose.

The shape will also cope best with having a fuck-ton of snow dumped on it. If I'm incorrect and the bastard thing does cave in during a snowstorm and crush me flat, then it won't matter because apparently, I'm a total waste of space.

I'm digging, using a blunt hand axe that I found discarded near the cave. A hand axe is more or less the size of a small frisbee. It's blunt and circular along the side that fits into your hand. The other side is the sharp cutting side. Your arm acts as the haft of the axe.

The owner obviously didn't want it, so I've managed to wrap it (with sinew begged from Greta) to the end of a straight stick. Kind of like a wide pickaxe. The ground is soft and loamy and without any large stones, so it's easier than it should be. It feels like I'm being let off lightly, like I'm being paid a favour I have not earned.

I'm thinking about copper, about where I might find malachite, when Raka strolls up and sits down on one of the stacks of bricks.

'Be careful of the bricks,' I say.

'I apologise,' he says, but he doesn't move. I turn my back to him and continue digging.

'Charlie, I wanted to say that I'm sorry about what happened.'

'Nothing happened that cannot be fixed,' I reply flatly, still bent to my task.

'The ceremony didn't go as expected, though. And it was very embarrassing for you. People –'

I cut him off, my voice dull.

'People can think whatever they want. The ceremony went better than *you* had planned. I'm sure you were very happy with it. I should congratulate you on a great success.'

This shuts him up for a moment. My back is to him, but I can almost *hear* him frowning.

'I don't know why you did not want to be joined with Freda. She is young, fresh –'

'I did not want to be joined with Freda because I am in love – is that the correct word – love? I am in love with Sara. You know this. I believe you enjoyed hurting me. I feel deeply sad that she is now joined with you. She will never be joined with me. I am sad the way a big river is wide. It hurts me here –' I turn to look at him and thump my fist against my breastbone.

I learned a long time ago how to annoy bullies. Speak the words they long to hear from you. It fills and rewards their desperate need to dominate. But bullies are as compulsive as gamblers – hand them their winnings and their pleasure evaporates, leaving them with a hole they will torture themselves to fill. Again and again and again.

That's dopamine, I guess.

'You win,' I say. I step out of the trench. 'You are more clever, more handsome, more talented, faster, bigger and better than me. In every way. And Sara is very happy to be joined with you. She will make an excellent mother. It is very clear to *everyone* that she, ah. . . she loves you *very* much.'

At the end of your speech to a bully, you hit them with a bunch of obvious lies, ending with the biggest of all. In this case, the cherry on top of this ice-cream sundae of whoppers is *she loves you very much*. A lie that they want more than anything to be the truth. But they know it isn't the truth – that it *never* will be. And this antagonises them more than life itself.

Treating them this way quickly teaches them that they will obtain no sense of reward from you. They leave the encounter feeling like they've just eaten something deeply unpleasant. After this they generally leave you alone.

In retrospect, I was too blinded by anger and jealousy to see that this would not work with someone so fucked in the head as Raka.

I'm still holding the pick. The hand axe is mounted on the end of what was once young and very stout oak tree. I walk towards him, slowly, slinging the pickaxe to balance it over my right shoulder.

'But you have made a big mistake,' I say.

He can't help but cower slightly. His eyes dart towards the caves, then to the pickaxe over my shoulder.

'What?' he snaps.

'You are still sitting on my bricks,' I say, pointing. When he doesn't move, I feint – sharply, like a boxer. He jumps, but he is seated, and this sends him clumsily backwards. He falls half on the pile and does this little jig with his feet but ends up on his ass. I swing the pickaxe off my shoulder and prop it against the remains of the stack.

'Thank you,' I say, examining my fingernails. 'You may go.'

He gathers himself up. Incoherent rage colours and contorts his face. I wonder if he will attack me. I rather hope he will. I won't defend myself very hard. Getting the tar whipped out of me would be a small price to pay for him being publicly censured by Tazak. A trial by fire. A bullet in the brainstem. I'm not bothered which.

I watch him march off, his head held high and his chest out; a walking billboard advertising a dented ego.

He walks in the direction of the river, through my row of transplanted hazelnut bushes. He snaps a few of the branches. Dickhead. I have twenty of the bushes (dug up from the woods and replanted here) in two very pretty rows near the stream. I think at some point I will plant numerous willows and train them into a fence. See if I can domesticate something in there.

I jump, almost out of my skin, at the sound behind me.

'Asshole.'

I whip round. Yaneck is standing next to my circular trench, peering at it. He's not looking at me.

'Goddammit, Yaneck!'

'What?' he asks, looking at me, his voice mild. 'Is that not your word for a person's shit-hole?'

'Stop creeping up on me!'

'I have been observing you, Charlie.'

I glance into the woods. I have not masturbated in the last week, thank God.

He follows my glance. 'Oh, I have not been following you around. Greta tells me things. Sometimes I sit and watch you. I have good eyes.'

'Like a hawk, it seems.'

'Yes, like a hawk, and I see much.' He points upwards. 'Being like a hawk and very high up, I see very much.'

'OK,' I say, grabbing the pickaxe and stepping into the trench. 'So?'

'So, I will say it again. You are being like this *asshole* of yours.'

'*I'm* the asshole?'

He thinks for a second, then nods.

'Why?'

'You know perfectly well. You continue to antagonise Raka. This is not wise.'

'Wait, you are saying that *I* antagonise *him*?'

'It does not matter that he took a dislike to you before he even knew you. It does not matter that his dislike of you is not based on anything sensible. Raka has always been this way about things. He is. . . unpredictable. . . he is not an easy person to like. But he is important to this tribe. He has invaluable talents. He finds things that most people miss. He is our best tracker. He is important to the tribe.'

'You said "he is important" twice, which makes me think you do not believe it.'

Yaneck moves over to a log that I dragged out of the woods some days ago. It's a nice place to sit and look out over the plain below. Or it would be if I didn't immediately decide to make my fire on the other side, so I was facing the forest instead. He sits now, facing over the plain towards the river, and motions for me to sit beside him.

He picks up a splodge of wet clay and moulds it into a ball. 'Charlie, this tribe – any tribe – is a complicated thing. It must be held gently, massaged, treated well, managed carefully.' With heavily callused fingers he delicately forms the ball into an egg-shape.

'I know, Yaneck, but –'

'But if we are *asshole,* then –' He snaps his fist shut around the wet clay. It squidges between his fingers and patters messily on the ground.

I prod at a lump of clay with my foot.

'About Tazak,' I begin. . . and then I stop talking. I'm suddenly desperate for approval. Yaneck might only be seventeen years older than me, but he's the closest thing I've had to a father since forever, since. . . like. . . my whole life.

'I understand why you told Tazak,' he says, looking at me. 'It was clever. It was all you could say to save your own life. But Charlie, you must understand that *other* people are living their lives all around you, all the time. Their own lives matter, they are just as important as yours.'

'I know, but–'

Yaneck holds up his hand and cuts me off. 'You remember what I said about choices? When you were lying covered in your own sick, half-poisoned, just a few days ago, with Tazak about to cut you open? Your choices led you there. Well, you are starting on a similar path now, yet again, by *choosing* to anger Raka.'

Yaneck is right.

When I swiped the bladders of birch wine and drank them, I knew that was unwise. And I knew it was unwise to wind up Raka just now. Both were the stupid choices, but I couldn't help myself.

Yaneck stands up.

'Thank you,' I say, though I'm not sure what about.

He flicks my temple. His fingernail raps against my skull. I wince, surprised.

'*Think* about these things.'

'I will.'

He flicks my skull in the same spot. Harder.

'Ow!' I say. 'I understand!'

'Better. And while you are thinking about these things, have some gratitude for the things that *are* good, right now, in your own life.'

Abruptly he walks off, making very little sound. I watch him go. He follows the stream past my orchard of hazel bushes, then stops, looks at them for a moment, and slaps his forehead, as if to say *what a brilliant and obvious idea*. He doesn't look back though. Down the slope he goes to the level plain, then he walks back towards the caves, disappearing from my view.

I'm about to get up and re-attack the trench when I remember the snap of his fingernail against my temple. *Think about it*, he said. So I sit, waiting for my brain to think. Below me, Willow is carrying his little sister over his shoulder. She squirms and wriggles, and her screams of delight and mock alarm bring a smile to my face. I sit on that log overlooking the plain and the river, with all those people sitting in caves underneath me, watching the sun set on a world that is fundamentally different from mine.

The dipping sun casts long shadows amongst the hazels. For the first time, I hear the low drone of the beehives – now not only with my ears. Now, the sound is woven into the tapestry of the moment around me. Somewhere, a baby wails. A woman is carrying water from the river. The smell of roasting duck wafts fat on the breeze that swirls pollen-drifts in the orange sunset sunbeams filtering through the branches of the willow trees that cluster near the river. *This is what I want, what I choose*. I hear the thoughts as hushed whispers. *This is what I choose*.

How? I ask myself. I have no answer. I sit and watch the day turn into night. I see stars. I see shooting stars; falling meteorites, turning and tumbling, breaking, splitting, burning up against the black backdrop of infinity. The moon rises, flying high above this spinning world that spins me with it in perfect time.

A ladder, I think, *that's what I need*. A ladder made of the same golden thread that emerges from the crown of the head and tethers the soul to interstellar space, to the universe.

We are actually upside down and we don't realise it. We think that our feet, on the ground, on this planet, are *beneath* us, holding us up. It's the other way around. We are kept standing, kept erect, by that thread that we dangle from, the thread that leads back to our *real* home. Among the stars.

Stardust thou art, and unto stardust shalt thou return.

I lie down on my back. I watch the sky, and I have no memory of closing my eyes.

23

A guy once told me that after he had gone through withdrawal from booze, he discovered that he had nothing. Actually nothing. Even the clothes he found himself wearing did not belong to him. He'd been pulled from a burning building – his house. He *had* been wealthy, but he drank away his bank balance. No mortgage on the house, and rather than applying for one and carrying on drinking he'd decided to torch the place with himself in it. That the house was uninsured didn't matter since he was going to die.

An alcoholic's logic, I guess.

It was actually worse than nothing because he was then charged with arson. But to hear his story, this criminal charge didn't upset him at all.

Once you're at the bottom, the only way is up.

By the time he appeared next to my bedside in a rehab clinic he'd been sober, and happy, for nearly two decades. I was twisted into a ball, not feeling very well. He had come in to talk to the patients, to try and offer them something that his own years of sobriety had taught him.

He told me his story and asked me for mine. I talked, filling the air with complaints and grievances. If ever you want to hear someone who is firmly in the category of *poor old hard-done-by-victim*, then I can point you to that moment in time where I gave that little speech.

After listening to me moan and groan about how awful my life was, he stood up and looked down at me. His tone was gentle, kind.

'You're not ready.'

'What?' I snapped.

'You're not ready,' he repeated. He smiled at me, and went to turn away, but I grabbed at his shirtsleeve.

'What did you do?' I asked him. 'After you found you had nothing?'

He shrugged. 'Someone else spoke to me, the same way I'm speaking to you now.'

'What did they say?'

'He didn't expect me to feel gratitude for where I'd ended up.' The man laughed with genuine humour. 'Who'd be able to feel that? Instead, he suggested that I *cultivate* gratitude. *Like a seedling.*'

I scoffed. 'How'd you do that?'

The man's smile was steady. 'The one thing that I realised I needed, that I could rely on, was the water supply. So, I went to the little shared kitchen, pulled a stool up to the faucet, and turned on the cold water. I stared at the gushing water for perhaps only five minutes. That was all it took to change my life forever.'

I wake up, with this memory bright and centre. It's dawn on a summer morning in the Ice Age. I lie on my back listening to the nearby stream. Gushing water. *So what?* I think. There's plenty of *that*. That long ago alcoholic – his smile was generous, like the stream, like Yaneck's smile.

I think about the two men. Side by side. Yaneck, and the alcoholic in his rumpled shirtsleeves. Is there much difference in their demeanour? Not really. Both seem to be the joint and supreme leaders of the cult commonly known as *getting over shit that doesn't actually matter.*

The Ayatollahs of Who Gives A Toss.

The Buddhas of Flying Fucks.

The urge to drink comes out of nowhere, hitting me from leftfield like some demented quarterback. I'm suddenly crying. I want to pour the flammable spirit of my life all over this world and myself and set the whole fucking thing on FIRE. I don't *want* to face anything alone. I want that bottle beside me. I want to take from it that calming power and have it *claim me* as a disciple. I want to hug it to me, drink from it. Love it.

Then.

Rage.

I want to fasten my fingers around Raka and Sara's necks and watch their faces *die.*

Half-blind from tears, I stagger to my feet and stumble to the log. I sit, twisting my hands and squeezing them into balls, breathing in heavy drags. *Calm down. Calm down.*

But I don't.

In the absence of anything comforting (the bottle) I reach back for the smiles of those two men, millennia apart in time, but side by side in their humanity.

Cultivate gratitude. Like a seedling.

His fingernail rapping against my head.

I get up and without thinking I stamp off towards the forest. I follow no route through the trees. Branches slap and flick me. I plunge on.

I find myself in the small clearing where I had come upon Sara digging truffles.

Am I surprised? Not really.

I turn to go, but the faint truffle smell catches me. I make myself turn around.

Sara lingers here, the faint earthy smell of the fungi still memorised in the cool morning air. My legs are weak. I sit down and lean my back against a tree. I watch the patterns we left in this clearing, something endlessly repeating. I see myself kneeling beside her, miming zipping my lips, I see her frown, then straighten, her mouth speaking words to me.

I close my eyes to banish the scene, but I can't help but breathe in the air to taste what was left of us that might still be here; a ghost hanging mournfully about the scene of a murder.

I try to convince myself that everything I have felt about her, I had made up in my own head.

That doesn't work. I become angry. I hear Yaneck lecturing me about consequences.

Consequences are not something I can control!

Fresh tears prick my eyes.

I cry.

I cry, but self-pity has a limit. In time, the tears dry.

There is a tapping sound, somewhere, filtering through the trees.

My gaze relaxes. I notice that my stomach is squeezed tight, as if I've got a cannonball wedged into my belly. I relax the muscles, and I find that it prompts a dragging breath of relief. *That's better.*

There is something making a noise, a tapping, tapping, tapping, in the distance. A woodpecker, I assume.

Tap-tap-tap.

It must be a woodpecker.

I was here, many days ago, whispering with Sara. Then we were both gone from this place. From there, a divergence from a close path towards futures that now seem mountain-wide apart.

But this chance meeting was so very sweet, so very *pure.*

Tap-tap-tap-tap.

I stare into space. Time passes. Tap-tap-tap.

Tap tap tap

The forest clearing becomes crisper, as if focus is pulled through a camera lens. The shade cast by the overhanging trees flickers, darkens, lightens.

Clouds pass.

The woodpecker stops. In the quiet of an inbreath, the silence dials up to nothing. The forest is crouched, humped in silence, like an animal that hides in a burrow as a human blunders and stamps by.

Now, the forest emerges. A finch alights on the ground, ignorant of me. I'm entirely still. I'm a rock, a stone, a leaf on the ground beneath the tree I have my back against.

Another finch, drab – the mate – flits down to the ground. The birds hop, they peck. Flit, tap, tap, flit.

Peace, here, smooths out the clearing and the trees. Something scuttles in the leaf litter, a brittle patter. A bird of prey screeches, far above on the morning thermals. The forest brightens, then dims, as clouds pass. Time passes, the birds depart, and I remain, an observer.

Above me, a scampering in the trees.

Time passes.

A family of pine martens descend the tree where the pile of dug earth has been flattened by wind, rain, and time. The three youngsters tumble and fight, the parents sniffing this way and that, smelling the human who is here and not here.

A deer picks its way through the leaves on the edge of the clearing. Its head dips: it nibbles leaves from a low bush. Other deer appear. One steps into the clearing and pauses, in profile. A black liquid eye reflects the forest like a curved mirror. I see myself in this reflection, and I'm surprised I am here.

It can smell me. It doesn't matter to me, and it doesn't matter to the deer. I don't move. It cannot see me.

The deer move off, pausing, nibbling, and the pine martens ascend the trees. The sound is fluid now, the forest moving like a river, unfolding, flitting, growing, being, happy.

What is this thing that watches? It's hardly a person. I own nothing, save the clothes I wear, the few tools I've found or made. I am a blank slate. The world offers itself to me. The forest offers itself. The stream and rivers of water offer themselves to me. The tribe offers itself to me. I have a home.

A tickle begins in my stomach, a surge of excitement, that flipping of the stomach. It doesn't surge. It suffuses. Moving into my heart. From there up the back of my head, over my scalp, and in – in, to the centre of my head, where it shines.

Joy. Pure joy.

And it's here, *right here*. Not in the future, or the past. It's here, in the present.

———

Nothing is ever easy. Even the present moment. I hear voices. Human voices despoiling this moment. The spell is broken, and I feel my cares rushing back in, like rude people jostling in, late, filling up the back of a packed meeting room. Which is my brain. You get the analogy.

I get up and make my way back to my sleeping spot above the caves.

I'm not at peace anymore, not like I was in the clearing. But something *has* shifted. My eyesight seems *new*. The world has been reframed. The royal-rich sky, the cool stream, the green grass. As if while I was in the forest, someone came along and gave everything brighter colours. I hold my hands up. They look like someone else's hands. The fingers are different.

In my chest, Charlie's heart beats out a different sound.

The next morning, I sleep in, past the dawn.

24

It's as if my body and mind are now giving off a scent. A scent that turns me into a homing beacon for humanity. I am sitting staring at the trench I have dug for foundations, suddenly not so sure if I actually want to live here, outside the cave. I realise I want to be *in* there, with them. I want to be near to Yaneck, to Willow and the assorted denizens of my cave.

Oh, but you fucked the adoption ceremony, remember.

I remember puking on Freda.

Like a hawk, like Yaneck, like an eagle, like Superman, I see the bigger picture. *Ok, so I got wasted and blew chunks on one of the brides. So what?* The feeling that *everything is gonna be all right* comes over me.

I puked on a bride at a wedding and told the assembled guests that they needed to go to hell and suck dicks. I wince. And then I laugh.

Yes, I laugh. What else do you want me to do? It's better than feeling sorry for myself!

Of course, I do feel *very* sorry for Freda, the poor girl. And Yaneck. And for everyone. Sara most of all. But it's time to start making things right. Time to pay the piper. Time to apologise. To *everyone.*

Including that asshat Raka.

But I've barely stood up when I see that Willow is approaching with his parents, Salanda and Deakel.

I can't help but feel sheepish. *Baaaaad boy - you puked on the bride.*

'I want to say I'm sorry, Salanda and Deakel. I'm very sorry about what happened.' Salanda looks at me directly.

'It was certainly memorable. I don't think anyone has ever made such a fool of themselves.'

'I am sure,' I reply. 'I am going to apologise to Freda and her family. And Tazak. And everyone else.'

'I've never seen Tazak so angry. I was scared just being in the cave near to him.'

'You drank too much,' says Willow. 'You vomited on Freda.'

Helpful.

'Why did you drink so much?' he asks me.

'Why?'

'Yes.'

I reach out and ruffle his hair. 'Another time,' I tell him. I can now see lots of people ambling up the hill towards us: a throng of hunters on their way out. I watch them coming. I can't recall ever seeing so many men go out at once. It seems to be almost all the men. Some of the women and the kids follow after them.

'You not going with them, Deakel?'

He shifts on his feet, seemingly embarrassed for some reason. 'They want me to go, but I really want to find some better flint.'

'Great,' I say, with no idea what the issue is. I'll leave that with him to figure out, I decide.

The hunters reach the flat above the caves where I stand with Salanda and Deakel and Willow. Culeg, Grease, Zavik, Tazak, the rest of the men, the whole crew. They look at the stacks of bricks, at the hives in the distance. Tazak, downright freaky in his mud-smeared camo war-paint make-up, looks at me.

'So, you are staying?'

'I...'

He gestures with his spear. 'All this. I assume you are staying.'

'Um, yes,' I say. 'If you are happy with that.'

'Not exactly happy,' rumbles Tazak. I see Raka coming up the hill, carrying his spear. He's joining the men. I'm not quite ready to apologise to him. Tazak steps close to me and puts one hand on my shoulder. I flinch slightly, as if he's about to crush my shoulder in his fist. But he leans in, down to my ear.

'Time to grow up, Charlie.'

The hunters go on their way (with Raka giving me a wide berth, thank God). A few women mill about, touching the bricks and staring at the foundations, touching the several clay vessels that I've made in that typical Roman wine amphorae-shape that you see carved on their statues and painted on their frescoes. I look at them now, feeling queasy. I had made them to ferment stuff in. Honey. Fruit. Booze.

Suddenly, I *need* to find Freda and her parents. I need to get that off my chest.

'Charlie.'

I don't see the speaker. I don't care. I look at Salanda and Willow.

'Where's Freda? Where's Hukel and Dera?'

'Dera went to the river,' says Salanda. 'I think Freda is with her. As for Hukel. . .' She points up the trail. 'But Charlie, wait until everyone gets together tonight. You can apologise then.'

'I'll look for them now,' I say. Before I lose my nerve, I need to go and get this done. I need to say my piece. For my own good.

'I'll come with you,' says Salanda. She motions for Willow to stop fingering the stack of bricks and follow her. Deakel has a backpack slung over one shoulder, a spear in one hand. He touches Salanda's cheek with the inside of his palm.

Leaving Deakel to go off and do whatever he's up to, the three of us walk to the stream and follow it as it flows down the hill past my very organised-looking hazel orchard.

Things are coming together. I have some hives, a house project, and I have a whole load of hazelnut trees. *I'm cultivating,* I think to myself.

As for Sara. . . well. . . I feel it cannot last, between her and Raka. Something will give, and soon. And I'll be there to help pick up the pieces. All in the fullness of time.

I see Dera, a long way off, by the river, about two hundred yards west. I'm about to head in that direction when I realise that bringing some form of reparation would be a start. One of my best clay bowls or pots. Something like that. I don't have anything else to give.

'You go ahead,' I say to Salanda and Willow. 'I'm just going to get something for them.'

I peel away from them and head into the cave, walking slowly, letting my gaze settle on all the comforting evidence of human life. The leather-wrapped flint-knapping tools lying neatly on a stone ledge, around which are scattered innumerable chips and flakes of flint and assorted stone. Racks of drying hides. A pile of clay. A cold, ashy campfire. The day is warm, but the caves are deliciously cool.

Yaneck is there, as I hoped he would be. He has some sort of foul-smelling brew simmering in a little clay bowl. It's clearly not for eating. It will be some potentially toxic shamanic Ouija-medicine.

I mean to ask Yaneck about tripping on magic mushrooms, which seems to be a feature of almost all emergent societies. Whether you're a Sioux Indian or South American Indian, or a proto-European or proto-African, it seems that getting mashed on mushrooms is an essential part of advancing your particular civilization.

I never took mushrooms myself, but by the time I left the 21st Century, therapist-mediated tripping had pretty much halved the cases of mental illness in Western societies. I suppose I never did it because I was afraid it would work. I was also scared of what I might see.

I watch Yaneck stirring and fussing over his brew. He looks across the cave at me and gives me a slight smile.

A rush of love for the man hits me, my skin crinkling with a semi-orgasmic sensation of pleasure. Like a thousand sneezes, a million itches, scratched all at once.

'Yaneck,' I say, realising that I'm going to use an English word since I don't know their equivalent, 'you are an absolute *legend*.'

'What's a *legend*, Charlie?'

I'm opening my mouth to explain when Yaneck suddenly holds his hand up. He goes rigid. He tilts his head.

'Urla!' he shouts. Urla moves, and I realise she's been here the entire time – sitting entirely still with her back against the cave, invisible. She looks up.

Yaneck scrambles to his feet and lurches towards me. Urla grabs a long flint knife.

'Yaneck?' I hold out my hands to fend him off.

He runs towards me.

'Yaneck what the fuck man!'

He tears past me, grabbing onto my arm as he goes past. As he pulls me out into the open air, I hear the screaming.

From all around. Upriver, downriver. From somewhere above the caves. Screams and shrieks of women and girls.

Back in the real world, where I came from, I would have thought someone was pulling a nasty practical joke. Not here. I understand, instantly, on some level that genetics has bred into me over millennia, what is happening.

Someone is stealing our women.

It's as hardwired into me as the genes that make my body produce the testosterone that makes my body grow thick muscle over the bones of my limbs.

Sara where's Sara

Yaneck tosses me one of the spears that lean against a frame outside the cave.

'Come!' he says. He stabs his finger at Urla. 'Hide!' he shouts at her.

A scream, nearer. Willow is pelting towards us from the river. Salanda is hard on his heels. And now I get my first look at the raiders. Their leather clothes are almost pitch black. Two of them are running after Salanda.

the men they're away hunting

The knife I've been using the last few months is in a leather sheaf on my belt. I grab at it. It's not there. It's with my things above the cave.

'Willow!' shouts Yaneck, as the boy nears us. 'Keep going, find Deakel, find the hunters!'

The two men chasing Salanda don't stop or slow. In their hands are hatchets.

Yaneck hurls his spear. Salanda doesn't duck. The spear goes over her shoulder. The man Yaneck aimed at doesn't slow; he pirouettes, twisting his body out the way, impossibly grasping the spear shaft as it whistles past him. He swings it around and hurls it back with perfect momentum.

It hits Yaneck where his throat meets his chest.

Salanda passes me.

I'm expecting the men to raise the hatchets and strike down, but they hit Urla and me like a tsunami, smacking their shoulders into us. Both of us go flat backwards. Winded. The man who'd thrown the spear passes us, headed straight after Salanda. The other is above me. He kicks me viciously hard in the ribs. I double up, sucking in a mouthful of his rancid stink. He raises his hatchet high over his head. I raise my arm above my face and cringe against the coming blow. It'll sever my arm, and then my neck.

The man grunts in surprise. I lower my arm and see a spear sticking out of his midsection. I reach up and grab the shaft and I push. The man goes backwards. I stumble to my feet. Urla is unharmed, but dazed. In the mouth of the cave, the second raider has buried his hatchet in Deakel's face. Salanda stabs the man in the shoulder, but he twists, elbowing her hard in the side of the head. She drops the knife but doesn't fall, and he grabs her hair.

He hauls her to her knees and drags her away as she screams and hits his arm. He doesn't stop or even slow down.

I pull Deakel's spear out of the raiders stomach.

Deakel saved me. He saved me, and now he lies, his face crumpled inwards, already dead.

I follow the other man and Salanda as he drags her towards the river. I heft the spear, trying to remember everything that Zavik, Culeg and the others have taught me. But I can't think. Salanda looks back at me, pure terror in her eyes.

'Throw!' she shrieks at me.

But I can't. I can't. The man keeps her close, a human shield, and I see for the first time a twisted smile of satisfaction on his face. He knows I won't throw the spear. His eyes glitter, greed and savagery in equal mix. I step forward. He brings his hatchet to Salanda's throat.

I can't throw my spear. But I can follow. Now I can see the other raiders. They are congregating at the river, herding the women and girls. The men prod them with spears and sticks. And now I see something sickly familiar: boats.

These raiders have come by boat. Twelve dugout canoes, each one much bigger than I'd ever seen or imagined, are tied to stakes in the riverbank. They load the women and girls aboard, several to each canoe. Then four men get in each one. And they pull up their mooring stakes.

I stand nearby, holding a spear, watching. The men look at me and laugh. Some have spears but they don't even bother to throw them. I'm no threat to them now.

I stand on the bank, useless.

I see Salanda and Greta, their hands already tied. I see Tazak's twin girls, their faces red, screaming with fear, clutching on to Sara.

Sara.

Two men in each dugout start paddling. They are going with the current.

As swiftly as they appeared, they vanish.

25

I sit with Urla. We stare at Yaneck's body. He had fallen flat on his back. The spear had passed through his upper chest and protruded a little out the back of his neck, giving his prone body a strange curl that looked like he was locked in the beginning of a sit-up. I had pulled up his cloak and covered his face, but Urla made me remove it.

'Father Sky needs to see,' was all she said. I didn't argue.

We sit. When I look at his face a feeling of fear and horror comes over me, so I find myself staring at his hands. I feel the snap of his finger against my skull, just a day ago.

Think!

An hour passes.

Urla makes a noise, points, then waves. A girl is running up from the river. It's Freda. She's followed by her mother, Dera. They reach us, still pasty with shock. This slowly wears off. Then they begin hollering and weeping. They'd been at the river and seen the raiders coming. They had hidden in the deep pocket in the riverbank – the pocket that has been made by all the recent clay-mining. I don't blame them for hiding. I would have done the same.

Two other women return. One is Grease's lady; a plain but very kind lady called Cela. She's newly pregnant, the bump only just showing. The other is a thin and nervous jitterbug called Rona who is partnered with a guy called Bazel. He's one of the not-quite-over-the-hill hunters. Maybe mid-thirties.

Rona was one of the intolerant shrews who had always been quite adamant that I be expelled. I don't hold it against her. I would probably have expelled myself.

In the late afternoon, the hunters return. Willow managed to catch up with them at some point in the day.

Neither Urla nor I have moved. Both of us have been unable to stop staring at Yaneck's body. The men rush around for a while shouting for their missing women and daughters. When Willow finds his father in the entrance to the cave, dead, he begins crying, and Urla goes over and leads him away. He sits with us now, the three of us made warm in the cooling air by furs that the men drape over us, by the fire they have built next to us.

Urla gives me Willow to hold on my lap, and then she speaks at length with Tazak. I don't really listen. Willow cries for a while and mercifully falls asleep. He sleeps, but his fist remains tightly clutched around my wrist.

I had developed a rather rose-tinted view of this world: it was an unpolluted Eden, free of disease and despair, where you didn't pay tax and where there was no social media. An Auellian paradise where everyone humped each other and made buddies of Neanderthals. What was there not to like?

The issue with Raka, in the light of this raid, seems utterly trivial. Getting drunk at a wedding and insulting everyone seems a silliness that I don't now feel any embarrassment for.

I thought this place was all full of tribes meeting up in the summer, free love, hunting mammoths, trading trinkets, having children, watching them grow and play, a man-woman world of relative equality. I thought that I'd run into some other Homo species; Neanderthals for sure, and probably several other that we didn't even have fossils for. Homo sapiens wasn't the only kid on the block. Most experts reckon we interbred with them, absorbed them, and/or killed them off.

I think I just experienced this potpourri of interbreeding and killing. It's a lot more painful than I'd envisaged it from my 21st century armchair.

Urla is forty-eight years old. Far too old to be bothered with. There's a horrible calculus to this place. There is cold logic that erases all questions of morality.

Morals are like swimming pools or speedboats: people only have them when they can afford them.

So, what is this place? Where am I?

Every form of life is based around resources. Whether it's a plant taking photons produced by the sun, whether it's a bear eating the leaves of that plant, whether it's a human killing and eating the bear, it's always and forever about resources.

The raiders – the men – haven't actually done anything immoral. They've simply appropriated stuff, in this case reproductive resources: the wombs of women.

That they have done so in a complicated way that involves a lot of planning speaks volumes as to the intelligence of a species of primate – but it says nothing about whether it's *right* or *wrong*.

With no real surprise I realise that I have no compunction about killing another human being.

There is no law here.

No police, no god, no judge.

There is only breathing and living, or not-breathing and not-living.

I feel as certain about killing as a child whose toys have been taken away, and who screams to get them back. Right and wrong is irrelevant.

I want my shit back.

I hear my name. I perk up from my daydreams of killing. There's a vague voice that's been nipping at my thoughts, saying that I'll be flayed alive for not having been – what – more effective? But I'm not very bothered. And anyway, Urla has argued my case.

Culeg, who was very close to Deakel, sits down heavily next to me. He looks grim, more *John Wayne* than I've ever seen before.

'Deakel would not have thrown the spear,' he says, his voice distant. His own missus, Ela, has been abducted. He bends and places his forehead in his palms; he stares at the ground.

'Yaneck has been teaching me since I was a young child.'

He's silent for a minute. Then his voice breaks.

'Father Sky. . . did he have to go?'

Grease and Cela sit on either side of Culeg. They put their arms around him. They bunch together.

My buddy, Zavik. His blue eyes, normally almost invisible beneath bushy blonde eyebrows, are wide with shock. His gaze catches mine. No tears on his cheeks, but his eyes shine in the firelight. The big Blondebeard pirate has lost Greta, the lovely, happy lady who always managed to be remain plump and jolly no matter what the food situation was. Zavik and Greta are my two proper buddies.

Greta brought me food every day that I stayed above the caves, sulking like a child.

You know what they'll do to her, don't you?

I shake the thought away. The urge to drink crashes like a wave. I want to drink, but I want something else a lot more:

I want my shit back.

That's better.

Tazak has not stopped. The moment they got back he organised a search party to look for anyone who had hidden or run away. Then he questioned all of us who'd seen the raid. I told him what I saw, what happened from where I was standing. He only nodded. Then he went back and questioned everyone all over again.

His lady, Vala, and their twin five-year-old girls are somewhere on the river, heading east, captives of vile and violent men. I told Tazak that I saw them being taken away. I didn't tell him that their faces were red, and they were screaming in fear.

I sit. Yaneck and Deakel are moved, taken away. Not sure where. I stare at the spot where Yaneck lay. Raka comes and asks me if I saw Sara. I say that I did. She was on a boat.

I tell him I'm sorry.

Sara.

I am angry.

I want my shit back.

26

Culeg officiates at the funerals.

'Deakel was from the Earth. Mother Earth. He is gone back now to lie in her belly.'

Deakel lies in a deep grave. He is dressed in his summer travelling clothes. Beneath his head is his backpack. Winter clothes, some seedcake, a little water, his fire-kit, his knife, his trinkets.

I help the men shovel the earth into the grave. The air is warm in my lungs and the earth is warm in my hands. Willow is between me and Zavik. Next to mine his little hands scoop the earth. He sniffles, drips fall from his eyes, shining strings of snot fall from his nose and pattern the black earth like wet spiderwebs.

In silence we claw the earth over the body of his father.

I wipe Willow's nose and cheeks. I pick him up and kiss his cheek. The salt of his tears stings my dry lips.

Urla, Deakel's mother, stands silently, watching. Only men do the work at a man's funeral. Only women work at women's funerals. I bring Willow, her grandson, to her.

'No!' Willow says, shaking his head.

'Go on,' I say. I put him down next to her. Yaneck is next.

———

Yaneck is laid on a pyre of wood on the flat ground above the caves. It's at his meditating spot where he had watched me while I got into trouble making tea with Willow.

'Yaneck was from the Sky. Father Sky.'

The sun is low in the west when Tazak puts a burning torch to the pyre. Like Deakel, Yaneck is dressed for travelling. Above us and all around the rim of the land, his home the sky waits, arrayed in celebration: the brightest stars nestle in royal blue and the clouds on the horizon glow red and gold.

'Yaneck goes home now,' says Culeg. The flames catch, warming the cooling air.

The flames rise, singeing my face. I can almost believe that Yaneck *does* belong in such a sky. But that would be *magic*. And I don't believe in that. Yaneck is simply dead and gone. I don't move, and I feel a hand on my shoulder. I shake it off, but it returns. I am pulled away from Yaneck's burning body. I turn away from the group of men and walk the short distance to the log where Yaneck and I sat talking – only a day or so ago. Flicking me on the temple, telling me to be better. As I sit, feeling the emptiness where he sat next to me, I *feel* the memory of it, and I *know* it will always carry the agonising bittersweet rush of that time everyone has when you remember your first kiss with your first love, both of you young, supple as weasels, tender as baby ducks, touching, kissing, and when you're older and slower you remember this, it's like a sunset, a warm sun touching the sea and shining from so far away, but so very bright.

Finally, after a day of digging a grave, of building the pyre, of holding Willow and wiping his tears, my own tears come.

I will not tell you about those.

Those tears are mine to keep.

27

L ike a wounded and mauled animal that crawls into shelter and draws itself inwards, we contract.

Fourteen females have been abducted, leaving five women: Urla, Dera, Freda, Cela and Rona. Two males are dead, leaving twenty-two.

Fifteen men. Seven boys.

A numbness settles over the humans who live tucked in this valley in Europe. We are alone.

Willow keeps asking me if I think his mother and little sister will be all right.

'Of course,' I tell him, trying to add brightness to my voice. 'Your mother and little Sela will be fine.' In truth, I'm just hoping the raiders are patient people who will wait until Sela is sexually mature before they rape her.

I remember her shrieking with delight as Willow carried her slung over his shoulders. Perhaps they are not that patient, and Sela is already dead, or. . . living. . .

I can't think about it.

The morning after the attack, Tazak ordered us to pack what we needed and leave the caves. He led us up into the forest. Near the north-eastern side of the valley there's a cave that I'd never noticed. I had passed the area in my wanderings and only seen an accumulated pile of deadfall and rock. It looked natural. But it was carefully done. It hid the entrance to a large cave that accommodates twenty-seven humans at a tight squeeze.

There is little chance the raiders will return. But no one wants to test that theory.

Willow wants to sleep next to me and Zavik. Distantly, I'm touched.

Grebel, the teenager who had smacked his partner, Yala, lies on his bedroll by himself, staring up at the ceiling. He makes no noise, but I think that he sometimes cries.

The only complete family is Freda's. Her baby sister, Hera, had a chest infection and was being cared for by Urla. She was safely tucked up in the cave, asleep, when the raiders came.

Two sentries sit outside at all times, even at night. In the day, three scouts watch from three points: one at the top of the forested valley where it meets the high steppe. One above the caves where Yaneck used to sit, and one near the river. They communicate every ten minutes with whistles – siren blast loud. Like snipers checking in on a radio channel.

Zavik sleeps next to me. Culeg as well. Two men follow each woman wherever they go in the day.

We contract. Instead of several small families and direct kin, we contract into one family. We eat together. We defecate together. We forage and hunt together. We sleep together. The men are grim; ferocity sizzles in the air like static. The women are scared, angry.

In our new cave, our injured body doesn't heal. It metastasizes. What regrows isn't human, isn't Homo Sapiens. As if the injury has awakened genes dormant from times when tooth and claw ruled over brains and nimble tool-wielding fingers. And the flesh that now stops up our wounds is not hominid, but lupine.

We move as a pack.

We have become wolves.

———

We leave in four days. Two men – Brekel and Zander – will stay with the five women and the seven boys. The women are more than capable of hunting and foraging and taking care of themselves, but Tazak says the older guys would slow us down. Personally, I think I'm more likely to slow them down.

The learning curve for me has become a cliff wall. Tazak snarls at me to practice with the spear. 'Practice every day until you can't lift it,' he says, placing it in my hands. I'm by far the worst in the whole tribe. The women all have some skill, especially Freda and her mother, Dera.

To hear the people of this tribe talk about it, I get the impression that raiding tribes and stealing people is an ice age bogeyman: something you hear about, but never experience. Travellers, who Tazak says are less numerous in the last few years, have brought notice of these raids, but they have been occurring "far far eastwards, near the salt sea."

I assume this salt sea is the Black Sea. The only river I know of that ends up there is the Danube. I'm only going on the fact that I was originally in Romania, and I'm guessing I'm still in the environs. The river that runs through our valley is *not* the Danube. It's too small. It must be a tributary.

But even though news of plunder and pillage has reached the tribe, no one has any tangible details. Who these people are, or where their home is, or how many of them there are. Nothing.

I'm given a backpack that is a leather hide stretched over a frame of deer antler, with shoulder straps. Exactly like a modern backpack. A bit boxier, but the space is generous. I watch as Culeg fills it with stuff: a fire-starter kit, a waterskin, a few nodules of flint, spare boots, a big packet of dry tinder and fluff, a cape of thick leather that looks waterproof. Food: dried meat (kangaroo ass is actually venison), dried fruit, dried fish, and fatcake (my name for the balls of rendered animal fat mixed with seeds and wrapped with a section of animal intestine). I heft the pack and try it on. It's not too heavy.

'Thank you, Culeg,' I say.

Culeg nods at me. He barely speaks, these days. The man has turned to iron. He could crush John Wayne like a bug.

Food. We sit outside the cave in the early evening, around a large fire. The women roast the whole carcass of some sort of enormous goat. Zavik turned up with it earlier this afternoon. He carried it slung over one massive shoulder, dropped it with an almighty *thud* at the entrance to the cave, and then stormed off down to the river. Even though I could see blood on his spear, if someone had told me he'd just beaten the goat to death with his bare hands, I would have believed it.

Worn out from my continual practice with the spear, and from trips down to the river collecting water, I sit and stare at this stripped and gutted animal as the outer flesh bubbles and cooks above the flames. A spit has been hammered through its hindquarters, emerging through its throat. It was grazing earlier, somewhere. Now it is suspended above a bonfire. The fat in its muscles liquidizes and drips into the fire. No one dressed it with the normal assortment of herbs they often do. It is fuel.

Fuel to feed a pack of predators.

Freda hands me a platter. An eyeball glistens atop the mound of meat. Brain matter puddles. My fingers spoon it all into my mouth. The only taste I notice is grease.

Wolves, we eat.

The women and the children are sent off into the cave. As I watch them go, I realise I can't remember if I did ever apologise to Freda. Or her parents.

Culeg taps me on the shoulder and hands me a bowl.

'Take a big mouthful,' he says. I comply. The tepid liquid tastes like dead earth and rotting leaves. Hands reach from my left and take the bowl. Raka is next to me. I don't care much. Raka takes the bowl and drinks. Passes it on. I watch the flames.

———

The hacked skeleton of the goat smoulders above the fire. Tendrils of dust – dust that is on fire – flow in lines up into the stars that glisten above us.

It's obviously fairy dust.

It could be spirit dust.

The meat that sits in my stomach smoulders. I notice the spreading warmth as the meat combusts and catches fire. It is alive, and it spreads from my stomach into my viscera, my flesh, my blood, my brain.

My mind.

It is alive and it spreads out into fiery points.

I listen to the person next to me. I reply. We discuss honeybees, about how fairies help them navigate.

My face is *sweating.*

I'm handed a facecloth. I pass this over my face, but I feel only my callused hands rubbing at the dry skin of my cheeks, my forehead, my eyelids. I look to the person next to me. It's Pooh Bear.

I've been discussing honeybees with Pooh Bear.

There's something wrong with me.

I push my finger into Pooh Bear's chest. The hallucination disintegrates.

There is only one feasible explanation for all this: I'm tripping my balls off.

Oh God. Now?

I turn and find someone sitting to my left. I prod them to make sure they are really there. I'm not sure who it is because I can't tell with the harsh light shining out of them.

My body is the size of the universe, my innards a vast black ocean, a void. Panic-dizziness closes my throat. I can't tell if I'm breathing.

On the oil-calm of this black void, a shark breaches the surface, churning a white wake.

The dead eye on the dead grey body swivels and fixes on me.

You're drowning.

Inside, in a faraway place, I scream. The shark turns both eyes upwards, into my skull. Where my brain is.

You're drowning and I'm going to eat your mind.

I can't breathe. I scream again. There's no sound.

The shark thrashes, excited.

An arm loops around my shoulder. I'm squeezed in a someone's arms.

The black ocean rises into my skull; the internal pressure of it breaches my skull, dissolves it into molecules, atoms.

I have no head. My head is now the world.

I'm the child of atoms.

Fairy dust.

My eyeballs are on a plate, and my head is upon a platter.

And the eternal footman holds my coat.

And snickers.

The arm around me squeezes harder. But I *can't breathe!*

I fight. Hands grab me. Wolf paws. Mouths around me say loud words.

My heart is gone with my head, dissolved, and flowing up into the night sky. I can still feel it beating, thrashing as it twists and turns in the thermals above the fire.

Stardust thou art, and unto stardust shalt thou return.

It'll take lifetimes to get it back. I'll end up stalking the interstellar fairy bases forever. Frost crackles my skin with the cold vacuum of space.

I'm being held, immobile.

I struggle. Yaneck is gone! Dead!

I will die alone.

If I'm put back together wrong, I could end up as a beaver's ass.

I am crying. I hear myself crying in the dark.

I lash out. Panic vaporizes the tattered remains of reality.

Impossibly powerful hands tighten around me.

I will snap myself into pieces like sticks of butter.

Someone is shouting.

'Charlie!'

'Charlie! It's Zavik.'

Blondebeard. I press my face against chest muscle, a scattering of hair. I wrap my arms around Zavik.

Dear, dear Zavik. I breathe in his spicy and musky scent. Old Spice. The aftershave of pirates. I find air, and gulp.

Shuddering breaths – mine – pushes the suffocating black away, out of my body.

'The lynx effect,' I say. 'Thank god.'

Zavik says nothing. He hugs me gently. I hear his heartbeat, loud as a drum in my head, but beating calmly, obedient to my controlling paws. I feel his paws, so much like hands, stroking my hair.

Blondebeard. Thank God.

His arms release me.

The shark circles in the blackness, in the night beyond the fire.

I'm going to eat your–

'No!' I shout. But a different man embraces me. He holds me, a mountain-thing, wrapping me in his arms. A mountain holds me up.

I will lift up mine eyes unto the hills, from whence cometh my strength.

A landslide rumbles in my ears.

'Focus, Charlie,' it says. It's Tazak holding me. 'What do you want?'

Before the searing white light of birth, before the pink-black pitch of the amniotic sea, before the first split of the egg. Before I was all these things, I was aware of the question. I've waited longer than my own lifetime to answer it. I see the words, lined like obedient soldiers, waiting for me to speak them aloud. I could dream in this language.

'I want to gather all our fairies,' I say. 'I want to get back all the shining lights that have drifted away.'

'Very good,' says the Tazak-bear. 'One more mouthful.'

That's the spirit juice. 'No,' I say. 'That's the mushrooms.'

'Charlie, it will help you to see.'

'See what?'

'Yaneck,' says Tazak. 'And Sara.'

I look up at Tazak. The zipping lights resolve chaos into a glowing ambience that comes from inside his body.

'I will help you see them,' says Tazak.

I can see into his chest and head. An ocean of gentle light, bathing the features of his grizzly face. Spreading out. Pure energy, pure power. From him comes strength.

Strength beyond understanding.

For us, Tazak is a god.

Tiny lines around his eyes. Little ant tracks. Furrows of the careworn. Furrows made by the heavy trudging worries and fears of his people. Of his world.

Tazak is the President of the United States of the Ice Age. He holds all our fears when we cannot. He keeps us safe.

He gives the night-time cocoa to all the little children.

'Tazak,' I say, 'you are glowing.'

A broad smile happies his wondrous face.

Inexhaustible beauty.

I strain upwards, on tiptoe, and kiss his lips. There is laughter, all around me.

Tazak doesn't react. He still smiles.

Zavik, his face clear now, his eyes a luminous violet in the falling of night and the firelight, holds up the bowl with the magic juice. Other faces float nearby. I am surrounded by friends. The night is warm.

The fairies are flying.

Love.

Love thrums in my flesh, in my skin, in the centre of my mind.

Love shudders.

Love goes supernovae.

Bursts in my mind, my heart, a dizzying bliss.

Fear falls away, a shed skin, fluttering and twisting in the air. The ripples of its impact on the black sea are far, far beneath me. I fly, far above.

I laugh, take the bowl, and gulp a mouthful.

The fungi inside me sizzles through the rivers and streams of my blood to every cell of my body.

The cells make the body, make the brain, make the mind, which reaches a hand, out towards the sky.

I am caveman no longer. I am an intra and extra-stellar traveller.

Tazak nods and turns away toward the forest. It shimmers, yellow with the light of fairies and the glowing grace of honeybees. Tazak holds my hand.

I go with him.

28

I wake up. I open my eyes. I gasp.

The inside of me, the numb interior flesh of my body, my brain, my organs, my muscles, my bones – all this is a crisp lake of clear blue from which I emerge into this day, impossibly freshened.

My life has been a hangover, and this is the first day of my new life. My thoughts. . . the trillions of neurons and synapses have been washed in the purest glacial meltwater. . . these now function in concert, where there was once conflict and discord.

It's a wanky way of saying that my mind seems to have been through a power-wash. It feels like it's been defragged. Like the Charlie Operating System 1.0 was crammed with errors and conflicts and in a tailspin towards the ground, and the last remaining un-fucked CPU decided to do a total power-down and a software re-build – from the ground up.

The mushrooms made me see. I *saw*, with icy clarity. Seeing comes with light, and that mushroom stuff launched me *into the sun*.

I push myself up. I feel a calm I last felt when my mother held me against her breast and let me suckle, her heart vibrating against my cheek, the skin of her nipple salty, and her milk sweet.

We eat breakfast.

We say goodbye.

We heft our packs and pick our way through the forest.

————

The pack of thirteen males travels in single file.

Here is their track, their trace.

Here is the path before they arrive, and here it is afterwards; plants tramped flat, a smell redolent of angry meat, of singed flesh, heartbeats a concert of purpose.

No sound except footfalls on the steppe, through trees, splashing across streams. No words but the few needed to adjust direction and route. There is nothing human here. I watch us, from high up like a hawk, moving across the landscape; wolves tracking prey. I see them, us, myself, each person scanning the ground, the trees, the horizon.

We move like a single entity.

The origin of mass hysteria; here shown in its original and beautiful inception.

'We are bee-wolves,' I say to myself, chewing kangaroo ass, staring east, downriver, whilst Culeg, Raka, and Tazak talk and point and decide.

Zavik stands, looking at the eastern horizon. I know better than to talk to any of them. Their cares and worries are now existential. They have lost their reason for being alive. I know this because I shared it with them. As they ran in the forest and howled at the moon and stars and gave voice to the abyss within them, I ran with them. I *joined* with them. Their grief was made into light I could see, into scent I could breathe into myself, as intimate a coupling as a sexual union.

The men ran, tearing their clothes and their hair, in a moonlit scream of fear and anger, staring into that absence of form, only their combined strength stopping each of them tumbling into madness.

Now in the sunlight, their minds together form single thoughts. These guys are not going gently into the night.

They are not taking it lying down.

Nor I.

I imagine a map, the image of where we are, and where the women might be. Where Sara is. I see the distance, my fingers tracing the map. Under the expanse of stars, I lie on my back, my eyes closed, my senses closed to the emptiness around me, and on this map I touch the place where I might find her. A distant, dark place. I see her face. In my mind, all the images that I've collected of her, I hold them up like snapshots, like pictures, like fragile film. I linger on each one carefully, aware they are precious things, existing only in transient brain matter, in neurons, in electrical impulses, chemicals.

Her head turned, looking at me, as she's led away by the women. The quiet smile on her face as she sees me looking at her as she stands, knee-deep in the shining river, naked, rivulets of water tracing her stomach, over her thighs. In the clearing, her lips parted, excited, her breathing almost ragged as she waits for me to reach out and touch her. For my fingertips to trace the taut skin of her neck, her cheek, to slide into her long blonde hair, to draw her to me. To kiss. The scent of her skin fills my nostrils, that scent I will get when I pull her close and taste the sweetness of her mouth, her tongue. Her arms around me, clutching, grasping, saying my name over and over, her soft skin *weeping*, a joy she can't keep in. I shiver as I see myself swim into her, as I see my soul enter hers, her embrace welcoming, wrapping me in *her,* in pure grace.

Ascending through space.

I need to be brave, as we move away from home, as we drift from the lights of home into the unknown. The days pass and my resolve weakens as both time and the landscape lengthen out. As the plains, hills and valleys become unending. I need to be brave.

I whisper her name, over and over. I lie on my back. I look at the pictures of her, night after night, and they grow in clarity, as if they are the opposite of memories, growing clearer and closer as time passes.

Sometimes I cry, though from the agony of love or from the fear of what might come, I can't say.

In that clearing, the only time I spoke to her alone, the only time we were alone, she touched the spot between her breasts and asked me: *when I think of you, why does my heart feel so bad?* The answer I should have given her was *love, it's love that makes it ache.*

It's love.

I need to be brave. I *must* be brave.

————

The pace is brutal. We start at first light, and we stop when it becomes too dark to travel. We have walked for nearly six days.

While the rest of the guys sleep, I sit watch with Raka. Not my favourite pastime, but I can tolerate the guy now. He still has a major beef with me, but I can't summon any greater emotion than a silent contempt that borders on not caring. Raka can fuck off and do what he wants with his life.

He's behaving strangely in a way that I can't quite put my finger on. He seems slightly manic. I suppose right now everyone gets a free pass for the state of their psyche. But I've seen him doing something that I am sure no one else does: stealing. At night, when he thinks everyone is asleep, I've seen him pilfer food from the packs of others, and then silently scoff it, I guess so there is no evidence.

I'm tired of having anything to do with Raka, and I don't want to get involved. I'm not some schoolboy sneak who's going to tell on him. Just let him carry on being an asshole.

The candle I hold for Sara – you've probably cottoned on to the fact that it is actually a Statue of Liberty-sized flaming torch. I fantasize about a life with her, constantly. I even entertain the idea of eloping with her. But the raw and basic violation of this fantasy is that I *cannot* leave this tribe. I can't. If we eloped, we'd probably last about a month – at most.

Yaneck might be gone but I have friends, and these people are as good as I'm going to find anywhere. They are *awesome* people, particularly given the competition that seems to be knocking about. If I'm to stay, I can't stand in the way of Sara being with Raka. She'll only suffer if I make trouble. And I can't exactly just kill him, can I?

While I sift through my pictures of Sara, night after night, I force down the pain that comes when I see that *she and I* cannot happen. I force it down. It is like swallowing a burning coal the size of a baseball.

It's what you have to do when you grow up.

You have to swallow it all.

I swallow it, and look up to the stars, and I lie on this land, in this cellophane-thin sliver of atmosphere as it drifts in space and time, and on my pictures of her I write words.

I will love you 'til I die. We'll float in space and time. Just you and I.

On the ground, in dreary reality, is Raka. The only way I can deal with him is to mentally separate him from Sara. See him as a singular human being. An asshat, yes. But nothing more than that.

This way, I *can* deal with him, though Yaneck being gone seems to have given Raka a license to be even more of a shithead to me. He bumps into my shoulder whenever he walks past me. He taunts me about my spear skills. Everything I express, he rubbishes. I don't react to any of this, though it grates more and more with each passing day. The galling thing is that he *is* great at tracking, he *is* fantastic at finding food – like he has some superpower sense of smell. He's slick, for sure. He's wiry and strong. At night, as I've done since last winter, I do push-ups, sit-ups, lunges, and I shadow-box, partly because it calms me, but mainly because I suspect I'll eventually end up in a fight with him.

'Charlie,' says Raka, breaking me out of my reverie. I look over at him, then at the sleeping men, lit by a small fire. No one seems to be awake. Perfect Charlie-baiting weather.

'What is it?' I ask.

'When we get the women back, do you think you will still want Sara after she has been with many different men?'

I say nothing.

'They will rape her, you know.'

I said I could deal with him. I take a deep breath.

'That's a sweet image, Raka.'

He ignores this.

'Some men will be unhappy their women have been treated like this. Some men find it difficult to forgive the women.'

'That's only if they are asshats,' I reply. I've taught him the word.

'I do not think I will mind,' he says, 'It will teach her some sense.'

I feel my hand spasm into a crushing force around the haft of the spear I hold. Burning hatred, sick revulsion. But I stay silent for a full minute. I don't move. In the flickering orange light from the fire I can see his little eyes on me, waiting. I wait for the wave of hate to ebb enough to allow me to speak without screaming at him. I take deep and slow breaths. My heart slows down.

'That is lovely,' I say. 'I'm sure if we speak to everyone tomorrow, we can agree to trade.'

'Trade what?' he asks.

'We can trade *you*,' I say, my voice soft. 'For Sara. If you think rape teaches people manners, then you should spend a few years with these men. We all know you would enjoy it.'

He stands up and takes a step towards me. He's suddenly angry.

And I was handling this all so well. I drop my spear and ball my fists.

'Charlie?' A small voice in the darkness. We both whip round.

Willow takes a step into the light cast by the fire. His face is a mask of fear, his high boy's voice is shrill.

'Charlie, you need to wake everyone up!'

'Willow!' snaps Raka, who stamps towards him. Willow scuttles over to me. Raka reaches us and clamps a hand on the kid's arm.

'Hey,' I say gently, putting what I think is a steadying hand on Raka's arm. 'Leave the boy alone.'

Raka shakes off my hand and pulls Willow hard away from me. I let him do it.

'You have to listen!' says Willow.

Raka shoves Willow towards the fire, and then whistles low. The men come awake in a single contorting spasm. Tazak rolls into a crouch, a knife in his hand.

Willow's eyes are wide with fear, but there's a determination in the lift of his chin. *Good for him,* I think. The little guy has followed us until it was too late for anyone to turn back with him. He wants to get his mum back. And possibly stick a spear through the guy who killed his dad. He's eight years old. Old enough to know which side he wants his bread to be buttered.

No one says anything. Some rub their eyes and peer. Raka can't help himself: he kicks Willow on the back of his thigh, dropping the kid to his knees.

'Raka, leave Willow alone, last chance,' I say, my voice rising slightly. Raka whirls around and advances on me, the butt of his spear wobbling in front of me like a club.

'You!' he snarls. 'You don't know a thing! You're not even meant to be here, you –'

'But he *is* here,' says Zavik, his voice level.

Tazak makes a noise, something between a hiss and a low whistle – the sound you'd make to a dog to tell it to shut up. Everyone pipes down. Tazak sits on the ground, crosses his legs, and motions Willow over to him. Tazak sits the boy on his lap and touches the outside of his hand to Willow's cheek. The touch is long. Tazak's two girls are only a few years younger than this boy.

'Willow,' says Tazak. 'The decision was not yours to make, but I understand why you have come.'

Willow ignores this. He points west, in the direction we have come from, in the direction he followed us from.

'Men,' he says. 'Four men. Scouts. Following you since home. I've been following them.'

Tazak is on his feet. I know what's going to happen. He's going to tell the men to spread out, into the darkness, to find the scouts. An image comes to mind, bright and clear: a middle-aged gunslinger, a bounty-hunter. I have an idea. I jump up.

'Tazak, wait!'

He looks at me, about to ignore me and signal the men.

'Wait!' I hiss this with a tone of command that makes him blink in surprise. Charlie, ordering the boss around.

'Charlie, this is not –'

'Shut up, Tazak,' I say, past caring about offense. 'I have an idea.'

––––––

I speak to Willow. I listen to him.

The four men, now watching the distant twinkle of our campfire, are scouts, left behind to follow us as we trek in pursuit of the kidnappers.

Our followers are thieves. They are predators. Looking for them in either the night or the day will only alert them, make them more cautious, skittish. Their design is obvious: to overtake us as we near their tribe; to warn them of our impending attack.

But Willow, watching from the steppe cliff as we departed the cave nearly a week ago, saw them pick up our trail. Willow tells me they stay well back, only coming within sight of us at night. They watch us strike camp in the morning, and they catch up with us when we make camp at night.

'I didn't want to risk them finding my track,' says Willow. 'I couldn't cross the river and overtake them until now.'

Willow assures me that the men didn't ever see him. I believe him. I speak to Tazak. A slow smile comes over his face. He looks dreamy. He likes the idea.

I resume my sentry post, sitting on the rock. Raka resumes his, whispering his nasty protests at my plan.

The plan preys on the gullibility of bloodthirsty men, on the it's-too-good-to-be-true cognitive bias. I remember reading about one guy, some cowboy in the Wild West, who was collecting bounties on a group of American Indians who had attacked a caravan of Europeans, murdering the men and children, and raping the women.

The cowboy came back with a bagful of scalps to get his reward at the sheriff's office. Of how he managed to scalp a retinue of mad Indians, he was quoted as saying: 'It wasn't good or honourable. There was no honour in it. It was the only way to do it, is all.'

———

Tempers are frayed. The next morning, there is a disagreement that breaks into a fight. Culeg loses his shit with Grease. It starts with an argument about food. Blows are traded. It takes several men to separate the pair. Grease's leg is broken.

We waste two hours getting it set and crafting some makeshift crutches. The men grumble about bad luck. Progress is slow. We cover about ten miles, tops, before stopping in the late afternoon, well before nightfall. We make camp on the riverbank, in a wide meadow that's been cropped low by horses – the animals are gone but their dung is spotted about, fresh.

A despondence settles over the men. Raka needles me more than usual. It is a supreme effort to ignore him. Even the deer that Bazel and Culeg brought down doesn't lift anyone's spirits. I watch them gut and skin it and build up a big fire. Out of character, Tazak snaps at everyone. He shouts at Willow, telling him he's stupid to have followed us. Culeg and Bazel argue with him. I retreat to a small hillock a stone's throw away and watch them go at it.

Raka can't help himself. He comes over to me.

'You!' he shouts, stabbing his finger at me the way I know he'd like to do with a knife. 'This is your fault!'

My patience, my carefully cultivated control, snaps. I stand up. 'Fuck off!' I shout.

The fucker socks me in the face. Well, he tries. Unthinkingly, I flinch, dipping my head, and his fist connects with the thick skull of my forehead. I've heard it said that it's like punching a wall. Raka shrieks and holds his injured hand. I'm stunned with surprise, more than injury. I simply stare at him for a few seconds.

'No, Charlie!' It's Tazak's voice. It's several of the men, all saying this. It has the opposite effect.

I launch myself at Raka, my hands going to his throat.

It's a rubbish fight. It's the opposite of what happens in the movies. We grapple with each other, muscles straining, trying to hit and strangle each other. We roll around, grunting like pigs. Hands seize me, lift me away, prise my hands off the slimy toad I was trying to throttle. Whatever fever has gripped these men, it's now blazing in my veins. I kick and scream in frustrated fury as I try to *get back* to Raka, to *finish* him.

They dump me near the fire, where the deer is roasting, sizzling and spitting. Culeg, Zavik and Bazel are still holding me. Tazak is shouting at Raka.

It's all going to hell.

———

It gets worse. It's not even nightfall before someone (I'm not sure who) produces the birch-tea. I watch, horrified, as I see them all get properly drunk. Apparently, several others had also brought supplies of the birch-sap brew. I pretend to drink. I don't know what else to do.

I can't drink. Not now. I must keep my head whilst all about me are losing theirs.

Songs are sung. Drunken voices roll gaily across the landscape. They eat heartily and drink heavily. This is the high. Then comes the low. There's another fight. Lots of rolling around. Willow comes over to me. He sits down and his small hand finds mine.

'Are we going to go home?' he asks me.

'I don't know,' I say.

Hours have passed. The men are winding down, finishing the supply of birch-tea. Some of them are already asleep, lying in random spots where they have passed out. The party is over.

———

The fire has burned low, to just a bed of baking coals that give off no light. Willow and I are the only ones awake. Near the remains of the fire, Tazak sleeps, still sitting upright, leaning against a large rock.

I roll out my bedroll and Willow snuggles up next to me. I close my eyes.

Two hours pass. I can't sleep. No one else stirs. There's just some incoherent sleepy mumbling from time to time. I watch the sky, counting shooting stars in the cloudless sky. The moon is a thin slice of sliver in the sky, giving little light.

Willow hears it first. He taps my leg with a knuckle, and he doesn't move. I listen, and then I hear it. The sound is barely audible: the sound of low grass being *bent* by a foot moving in slow-motion, then a squishing sound as a human weight comes over the foot.

My heart is thudding in my chest, blood rushing in my ears. One hand lies on the hatchet that I took from the raider who Deakel killed. The other hand is curled against my chin, index finger and a thumb resting against my lips.

My eyes are open. I tilt my head slowly. Against the stars I can see the humped shapes of the scouts, moving slowly, almost silently, perhaps six feet away. Moving amongst the scattered forms of the prostrate men. With my thigh, I nudge Willow twice. I put a finger and thumb in my mouth. I take a final steadying breath.

Willow pushes a tall stack of dry twigs so they topple onto the roasting coals.

I whistle, sharp and loud.

There is a scream of pain. A sound of running feet. There is shouting, screaming, as the intruders encounter Culeg's posse who an hour earlier snuck off into the night and circled wide to make a perimeter.

Every one of us is shouting our own name so that we don't accidentally stab or spear one another by accident. The flames flare up around the stack of twigs, absurdly bright after the near pitch-black. Tazak runs past me, moving with that weird bear-speed he has.

One of the raiders lies on his front, a spear stuck into his back, between his shoulder blades. He flops pathetically, both hands reaching behind to try and get hold of the spear.

It's no contest. The game was rigged from the start. Inside a minute, three of the scouts sit in front of the fire, their hands tied behind their backs. Spear points bristle against their chest, their faces, their backs. Tazak goes from man to man, tying their ankles together, tugging the knots viciously tight.

Grease didn't have a real fight with Culeg, and he doesn't have a broken leg. There was no birch-tea. No one got drunk, and no one was asleep when the raiders entered our campsite. The only thing that was unplanned was *my* fight with Raka.

The guy, the bounty-hunter who killed the six Indians and took their scalps as proof for his reward admitted how he'd done it. He'd tracked them for several days. He waited until they were sitting around their campfire, incoherently drunk off their ass on whiskey, and then he walked up and shot them all dead.

We laid a sneaky trap for these four men. A false-flag operation.

We gave them a too-good-to-miss opportunity to dispatch a gang of drunken hostiles. We played possum.

There's no honour in it. I know that. But honour can go to hell. It was the only way to do it, is all.

29

I sit down on the ground. I'm dizzy with relief. I've spent the day nervous as hell. I've been in the grip of gnawing fear and near-panic for the last two hours.

If someone gets hurt, if it doesn't work, if. . . if someone gets killed!

Finally, I can let go. The tension leaves my body in a shaking flood. Tazak is jubilant. Everyone is fucking ecstatic. Everyone is clapping me on the back. Well, everyone except Raka who seems happy but doesn't come near me. The men are so happy there is a big hug-a-thon going on. Everyone's as giddy as schoolgirls.

Everyone except the three muppets trussed up by the fire.

The guy with the spear in his back has stopped moving. I think he is still alive but the amount of blood that had pooled around him is quite astonishing. The spear must have punctured an artery. He probably has a minute or two of life left.

The three men look like us. Different style of clothes, but they are definitely Homo sapiens. They are big specimens, like my tribe is. They are handsome, and I'm reminded of the Slavic/Malaysian look that seemed to be *the in thing* on social media. The sort of look you'd get if everyone in the world fucked each other, and a single kid was produced from all that fucking.

The three men are mute, unmoving. They stare at the fire, their faces blank.

I've suggested a method of interrogation to Tazak and Culeg. They follow it perfectly. Tazak, sitting next to me, signals for silence.

'Culeg, there's no sense questioning them if they can't understand us.'

'I suppose not,' replies Culeg gruffly. 'It's a shame,' he says. 'If only we could trade these lot for the women. But we can't make them understand that.'

'I agree,' says Tazak. 'So, which one do you want to kill first?'

I watch the men. One of them doesn't react. Two of them go stiff, lock eyes with each other, only for the briefest moment. Then they look down at the ground.

This charade between Tazak and Culeg accomplishes two things: these dickheads now think that we aren't messing around when it comes to offing them – but we would be open to negotiations.

A bit of *give and take.*

But the thing is, I expected them, upon hearing of our willingness to kill them, to just start gabbling. They don't. They stare at the fire. Are they really going to keep silent and let us kill them?

Like a hawk, high up, I look down on this scene. I see very much, too much. A cold horror crawls over my skin. I speak in English, to myself. There is no real way of saying this in my tribe's language.

'I'm a child of the atom.'

Willow looks at me.

'What?' he asks.

I swallow hard. Even though he hasn't understood the words, I feel like just hearing the phrase has contaminated him, like I've just upended pure filth into this world and it's spreading like a rushing tide across all of us.

'What?' repeats Willow. I shake my head, clearing it. In truth, I've realised a terrible thing. It's my design that has brought us to this juncture. It's my sneaky 21st century self, steeped with the knowledge of unending human trickery, warfare, and strife. It's because of me that we have three captives in front of us. Captives that we may well have to torture if they don't cooperate.

We could have ignored these scouts, could have pressed on, and come up with a different plan. A plan involving simply abducting our women, with no casualties.

But that makes no sense. That's a stupid plan. One that wouldn't work. We'd just get ourselves killed.

I think of Yaneck talking about *choices*.

'Charlie?' It's Tazak who says my name. I blink a few times, coming back to myself.

'Yes?' I say.

Tazak nods at the men by the fire. He means *now what?*

'Let's take a walk,' I say.

I go with Tazak past the men, to the edge of the firelight. Culeg joins us. Raka is on sentry duty, staring out into the darkness. I lower my voice so there's no chance the hog-tied men by the fire can hear.

'The two on the left,' I say. 'They understood you and Culeg. So, kill the third man. These two will talk and tell us everything.'

Tazak looks at me. His eyes scan my face, then they drop to look at his hands. He rubs his knuckles, the way I've seen him do sometimes when he's deep in thought.

'Good idea,' says Raka. 'It will make them talk.'

I look at Raka, something sparking in the back of my brain. Something that doesn't make sense. He doesn't sound sincere.

(he's lying he knows they won't talk)

I shake my head minutely. *Bullshit,* I say to this voice. *It's just that I'm not used to Raka agreeing with me. Ever.*

'You want to kill this man?' Tazak asks me this.

'No,' I reply. 'But I don't see what choice we have. They killed Deakel. They have the women.'

Tazak turns and speaks quietly to Culeg. Then he walks back to the fire. I follow. Tazak sits down facing the men. I sit next to Tazak.

Tazak nods. A moment later a spear tip erupts from the throat of the captive, the third man. He man pitches forward, making a gurgling sound. Culeg stands behind him, one hand on the spear shaft.

Incredibly, the two remaining captives don't react.

What the hell?

We all watch the man die. It takes a few minutes.

I lean and whisper to Tazak.

'Take this one.' I point. 'Hurt him, but don't kill him. Hurt him badly. Make him talk.'

Tazak is silent for a long moment. The fire crackles. The blood of the dead man is still spreading in a wide pool. Then Tazak rouses himself.

'Culeg,' he says, 'break two of this man's fingers.'

'Me?' asks Culeg.

'Yes, you.'

Culeg pulls the spear out of the prostrate corpse. Killing something is one thing. Torturing is evidently another thing altogether. He hesitates.

'I'll do it,' I say. I hear the words come out of my mouth before I can even compute what I'm saying.

Everyone looks at me. Including the guy who's about to get tortured. His gaze is blank.

'Fuck's sake,' I mutter. 'Zavik, Culeg – hold his arm out.'

They grab the guy and cut his hands free. Culeg and Grease wrap their arms around the guy's chest and one of his arms. Zavik grabs a wrist and wrenches the guy's other arm forward. My stomach is already swimming sickly. I take the man's little finger and push it backwards. It gives with a sharp snap. My stomach heaves.

The man grunts, his body spasms.

'I know you understand me,' I say. 'Tell us where your people are.'

He shakes his head. I break another finger. No response other than a muffled grunt of pain.

'This is going to get worse. Much worse. I will not kill you. I will just keep hurting you. It will be worse than death.'

The man says nothing. I feel like throwing up.

Suddenly I see myself. From a hawk's view, high above: I'm leaning over a man, breaking his fingers, telling him I'm going to torture him until he screams and screams and screams.

I had this evening all planned out. It wasn't supposed to happen like this.

Choices. Consequences.

I thought if the captives simply *believed* we were down with some ice-cold murdering, then they'd sing like canaries. I didn't expect them to be so darned obstinate. Their silence makes me angry.

I want to know where Sara is.

I think of Yaneck. I think of Greta. I think of my plans; my little house on the prairie, a merry fire burning in the hearth while snow falls silently on my hazel and fruit orchards and on my beehives. And these men had to come along and *fuck it all up.*

People talk about *seeing red.*

'Put his arm flat on the ground,' I say to the guys.

They shove the man forward so he's on his belly. Zavik puts a foot on the forearm. The palm is flat on the ground, the two broken fingers lying limp at a dizzying angle. I take a thick branch from the fire.

'Tell me,' I say to the man. He remains silent.

The tip of the branch is a solid glowing coal. I lay this on the back of the man's hand. He screams. I keep it there for a long two seconds. Zavik steps down on the man's arm. I hear a snap.

I hunker down so I'm near the guy's face. His eyes are tightly shut, ragged breaths coming between gritted teeth. I push the hair back from his face. It is already wet with sweat.

'Tell me,' I say, my voice gentle.

He opens his eyes and looks at me. He spits in my face.

'We can trade you,' I say, wiping my face.

He starts to laugh, manically. This noise turns to a blood-freezing howl of agony as I press the glowing coal into the back of his hand, *hard*. I keep it there, smelling burning flesh that smells like frying bacon.

He doesn't even sound human anymore, he doesn't seem human, maybe he's not human...

Someone takes hold of my hand and lifts the branch away. The spell breaks. I stand up and walk away from the fire, into the darkness. I'm dizzy. I go to the river and bump into a hunk of driftwood. I sit on it, part my legs and vomit between them. Torturing a man is. . . difficult. I close my eyes and for a few seconds all I can hear is my breath, panting, and my pulse throbbing in my neck, a rushing in my ears.

Tazak speaks from behind me.

'Now what?'

I wipe my mouth on my sleeve. 'If they won't talk, then it's your decision.'

Tazak comes over to me and sits on the ground. He is so big that his head is level with mine. 'Are you all right, Charlie?'

'No,' I say. 'I've never treated a man like that before. I didn't know I could, until I was *there*, next to him, asking him questions I need answers to.'

Tazak doesn't say anything.

'I am some sort of. . . savage animal.' I want to say *monster*, but I don't know their word for it.

But Tazak understands what I mean. He puts a hand on my shoulder.

'Charlie. . . these people attacked us first, days ago. And these four men came here tonight to kill us.'

'But Tazak, you don't know what I know.'

(twisted metal, burning)

'And what is that?' he asks.

(the skyline's on fire I saw it)

Tazak shakes my shoulder gently.

(castle bravo little boy fat man)

'Charlie?'

'Huh?'

'What do you know that I do not?'

I take a steadying breath.

'There is much death, where I come from. . . I never imagined I could do bad things – things truly bad people did. I *hated* those people. I thought I was a good person, one of the good people.' I take a deep breath in.

'But I think I am not. I am just as. . . filthy.'

'Charlie, you have saved us from a certain trap. If these scouts had gone ahead to warn their people. . .' Tazak smacks a fist into his palm. 'It would have been the end of us, Charlie. You have done what you needed to do.'

'Yes,' I say. 'I did. But Tazak, human blood has a way of sticking to your hands.'

Tazak shrugs. 'What do you want me to do? Leave the women with this tribe? Abandon them?'

'No,' I say.

'Good.' He gets up. 'At least we are sure they are not going to tell us anything. If it makes you feel better, I was going to hurt them too.' With that he tramps back to the campfire. I stay where I am. I don't want any part of it.

(but you started it)

Tazak will never understand. He won't ever grasp just how pernicious violence is. He's never read a history book. He's never watched the news. Imagine trying to explain the Crusades, the Inquisition, anthrax, sarin gas, nukes, the Holocaust – to Tazak? His brain would just squish flat under the sheer weight of the numbers.

I stare into the darkness above the river, and I listen to the brief sounds of two men being killed.

Thankfully, it's quick.

30

We follow the river east for fifteen more days.

The first day or so after killing the four scouts, the oppressive sadness and loss that had kept us crushed was lightened. I put it down to a cathartic bloodletting, a levelling of the score. But whatever it was, it didn't last long. The days of travelling that follow are a dispirited march eastward.

Always eastwards. Following the river. The kidnappers had to disembark *somewhere*.

The landscape barely changes. On the brows of the low rolling hills we stop to rest: to snack on something but mainly to scan the horizon. As far as we can see in every direction is more of the same. It is like a greener version of the African savannah: plains ringed by hills and the flat horizon only, the river lying twisted out, coiled in places, but draining always eastwards.

I sit in the shade of a rock, or a lone tree, a bush, and stare beyond the river to infinity.

This view, this *openness,* this big sky above a vast continent – it would once have made me tremble and have some kind of agoraphobic panic attack. Now, it is not frightening.

Best I can figure it, it's because not so long ago, I *saw* infinity. I saw the *distance* of everything. I saw where the fairies hide their gold under the rainbow. Far, for sure, but reachable.

My brain was scrambled and rebuilt by mushrooms. When I have this thought, I laugh out loud.

I sit in the nook of a red rock and watch stars glitter above emptiness.

We plant a foot on the ground, tilt forward and plant another foot. Like this we make our way across the infinite earth, towards where fairies hide, and men keep stolen women. We follow the river, the signs of these marauders' trail as thin as vapour, a mark made by a cloud that has outwept all rain.

And on the low heights above the plains, we look ahead. For anything – for any sign of human activity or habitation, and for herds of animals to prey upon. Many of the species are what fossil-hunters millennia from now will call "megafauna" – the large animal species that didn't make it past the mass extinctions that occurred during the latter part of the last ice age. The word *mega* is apt: the animals look like they've been injecting steroids, testosterone, growth hormone and possibly some radioactive waste. They are *mega* in every sense.

We see woolly rhinoceros. We climb trees when a family of these grumpy bastards get protective of their young ones. This involves trying to stab and stampede us. Rhinos, furry ones. In Europe.

The giant deer (from a family called Megaloceros if my Latin is correct), are insane, their shoulders about the height of Tazak's head. They are like stocky adolescent giraffes. We see them in herds. Their antlers are a weird saucer-shape – solid in the middle, flaring out into points. The racks on some of them look the size of a dining room table. I think these are last recorded as having died out around about the time humans were discovering agriculture.

Though some folks in the 21st century bang on and on about climate, a sober look at the evidence shows you that wherever humans went, they killed off all the large herbivores; mammoths, giant elk and deer, straight-tusked elephants. They did a pretty good line in extermination, without the help of global warming.

The mega-carnivores like cave lions and sabertoothed cats that depended on these – well, they popped their clogs en masse.

Even when armed with only fire and flint, technologically a young species, we are as dangerous as a novel virus. I suppose you could say that by the 21st Century AD, the virus called H sapiens had a near 100% fatality rate. And an R-0 number well into six figures.

Between the trees, in the open grassy meadows that line the river, our passage often flushes some kind of hare, but again, it's like the hares are also juicing the steroids. A medium-sized dog is about the same weight. Is it a giant *jerboa*? Something like that.

These are pleasing distractions. But these are only giant herbivores. There are also giant animals that are a lot more aggressive and much more up for a ruck with a bunch of tasty two-legged apes. Cave bears. Cave lions. Sabertoothed tigers. Leopards. All this madness existed in Europe during the last ice age.

Raka is leading. Taking point, as the military would say. He turns and makes a signal, which I've been taught means *lion*. We walk carefully and congregate around Raka. A massive poo lies on the ground in front of him. He points at the ground around it. The men are nodding. I don't see anything, but evidently there are tracks. Paw prints.

'How many?' asks Tazak.

Raka fusses about in the grass.

'Seven,' he says eventually. 'Maybe more.'

Christ on a hellhound. *Seven* cave lions.

Christ. Ok.

I don't move or say anything. But I feel my skin go cold, and clearly I have gone pale since Raka nods at me and grins.

'Do you feel well, Charlie?'

Asshat.

I don't bother to reply. I *am* scared. I've been told repeatedly that cave lions are huge, and the best thing to do if I see one is run away.

'The boundary is here,' says Raka, scuffing the earth with his heel. 'It will take days to cross.'

He means the lions' territory. Tazak sucks his teeth in annoyance, looks this way and that, then faces forward and nods to a rocky outcrop ahead of us.

Culeg motions for quiet. He makes a sign: *continue on, keep low, nobody make a fucking sound, and if you have to squeeze cheese then do a super-quiet sneaky one.*

If I don't go with them, I'll be left behind. We scuttle a hundred yards to a spine of rock. The river runs to our right, and it has carved its way through this stone over countless millennia, though here the erosion is slower: there's a small waterfall.

I'm taking note of the direction of the wind, I realise, as we pile against the rocky slope. It's blowing in my face. So technically we are downwind of the lions' territory. This, at least, is comforting. We scramble up the slope, the guys looking at me disdainfully as I'm the one making all the noise. I peek over the top.

And my testicles contract into little grapes.

The lions are on a rise about a quarter of a mile distant. Several females, four or five cubs rolling around. I'll dispense with the hyperbole. These things are bigger than my worst nightmare. One female, standing in profile, looking south across the river, seems the same size as a three-person sofa. But the male... the male. He is as big as a bastarding racehorse. Ok, my words are screwy. But this thing looks like it eats grizzly bears for breakfast.

I don't deal well with danger. I get scared. I've always been somewhat scared of animals, particularly large ones. As a kid I was afraid of things like horses, big dogs, even cows. I got over it, mostly, but I suppose I never got the chance to test my personal phobias through exposure therapy with cave frigging lions and lorry-sized rhinos.

I let myself slide down the slope, and when my feet touch the level plain my legs almost fold under me. Willow follows me down.

'I'm very scared, Willow,' I say. I fan myself theatrically, but in truth, I *do* feel like fainting. I *do* want to run home, screaming.

Willow puts his hand in mine. He looks a lot less anxious than I am.

'I'm scared too, Charlie.'

Willow. Bless his little cotton socks.

The men climb/slide down the rocky slope. Tazak looks at the sky. It's late afternoon. Still many hours of daylight left. Many hours of travelling time.

I sidle up to Zavik.

'What happens now?' I ask him.

Zavik just nods at Tazak, who is deep in conversation with Raka. They point in various directions. Hammering something out. Tazak eventually turns to us all.

'We will go back the way we came. Half a hand.'

A hand is a unit of time. Stretch your arm out and place your hand horizontally against the sky as if shielding your face from the sun. *A hand* is the time that the sun takes to travel across your hand. For me it equates to about half an hour. It's relative, of course. If you're sitting there watching a pot of water, waiting for it to boil, or if you're stalking a buffalo, time dilates or compresses, respectively.

So, it's a fifteen-minute walk back the way we came.

One lonely evening, I'd made a small hole in a pot and counted three thousand, six hundred seconds (an hour) whilst I watched sand pour out and fill a lower receptacle. Then, that amount of sand, in that lower pot, would always take the same amount of time to fall through the hole in the upper pot. I reckoned I might at most be a minute or two short or long. But I invented a timer!

Then I realised it was pointless unless I also invented a gas oven and needed to follow a recipe for cheese soufflé.

We retreat, and pitch camp. We make two fires. One of them burns, lonely, a stone's throw away. More fires equals less lions. That's the theory.

Even so, the men are all on edge. In part because of the lions, in part because the need to keep travelling is so urgent.

Sleep is long in coming. I think of those cave lions, those *apex* predators. Top of the food chain. We might as well be swimming in a lake with a bunch of great white sharks. Two fires are the equivalent of double locking your doors in a rough neighbourhood. I sit cross legged on my sleeping roll, holding my spear: a slim staff of ash wood tipped with a four-inch flint point. I feel incredibly silly. Stupid, even. To think that being out in the middle of fuck-knows-where was a safe pastime.

To a cave lion, we are fantastically fragile things. Our hides are as thin as cellophane, holding in litres and litres of very spillable lifeblood. Puny twig-like bones and ribs, pathetically covering a heart. A thin papier-mâché skull encasing a delicate and critically important blob of grey jelly. Cave lion – cave bear – cave werewolf for all I know; all these things can rush through our toothpick spears and start snapping up all our shit: our skulls, legs, faces, arms, asses, balls. Everything about us is removable. Breakable. Spillable.

Evidently, a mind-meld with mushrooms doesn't extend to banishing fear about getting eaten by a Volkswagen-sized carnivore.

But fear and anxiety *have* to give way before the sleepiness brought on by a twelve-hour march.

I open my eyes to the dawn, the first flecks of lightness against the small ripple-trail clouds, I nod off, to be awoken probably only minutes later by someone shaking my shoulder.

I stand up. I'm enveloped by a mild smell of myself. The smell is healthy. Earthy, alive. I might as well be just another denizen of these plains, migrating, making my way from here to there, wherever *there* might be.

I stretch, yawning so wide that the joints of my jaw almost pop lose. Another day's march ahead. But I'm getting used to it. My boots are soft leather, wrapped and tied firmly about my feet and ankles, moulded by my feet, for my feet.

Sunlight glints over the tops of the distant hills. Dawn on the wide plains of Europe. I brush grass from my hair and drink from my waterbag. No one is bothering with breakfast. We'll eat later. The knee-high grass is green, with spikes of golden flowers that will turn to seed and drop come autumn. I should look for ancient wheat. Wild oats.

Another time.

There is only the sound of the steppe, which is the river, the honks of massive elk and the rolling-thud calls of the straight-tusked elephants, the screech of buzzards and the soft rush of the wind. The smell is of grass fields, earth, animal, air; so pure that scents are acute as they mix and enter my nose. Sight is enhanced, the distant views incredible in clarity, like you're looking through a wide-angled telescope at the hills and horizon.

In this purity, this emptiness, time dilates. The fastest change is the course of the river that curves and digs through the landscape over countless millennia. The sun rises, sets, rises again, shadows stretch out into darkness while animals are born, live and die and evolve, stretch their wings, and become different things.

I glance at the fire, at the blackened and twisted branches. The pace of change is now forever altered. I look at my hands, my fingers, accusingly, like they are the dirty from some cosmic crime. Now humans are here, this place is on borrowed time. Fire comes with us. Then machines. Concrete, metal, asphalt.

Stop it.

I shoulder my pack and fall into line, moving easily, my body used to the motion. Willow and I bring up the rear as we crest the rocky bluff from where we'd seen the cave lions yesterday afternoon.

The lions are still there.

Raka leads us onwards. We hug the river. Apparently, cave lions have no problem swimming. They will cross a river this size without hesitation if it means an easy meal. So even if the men could swim, simply hopping over the river won't make any difference. Several of the men have made torches – thick branches with their ends wrapped in scrap leather that has been soaked in animal fat they rendered last night. The flames send up a black smoke.

The lions pay us interest. We come parallel with their spot, perhaps a quarter of a mile between us and them. I see them perk up. A few of the females pace back and forth. The enormous male doesn't stand up, but when he roars, I feel a spike of fear that sends my stomach flipping over like a triple-somersaulting Olympic high diver. I scoot forward in fright, bumping into Zavik's back.

Our pace is steady. Walking, we put miles between us and the lions. We eat, walking, only pausing for a minute to scoop some water from the river. Willow sits on Culeg's shoulders, then he walks, then sits on Tazak's shoulders. Then he walks again. He's strong but he's only eight years old. Everyone enjoys carrying him. It almost makes this whole thing feel normal. I carry him on my shoulders for an hour.

The light is fading when we stop to make camp. I reckon we put fifty miles between us and the cave lions. I'm so pleasantly exhausted that I just sling my pack down and lie on the ground. It's a bit naughty: I should be helping gather wood and getting stuff sorted. But I close my eyes and I fall asleep instead.

I'm woken by Willow. I open my eyes. The moon is above me. Growing fatter every day. A few days until full moon. No clouds. Good. No rain tonight. Just the brighter stars visible behind the milky-white cast of Earth's daughter. That's what they call the moon, though their proper word for her translates into English as "Gone Daughter". Most just refer to her with a short word that means *sky-daughter*. The reason she lives alone is because she eloped from her mother, the Earth, to visit her father, who is the sun and whose domain is the sky.

Angry at her disobedience, he refused to take her in, and so now she exists in limbo, her body bleeding itself into almost invisibility before being fattened when her father relents and feeds her back into fullness.

Mother Earth remains unforgiving and will not have her daughter come home, so she lives in purgatory, starved and bleeding for half her cycle, then fed for the other.

My rough guess is that the menstrual cycle has a lot to do with the whole story. Life and death. Plenty and scarcity. Bloom and decay. And a moral lesson thrown in: listen to your parents or spend half of every month being starved nearly to death. All that stuff.

I watch the daughter, swollen. Perhaps every month she has sex with one of the characters from the stellar constellations? Orion. Taurus, Scorpio, Capricorn? And every month she becomes pregnant, and the stars are all her children? That'd be kind of neat. If that's not weird enough, it gets a fair bit stranger when you start dealing with The Plough.

I'd best keep that celestial observation to myself. I don't want to feed them any more bullshit than they already have to deal with.

'Charlie,' says Willow, 'I brought you some broth.' He holds out a steaming bowl.

I sit up against my backpack. There's a single fire burning with a pot hanging over it. The men have settled down, all around me.

'You're a *sweetheart*, Willow.'

'What's a *swet-eert*?'

'It just means you're a good boy. The best.'

He nods, simmering with the praise.

'Tazak says we must eat plenty,' says Willow. 'He says we need our strength.'

'I am sure we will.'

'What will happen? When we get there?'

'You've heard the men,' I tell him. 'You've heard Tazak. We will get your mother back. We will get everyone back. First, we watch them, and then when we can, we go in and free the women and girls.'

'Raka and Tazak and everyone says we will have to kill some of the men.'

I don't say anything. I look at him, at his wide eyes, his pupils dilated in the flickering firelight. The weight of this has been pressing down on me, getting heavier every day. In truth, what option do we have? These people, these killers, these kidnappers, are predators. Predators who will simply return to our home again and again.

Especially if we take back what was stolen and especially if we harm any of their tribe.

What option do we have except *extermination?*

Many of the men do not want to spare the women and children of this tribe. They argue, sensibly, that if we kill their men and take their women, then what is to stop these women one day in the future cutting our throats in our sleep? And if we just leave the women alive, what's to stop them just following us home and waiting until we are asleep?

If we kill the women, who will take care of their kids? These are kids who will remember their parents killing their original parents. They would be traumatised. What's to stop them turning on us once we are old and frail?

I can't fault their logic.

I can't fault our logic.

It makes me feel sick.

I'm going to commit genocide.

I look at Willow and tell myself that this is what I need to do to keep this child safe. And since I know that the murdering of an entire settlement of humans will not result in the extinction of humanity, then I guess it's not the end of the world.

Keep up with the positive maxims. Plenty more fish in the sea. Have to break some eggs if you want the omelette. What goes around comes around.

Payback's a bitch.

But, damn, killing people?

I take the bowl from Willow, and the feel of my fingers brushing his small hands makes my heart throb painfully.

His little-child hands. If I can help it, they won't ever be coated in human blood.

I've even thought about arguing to turn around, to go back home. Maybe in time try and meet other tribes, friendly ones, and find some female partners for the men. But I've kept silent. That idea would fly like an iron glider. These men want *their* women back. Those who they've shared their hearths with, their bedrolls, their children, their lives.

Even *I* wouldn't listen to *me.*

I want Sara back. I don't care about me or Raka. I just want that girl back home.

Safe.

What choice do we have if we want to live safe and happy, and free of fear?

What choice do we have except to turn up and kill everyone?

31

We are twenty-two days out from home. When we made camp last night, I lay on the ground and I was sure that I could smell the sea. Well, not consciously. I mean that the idea of *sea* kept popping into my head, and I assumed that it was a scent so mild as to be beneath conscious appreciation of salt, but nevertheless tickling the sensory apparatus in my nose and sparking off something in my brain.

The sea.

This morning I still can't smell salt, but the sea was the first thing that came into mind when I awoke. The wind is still coming from the east. The Black Sea should be somewhere in that direction. But as I scan the horizon, I see no evidence of anything that looks like landscape becoming coastline. And if memory serves me correctly then the Black Sea is not particularly salty. More brackish, than true seawater.

Correction: it *will* be. Perhaps if a lot of freshwater is all locked up in the glaciers, then the ice age Black Sea might be as salty as what I think of as a normal sea.

The steppes have given way from grassy plains to a light forest. Must be the moisture coming off the sea. If it is the sea.

Raka is on point, as always. My animosity towards him has largely abated. I can't give Raka any mental space. I've bigger fish to fry.

It's early evening. The sun is going down in the west. The planet Venus sparkles in the cooling purple sky. I see it through the breaks in the trees. I wonder if Sara sees this. I wonder how she'd react if I told her what stars actually were. If I told her that Venus is a planet. That would bake her noodle. But I think Sara would –

Raka throws himself flat. Everyone hits the dirt. I half expect the treeline to light up with machine-gun fire.

But all I can hear is the slight breeze in the trees and a few birds tweeting. I raise my head. Tazak and Culeg crawl next to Raka. Together they crawl forward to slightly higher ground. They look about, their heads going in all directions. Slowly, quietly, they stand up and Tazak motions for us to do the same. We move and clump around him.

'Tracks,' says Tazak quietly. 'People.'

'Hunters, probably,' says Raka, 'but the tracks are older than I thought. A day, maybe two.'

Tazak takes over. He directs us into a small depression surrounded by trees. We are hidden from casual view. We settle down.

'No fire, stay quiet,' says Tazak. 'We move at nightfall.'

I can smell the sea, distinctly.

We huddle together, chewing kangaroo ass and eating a little of our fatcakes.

Fuel. For the fire in men's veins.

———

Skydaughter gives us the little light we need. We move through the trees, a hushed rustling of leaves as thirteen men and one boy move from tree to tree in soft leather-clad boots.

There are spears. And knives. A hatchet.

Across the open centuries I feel my youth flowing back into me. A scent stronger than the salt fills my mouth and nose. It comes from the open pores of men *on the hunt*. Sweet and heady, a dizzying power makes my heartbeat slow and strong. My palm is damp around the spear I hold. I smell the air, I lick leaves. I breathe deep. I follow.

Wolves, we move.

When we collected Yaneck's skull and his bones from the ashes of his funeral pyre, we laid them out so his spirit could see that it had no earthly body left and would go willingly – happily – to Father Sky. The men had all cut their palms and grasped the hand of each other, mixing blood, swearing to travel, to return with their abducted women, swearing to avenge Yaneck and Deakel.

I press my fingers into the small cut that is almost fully healed. I thought it was a bit pointless, pretending at magic, sharing blood, and possibly passing diseases, but now I understand why. I swore to be blood brothers with these men. My skin prickles deliciously as I sense a power flowing into me – from then. I grow young again.

This is their magic.

We move as a pack.

Here. Something. . . smoke.

Smoke!

Faint but unmistakable.

The trees thin at a small escarpment. We unshoulder our packs and crawl on our bellies to the ridge. The ground slopes away. The sea is visible, two miles away, a quicksilver spreading away to infinity. The land between us and the sea is lightly forested, patterned with open meadows.

In a small smudge along the coast are the yellow twinkling lights of fires.

Fires.

Built by human hands.

A hushed, excited jabbering breaks out amongst the men. I punch the air.

Fuck yeah!

See, you walk for nearly a month across the plains and valleys of Europe, inescapably alone but for the man at your side. You sit at night looking out onto. . . nothing. And you *know* that there is nothing sentient out there, for days and days in every direction. You and the others huddled with you are the only lights of consciousness in what feels like an entire world. There is no help, anywhere. I've been scornful of religion, all my life, but I think I understand now why it is necessary: it's there to stop you from going mad. If you can populate a lonely world with other consciousnesses – that of the deer that watches you warily and runs from you, that of the secret river and tree spirits – you don't feel so alone, so fragile. You know that something *else* sees *you*, and this confirms your existence as fact, not a fantasy. Even the devils, the malicious spirits; listening to the guys I get the impression that even *they* provide some comfort. Even evil is a good thing if it allows you a point of orientation in this universe, a point about which to provide your mental and physical body with an anchor in reality.

The sight of *other* humans. . . it snatches away reason, sense, even your breath. Even hostiles, they *still* count as people.

You only comprehend the existential terror of solitude as it departs, and the constriction around your heart and mind relaxes and you find yourself gulping short breaths of relief. Like coming up for air when you didn't know you were holding your breath.

We walked for nearly a month to cover on a map a distance that's the size of a fingernail.

I look at the men, all of us flat on our bellies, peering over the ridge, and I'm suddenly amazed that we all made it here alive, uninjured. Days and nights across raw wilderness. Cave lions, men with spears in the night, any apex predators that might have been stalking us, unseen beyond the ring of light from our campfire, deciding in the end *not* to pick off the man sitting at sentry duty. It is pure luck we are all still here. And maybe magic.

My throat cramps, and I feel tears on my cheeks.

Seeing these lights, seeing *a home*, is a greater joy than scoring the winning goal in the final seconds of the FIFA world cup final. It *has* to be.

It feels like you've cheated death.

Euphoria.

Fuck yeah.

But we're not here for a seaside vacation.

We're here on business. None of us have forgotten that, even in this moment of small triumph. It's not chilling-out time.

It's business time.

For *wet work.*

All we need to complete the image are suits and ties, dark glasses, and attaché cases stuffed with machine-pistols.

'Charlie,' says Tazak. 'What do you see?'

'Why are you asking me?'

'None of us know this place. You came from the east. What do you know about. . . this?' He looks at me, a pointed look writ on his face. What he's asking me is: *since you're a time traveller, do you know anything that could help us here?*

I look at the settlement. There's nothing to see. Just a few small fires. Perhaps I can see the dark shapes of. . . what? Dwellings, on the coastline? I can't be sure from this distance.

'Well, I would think that they are fishermen. They live off the sea.'

'Yes.'

'And. . . I don't know anything else that could help. We need to get closer.'

'Very well.'

'Now?'

'Can you think of a better time?'

I can't. Tazak speaks to the men.

'Raka, you lead. Single file. No sound.'

We shuffle back from the ridge and stand up. I sling my backpack on my shoulder and pick up my spear.

'Raka?' asks Tazak.

'Raka?' asks someone else.

'Where's Raka?' asks Tazak. The guys look at each other.

'Everyone, line up!' he hisses. He does a headcount. Twelve men. Not thirteen.

We go back into the trees.

'Raka?'

'Raka?'

Puzzle pieces slot together in my brain. When we caught the scouts, Raka was not as pleased as the rest of us. He smiled and said words, but they sounded *off*. He didn't go near the men when they were in front of the fire.

He didn't let them see his face. He knew they wouldn't talk.

'Tazak,' I say, catching the big man by his shoulder, 'Raka has gone.'

'Not *this* now, Charlie.' He shakes off my hand and raises his voice higher. 'Raka!'

'He's gone, Tazak.' I point eastwards, towards the settlement. 'He knows these people. He planned this with them.'

'No, no, no,' Tazak shakes his head, back and forth, back and forth. 'No!'

'Who planned the hunt, that day?' I ask him. I already know the answer. 'Who organised it, took charge?'

Tazak is silent. I press my point.

'It was all of the men who were able to hunt, wasn't it? Strange. Except for Deakel.'

'He wanted to look for flint. He insisted.'

'Raka took you *all* away on that day. Not a coincidence.'

Everyone is listening. They huddle closer, the way people gather around at an emergency, a traffic accident. When something has gone seriously wrong.

Bazel says, 'I wanted to fish. Raka urged me to come.'

Other voices. *Me too. Me too.*

Raka's sudden desertion is the final and damning proof. It starts to sink in. The men curse. Several, stunned, can do nothing except sit heavily on their asses, silently grappling with this revelation.

Tazak looks at me for a few seconds. Then he turns to look eastwards. He doesn't move or blink for half a minute. A man, computing a mindfuck. Finally, he blinks, and lets out a breath that he must have been holding the whole time.

He sees it. He digests it. He can't fall apart, though he must feel like it. He basically saved Raka's life and the only reason anyone puts up with Raka, in truth, is because of Tazak. And now Raka has taken a spear and thrust it squarely into Tazak's back.

Of course, let's not forget everyone else. Me, Sara, Deakel, Zavik, Willow, Salanda, Vala, Greta, Cela, Grease, Culeg, the whole tribe. The entire fucking crew.

In 21st Century parlance, he's fucked us all. In the ass.

I was calm when I first realised. It was like solving a maths problem. Now, I get it, emotionally.

'That... that... dirty motherfucker.'

Willow hears the English words.

'What is *dertimotheerforeer*?'

I look down at him.

'It's not good, Willow. It's not good at all.'

It really doesn't end with this asshat. But this behaviour is like rope-free rock-climbing or drink driving. It has a timeline attached. You can run on being an asshat, but sooner or later God will cut you down. Up here, a stranger in a strange land, this is cold comfort.

The hostiles must be fishermen. *People-stealing rapist* fishermen, but still fishermen. They have boats – dugouts. I look east at the twinkling lights, at the coastline, running north to south. On the sea, the ripples of waves show me the movement of the current. I think, *hard*. I snap my fingers.

'Tazak, can we cover our tracks from Raka? Can we travel so that he won't be able to track us?'

'In the daylight, we couldn't hide our tracks well enough. Not from Raka's eyes. But at night, yes.'

'Then we have to do it now. Raka left less than half a hand ago. It won't take him long to get down there and tell everyone about us. We need to leave, *now*. We will go there.' I point southeast to a spot on the coastline about a mile south of the settlement, to what looks like a rocky promontory.

'Now,' I repeat, looking at Tazak. He gives the signal. Culeg leads.

32

W e reach the coastline a hand or so later. I check Skydaughter. The little hand says it's a few hours to sunrise. The big hand says it's time to rock and roll.

We keep to the scrubby growth and follow the coastline north. We are about a mile or so south of the settlement. We move in stops and starts. Raka would have made it to the settlement even before we'd hit the coastline, so we are expecting. . . something. Sentries? Patrols? We don't know. We don't even know how many people are in this settlement. My guess is *a lot more* than we currently number.

Dread creeps over me, replacing the mania of *the hunt* that had gripped me earlier, the manic confidence that had inspired me to come up with this daft plan: just going to the coast and waltzing in.

What choice do we have? Run away? Or wade in, balls swinging, like Rambo without a jockstrap? There are no police we can call. No cops, no feds, no CIA, no SAS, no SEALS.

Nada.

There's no one else who's going to help us get our people back.

Just us.

We keep our eyes on Culeg as he shifts forward, motions, stops, shifts, motions. Small clouds cover the moon, our Skydaughter, sending creeping patterns of shadow that freeze us stock still whilst Culeg motions.

stop!

move!

stop!

down!

Willow is in front of me, one hand holding onto the back of Zavik's shirt. He's eight, but what are we supposed to do? Leave the little fucker alone on the beach, on the off chance we will come back? Not likely. He comes. He can hold a spear. He can hold a knife. He knows what the score is. He knows it's business time. His breathing is ragged. He's not out of breath. He's scared. Petrified.

As am I.

What else are we supposed to feel?

'Charlie!' hisses Bazel, behind me.

Shit. I was deep in thought, examining the size of my fear. I flatten myself on the ground. Culeg scuttles back to us.

'Four men,' he says, his voice eerily calm. 'Standing guard.'

Can we sneak up on them, take them by surprise, kill or club them unconscious before they have a chance to scream or shout? If we fuck it up and they raise the alarm, we're screwed. It's too risky.

I move into a crouch and peer around some scrappy bush. A quarter mile north, I can see some type of longhouse that seems to be built right out onto the beach. I can't quite tell in the low light, but it looks like it's on stilts.

Stilts. Like a pier.

'We go back one finger,' I say. Five minutes, roughly.

When I'm sure we are well out of sight of the guards, I call a halt.

'I'll swim,' I say, pointing out to sea. 'I'll swim out and around the guards. I'll come in from the sea.'

The guys look at me like I've lost my marbles. They shake their heads.

'None of you can swim like I can,' I say. 'And It won't be guarded there.'

'This is not a plan,' says Tazak.

I don't reply. I start to tug my clothes off.

'Charlie, what are you doing?'

'Give me a fatcake, someone,' I say. I'm handed one and I cram the entire thing in my mouth and chew ferociously, like a wolf gone mad. A mad, very naked wolf.

'Give me a knife.'

One is handed to me. A bone handle with a razor-sharp blade of flint.

'Swim quicker,' I say, motioning to my clothes. In truth, going in there with all that leather on and I'd drown. Naked, I can swim for probably twenty miles. I grew up on a beach, for Christ's sake.

'And what in Earth's spunk will you do when you get there?' asks Tazak, verging on anger.

'I don't know. I'll do something. When I do it, you'll know. You'll know what to do. You can leave me and run away, or you can come and get me. It's the only way to get closer. We need to know more before we all go in.'

I take a step forward. Then as an afterthought, because I have to leave them with something approaching an idea, I say, 'If you see me waving a light – fire – come up the beach as fast as you can.'

And with that I scuttle like a crab the thirty yards to the sea. The waves are a foot high. Calm. Silently I thank Skydaughter that I guessed the direction of the current. It goes north, towards the settlement.

I put the bone handle of the knife between my teeth, like a naked pirate going for a quick dip. In the middle of the night. Standard.

The water is cold, maybe 65 Fahrenheit, 20 Celsius. Warm enough to keep me from freezing, but cold enough to give me a seriously small willy and nutsack. I swim directly away from the beach for a hundred yards. Then I turn north and follow the coastline. I shudder in the cold water. I gasp, breathe, gasp, breathe again.

I have an irrational fear of sharks. I've always been scared of them. I hate being in deep water where I can't see beneath me. Which is the case tonight, no matter how brightly Skydaughter shines. The depths are black beneath me, and the thought of the mega-fauna that might be underneath me, cavernous jaws of razor teeth about to snap down over my naked wriggling legs. . . I almost turn tail towards the shore.

But the faces of Sara and the women and the girls keeps me on target. On mission. The faces of all the guys. And Raka, that slimy little two-timing asshat. Pointlessly fucking everyone's lives to satisfy some weirdness about him that I don't even have words for.

Raka. I bite down on the bone handle between my teeth, and I keep swimming, expecting the jagged jaws of some giant prehistoric lizardfish to shear me in half – anytime in the immediate future.

It takes me twenty minutes to come level with the structure that juts out onto and over the beach. As I surmised, there are no guards or sentries anywhere in sight. All the men must be guarding the perimeter, or even heading out in the welcome wagon for their uninvited guests.

Perfect.

Or it would be perfect if I knew what I was doing. If I knew anything at all.

I swim in and let the small waves deposit me on the beach. I lie flat in the gentle surf, scoping the environs. Definitely no guards. I stand up slowly, feeling much colder now the night air breezes over my wet skin, which is so raised with goosebumps that it feels pebbly as I flick the water from my arms and legs. I squeeze the water from my hair, my beard.

I pick my way across the rocky beach. The structure is definitely what you'd call a longhouse. It's a massive, rectangular structure that has wide barn-like doors on the end that faces the beach. There is a ramp made of slim tree trunks lashed together with rope or cord. The doors seem to be panels made from the same slim tree trunks tied together. A stout pole lies across the door, securing it. The smell of fishy decay is strong.

I'm looking at a prehistoric version of a. . . a what? A whale station? A walrus processing house?

As I come closer, I see the ground is littered with dry bones that glow bright in the moonlight. The smell is awful. I imagine these people must just gut their catch and chuck it out onto the beach. Not very sanitary. The longhouse is on stilts – tree trunks.

Drawn up near the base of the ramp are the massive dugouts that they came raiding in. Fourteen of them here. I move closer, thinking that the men who propelled these things must be superhuman. Must be, to propel these heavy boats all the way upstream to a tribe far away inland. Then I see it. A mast, lying in the bottom of each boat. I poke around. There is a strut and pulley system that raises the mast. I touch the sail. Skin of some kind. Sealskin?

That's how they did it. When I recall the wind on our journey – it blew mostly from the east. We were *downwind* of the cave lions, before we passed them.

These people sailed *up* the river, stole our women, and just drifted back on the current. Happy as Larry.

Cheeky fucking thieving bastards.

I walk under the fish factory, into shadow. No light comes from the cracks in the floor, but this doesn't seem strange, since this structure is clearly not for human habitation. Distantly, I'm impressed. A fish or seal processing station. These people must eat very well.

The ground rises as the beach gives way to earthy land. I have to bend down, lower and lower. When I can't move further forward, I emerge from under the structure. I'm in shadow, and I inch my way along the wall until I reach the front of the building. I peek out. One eye, then two.

I look into the heart of their. . . village. A fire burns, casting a wide circle of light amongst their dwellings. The fire has been recently fed; several branches lie on it, burning and smoking as they catch. Someone was just there.

Their homes look like yurts. I count perhaps twenty of them. Round things made of a supple material, probably sealskin, which I imagine to be quite waterproof. But seals, as far as I'm concerned, are off-limits. Seals are basically the aquatic version of dogs.

Seal-killing, women-stealing, rapist wankers.

A flap opens on one of the yurts. Three women and one man emerge. I can't see their features properly in the firelight, but I know none of the women are ours. Their clothes are similar to the scouts we left dead on the steppes. Their leather is the same black.

They move away from the fire, in my direction.

I take a few steps backwards, sliding against the wall, trying to stay in shadow. I hear their voices, foreign, growing closer. I step back until I can scuttle under the fish factory where I'll be well hidden and where no one in their right mind would want to go and hang out, what with all the fish guts, and what smells like urine.

I slip. My bare foot slides on something wet and gooey and I go down on my ass, a rock jabbing into my left butt cheek. I make an *oouuff!* sound as the breath shoots out my lungs.

The voices stop abruptly. I sit where I've fallen, my hand over my mouth, aghast at what I've done. There is silence. Then footfalls, coming closer. I grip the knife hard in my right hand.

Suddenly there is a pounding, smacking sound, again and again. It's one of the seal-killers, banging on what must be the entrance to the fish factory. Then some words, shouted. More banging.

A little laughter, and the four move off. I stick my head from under the building and I watch them move off into shadow.

What was that all about? They thought the noise of me falling on my ass came from the room above my head.

Aha. The penny drops.

If you have a bunch of troublesome women that you've recently stolen from another tribe, and you happen to have a fish factory that you can lock up securely, then it would make sense to imprison these women in such a building.

It's risky, but I can't help it. I reach above my head and with a knuckle, I tap softly on the wood, three times. There is nothing, for about a minute. I wait. Then, a shuffle of feet. An answering knock, hesitant, barely audible above the gentle sound of the sea.

I tilt my head upwards and stretch onto my tiptoes and almost kiss the wood above me. 'It's Charlie,' I whisper to the unknown person.

There is an immediate and audible squeak of surprise.

'Quiet!' I say, as loudly as I dare. More feet on the floor.

'Charlie? It's Greta.'

'Greta, I am under the floor.'

No shit, Sherlock.

I suddenly realise that I have no plan at all. Shit.

'Listen, do you have any weapons in there?'

'None!' comes the harsh whisper.

Ok. Fuck.

'Stay there,' I say. Then even more stupidly I add, 'Don't move.'

I duck out from under the stinky building. My heart hammers. Fear, sweat, seawater, excitement, more fear. If I don't win this – totally and perfectly – I will die. Probably horribly, if Raka gets his way.

I peek out from the side of the building. Skydaughter blesses me, hiding her light behind a cloud. The shadows shift and deepen. I take a deep, almost-panic-breath, and step around the building to the front door. Big barn-like things, same as round the back on the beach. I'm in a direct line of sight from any number of yurts. I expect a spear or a shout, any second now. I'm wandering around a village of savages, probably fucking cannibals. And I'm naked. If I get caught, I can't exactly appeal to gooey sentiment. Nor morality. Socrates and his ilk won't be around for a while.

I'm on my own.

I have my knife ready to sever all manner of knots and chains and stuff. But all that confronts me is a long wooden bar that prevents anyone inside from sliding the door panels away. I stare at it, suspicious suddenly at how easy this is becoming. I'm about to heft the bar when I realise my stupidity.

Open it from the back, you numbnut. Lead the women out and along the beach.

Ok. I slip back along the side of the building to the far end. The empty beach is between me and the sea. Better. I walk up the ramp and lift away the bar. I try to slide open one of the barn-sized panels, but it's heavy and it only budges an inch. Fingers protrude through the tiny gap, from the top of the panel to the bottom. I lift and slide. With the help of the women, I slide it open several feet.

A child rockets out like a jack-in-the-box. It's Willow's little sister Sela. I reach for her and manage to grab her wrist. She cries out weakly, but I hug her to me and roughly clamp my hand over her mouth. She struggles. I hold her tight. Salanda tries to follow her daughter out, but I block her way. I shake my head and urge her back into the fish factory. Inside, I hand the girl to her mother. She's stopped wriggling once she's understood it is me.

I stand in the shaft of moonlight, blocking the door.

'Quiet!' I snap this at the rising mutter of excitement. 'Tell me what's happening.'

I hear the sound of spontaneous weeping. 'Who's alive?' I grab Salanda's arm, and I shake her roughly. 'Who's here?'

'Charlie, I –'

'Quiet! Is anyone hurt, anyone missing?'

Please God don't say Sara please God

I hear Greta's voice. 'Everyone's here, Charlie, everyone who was put on the boats that day is here.'

Thank *Christ*. I want to ask for Sara, to see her face, anything, but my mind is shouting at me *you don't have a plan and there is NO TIME!*

'I don't know what to do,' I blurt. I truly don't. I see that if I free these women and run off with them. . . then the whole affair will end up in a pitched battle on some terrible hillside a day or so from here. Cannons. Muskets at dawn. Spears and probably harpoons. Fuck *that* for a game of soldiers.

I raise my voice, slightly, to address the women and girls in the darkness.

'We can't just run off. They'd catch us, kill some of us. We have to be smart, and be brave. Let me think. How many men live here?'

Greta replies immediately. 'We think about twenty-five. We counted. There are more women, perhaps thirty of them.'

'Children?'

'Twenty-two, maybe.'

'If there are more women than men, then why did they take you?'

Greta looks at me squarely. I step closer. She leans close so that her words don't carry to the others. She whispers.

'They *trade* people, Charlie. They *trade* women.'

I grab her shoulders and look at her closely. Is she mad? I can't immediately compute what she's saying. 'What? How do you know?'

'I hear them talking. I don't understand much, the odd word here and there. A few days ago, two strangers arrived. They look strange even compared to these people. They showed all of us to the two strangers. . . They argued and didn't appear to agree. The men went away. But Charlie, I *know* a trade when I see one.'

Jesus Jumping Catfucks.

Slave-traders.

Scum of the earth. Lower than low.

I don't believe in the concept of good and evil, but *selling* fellow humans into bondage? That is about as low and fucked up as you can get. A few notches further down that ladder into Hell is selling *women* and *girls* into. . . I don't even have the words.

Beneath even all that is the act of conspiring with hostiles to sell out your own family, to sell them into slavery. That's where asshat bottom-feeder Satan's bitch-in-chief Raka comes in.

I really don't know what goes on in that dude's mind.

'The women are just as bad,' Greta says, whispering. 'They spit on us and hit us with sticks, they piss in our food, they –'

'Shut the fuck up Greta,' I snap in English. I'm furious. *Livid.* I've probably gone purple with pure unbridled rage. But I'm also thinking – hard.

Priorities.

Side-missions.

Benefits.

Cost versus reward.

Risk.

'Can anyone make fire?' I ask.

'I suppose, but Charlie–'

'Make it right now. I need to make a torch, to signal Tazak.'

I stand aside to let Greta come outside and go down the ramp. She pokes about on the ground. Thank Christ it hasn't rained recently. The beach is littered with bone-dry driftwood and half rotted branches, dry as tinder. Greta goes inside with the bits of wood, and sits just inside the entrance where she can see by the moonlight.

I stay silent, shivering with cold, crouched down in the entrance, turning my gaze slowly north to south, scanning the beach for any activity. It's all I can do to stop myself from calling Sara's name. The urge to touch her, to see her, is a burning in my veins. She's close, so close. But I *must* keep a clear head. Stay on point. Keep my focus. Stand guard.

Minutes tick by. The sound of the firestick twirling, grinding, is audible above the soft lull of the sea and the salty breeze coming off it.

The wait is excruciating. I smell smouldering tinder. I see a tiny glow in the darkness, the size of a grain of sand. I hold my breath.

Raka and his butt-buddies are probably scouring the uplands where he left us. When they don't find us, and can't track us in the darkness, they will return home. Here, where we are busy jerking off and making a campfire.

We might as well just invite everyone up here right now. Chuck some seal steaks and shrimp on the barbie. Crack open a keg. Shoot the shit. Get lynched. Stabbed repeatedly.

Fuckballs.

The grains of burning tinder spread and glow bright.

Hold on. I was thinking about Socrates. . .

I speak to Salanda, who is sitting, helping Greta.

'Salanda, do these people eat together at night? In a big group?'

'Yes,' she says, her voice shaky. 'They eat their fish stews and drink something fermented. They let us out and make us serve them. They laugh and kick us and *touch us*.' She spits these last two words.

Perfect.

I step forward and put my bare heel on the few licks of nascent flame. I grind them out.

'Charlie! What are you doing?'

'Listen,' I say, looking into the gloom where I know the women and girls are. 'I will be back. Two days. I will bring you something. You will put it in their food. Can you do that, Greta? All of you?'

'Yes,' she says.

That's the only answer I need. But there's an immediate hushed uproar within the building. The women surge forward. I stand in the doorway, filling it.

I can't let them out. I won't.

I wedge myself in the opening and fend them off. I speak in a hoarse whisper.

'Quiet! All of you! Quiet! Now!'

Sara's face emerges into Skydaughter's light. Her blond hair is dirty, her face is dirty, her eyes swollen with crying. Impossibly beautiful. My heart caves inwards, and I nearly move out of the way, nearly let them all stream out onto the beach where I'll load them up into dugouts or let them run madly south towards their waiting men.

Risk versus reward.

Delayed gratification.

Triangulations.

My heart breaks. But I swallow the injustice, the gall, the bitterness of having to leave them here. I swallow it all. I reach in and take Sara's hand. It is warm, small, strong. 'I can't risk you – any of you – or your men – getting hurt. I will come back. I promise you.'

She looks at me, her green eyes a deep jade in the pale light. She nods once, a single movement. She squeezes my hand. And then lets it go.

'Charlie,' she says, 'you forgot your boots again.'

'What? Oh.' I look down at myself and realise I am buck naked. Well. Needs must.

'I will come back for you,' I say. 'I promise.'

'Go,' she says.

My heart breaks.

But not my mind.

I slide the panel back into place and secure it with the wooden bar. I go down to the sea and slip into the cold water. I swim out a hundred feet. I turn south and churn my way against the current, swimming a flat-out front crawl against the current. As fast as I can go, desperate to get back to the guys and stop them from getting itchy feet, offing the guards, and wading in, Rambo-style.

I come out of the water, my breath ragged. I run up the beach. I can't see them.

'Charlie.' it's Zavik.

Just like I first met them, I've gone past them. Damn, these people can *hide*.

I slump onto my knees, my chest heaving.

'We need to leave, *now*. Tazak, where's Tazak?'

'Here,' he says.

'Too many people. Over fifty adults. Too complicated. Too dangerous.'

'Plan?'

'We poison them.'

'*Poison* them?'

'Yes,' I say. 'It looks like wild carrot. You know it. I don't know your name for it.'

Zavik, bless him, is rubbing my chest and back with a pelt. I realise that I'm freezing. I take it from him and stand up.

'The women, they are made to do things for these people. They have to serve them food. Everyone who was taken is still there. Greta, Salanda, Vala, Ela, Sara, and the rest. I can bring them the poison. One day, two maybe.'

I'm not going to hit them with the fact that their women are to be sold as slaves. That would probably fry anyone's noodle. Fry it crispy and see them just go buck fucking crazy.

'Poison,' I repeat.

'I like it,' says Culeg suddenly. 'The plant has berries now. The berries have the strongest poison.' He looks at Tazak. 'I like this plan.'

Tazak doesn't say anything. He looks at Skydaughter. He looks back up the beach where the longhouse is a dark hulk. He looks at us.

'And Raka?'

Culeg scratches his beard and kicks his heel into the ground. 'Raka can't track us, not on this rocky ground.'

Tazak looks at me. 'South?' he asks.

'South,' I say.

He makes the signal.

We turn south.

33

W e run south, keeping to the coast of the Black Sea. We run until the sun rises.

We stop for a few minutes to eat and drink. Then we run until the sun sets. Willow keeps up with us, but when he tires, we all share the burden of carrying him. I think he even sleeps, slung over my back, as I run.

At sunset we eat and drink and lie down and sleep for a hand and a half. About an hour. When Willow wakes us, we walk onwards under the light of the full moon, the fully pregnant Skydaughter. I'm so tired I feel delirious.

Skydaughter. Skywalker.

We walk until mid-morning.

There's a hundred miles between us and the settlement of slavers. Finally, Tazak and Culeg are satisfied that we are out of any search radius that Raka and his slave-trading buddies might cover. When we find a river that flows into the sea, we turn inland and follow it westwards. By noon we come across the plants. They grow near streams and rivers. I saw them frequently next to the river along which we came east.

Water hemlock. Socrates drank a preparation of a closely related species. This one is even more poisonous than Socratic hemlock.

It is at this point that I explain to the guys exactly what the situation is with the women. They all stare at me. Two guys lunge at me, but Zavik, Grease, Bazel and Tazak jump on them before they can get to me.

Eventually Tazak speaks, his voice quiet but ice-cold. Like the sound a glacier makes when it crushes mountains.

'You were right to tell us this now.' He gestures to the men, whose faces are a horrible caricature of *aghast confusion*. 'I could not have stopped them, back there.'

We all pick the berries. It doesn't take long to fill a large pouch. Enough to slay the entire Trojan army.

They rest, finally. Culeg and I crush the berries into a runny paste and decant this into a waterskin. Tie the top with sinew.

Perfect.

It's ready.

Except for Culeg and me, everyone is asleep.

'Rest, Culeg,' I say. He looks at the poison for a long moment, then looks at me for even longer. This is the tribe's holy man, the shaman – now that Yaneck is gone. I wonder what Yaneck would make of this situation, this poison.

But Culeg puts his hand on my shoulder.

'Thank you, Charlie,' he says. His John Wayne eyes hold nothing cryptic. The look is clear: his eyes say *let's go kill them*.

'Please don't thank me now. Thank me when you have Ela and all the rest back safely.'

Culeg shrugs and turns away. I watch him lie down on the grass and close his eyes.

I sit and place the skin in front of me on the ground. It looks like any other liquid-filled waterskin. But it is anything but normal.

It is pure death.

I've just made the world's first dirty bomb. The world's first chemical weapon. The first weapon of mass destruction. It's not a comfortable feeling.

But slavers?

Even if they had nothing to do with us, I'm not sure I wouldn't be trying to kill the whole rat-bastard nest of them anyway – on pure principle. Torturing and killing those scouts made my *soul* feel dirty. It doesn't feel dirty now. I feel a righteous bloodlust.

If I was sitting on the fence before, I'm now in the middle of the field that is signposted: "Kill anyone who tries to sell people."

The ends justify the means.

Do they? Do they really?

This world might not have internet, mass surveillance, or social media, but it still manages to fuck you with some serious moral choices.

I'll come back for you. I promise.

I promised Sara.

I lie down on my back. Within seconds I feel a heaviness steal over me as my muscles go flaccid. Running, for two days. Talk about hitting a wall. I put my hand on the bag and curl a finger through the loop of sinew that ties it shut.

My brain goes limp and I fly towards sleep.

I promised her I'd come back.

––––––

The next day we follow the river back to the coast. Now we've made the warhead, we need the guided missile. The smart bomb. Which is me. I'm going to repeat my night-time skinny dipping trick and deliver the hemlock juice.

Tazak and the boys are going to sneak up the beach and hide under the fish factory. Wait until it takes effect.

It takes us three days to get back. We don't run, but we don't dawdle either. I'm assured that Raka – or anyone else – could not follow our tracks when we went south.

'He won't know how to look,' says Zavik. 'He knows the signs on the steppe and in the forests, among plants. Not here. Too rocky, too windy.'

'I told them two days, Zavik. It has been five days now.'

He says nothing. That's Zavik. There isn't anything sensible to say. Have the women been sold? No one dares discuss this.

Are they still there? God only knows. But even if our people aren't there, I'm still going kill the whole fucking lot of these asshole slavers.

I swore.

––––––

It's still light when I creep from the shelter of the scrub and onto the beach. I want to make sure the women have the juice before everyone starts eating dinner.

The sun is still above the western horizon. The moon, a little slimmer, floats in the deep blue pool of early evening. We are a mile further south than we were last time, and I swim out twice as far before turning north to swim along the coast. I swim gently, quietly, trying to look like anything other than a naked man doing breaststroke with a knife between his teeth and a skin full of poison strapped to his torso.

You really couldn't make this up.

I'm not scared of deep-sea monsters this time, but I'm not enjoying myself, either. I *am* scared. Petrified. Going back into the lion's den, towards savages with knives and spears, savages who think nothing of killing. But the only other option is to take a backseat while the people you've come to love are sold and raped and experience whatever the fuck it is that slave-owners get off on.

Taking a backseat whilst that shit goes down is *not* an option.

It takes a good half-hour to come level with the fish factory.

Feeling exposed and mildly crazy, I exit the sea and scuttle up to the building. The light is failing, slowly, too slowly. Skydaughter floats in dark blue, waiting to take over from Father Sky.

I tap lightly on the wood panel. There is nothing, then an answering knock, and then a voice.

'Charlie?'

Thank God.

'It's me,' I say. I lift away the bar and together we shift the wood panel back a little. I untie the cord around my waist and disentangle the skinful of hemlock berry-juice. It's the size of a large tennis ball.

Salanda, Greta – their faces fill the gap. The same mad urge to shove the panel wide open and run off with everyone grips me, but I only hand over the skin.

'Hemlock,' I say. 'Can you do it tonight?'

'Yes,' says Salanda. 'Something is happening tonight. A stranger came, they looked at us. It seems they might be having some kind of feast.'

I love it when a plan comes together.

'Perfect. Tonight, then.'

'But Charlie, the man. . .'

'What?'

Salanda looks pale. Panic rises inside me. I grab the front of her shirt and I shake her, panic whistling, kettle-hot, filling my head.

Where's Sara why isn't she here?

'Speak,' I hiss this, and shake her again.

'Charlie, the stranger has traded for Greta. . . and he is leaving with her and Raka. They are leaving with Sara.'

I let Salanda go, and I just stare at her.

'When?' I whisper. 'Where?'

'They are still here. Raka came in with the man earlier today. They leave tomorrow.'

My head is spinning. I lean against the side of the building.

'Raka said you had abandoned us. That you had run away.'

'Just put the juice in the food,' I say, unable to think anything coherent. She begins speaking but there's a noise at other side of the building. People talking, moving the bar that keeps the front doors shut. We slide the panel back. I lift the bar back into place. I slip off the ramp and slither under the building.

———

I wait in the shadows, naked and shivering, amongst the bones and the seal guts.

I wait in the darkness that deepens as Father Sky dims his own light.

I wait for the coming of night.

Raka said you had abandoned us. That you had run away.

Perfect. What an asshat. If it's not obvious to him that we'd *never* abandon our people, then his perspective on human decency is even more fucked than I gave him credit for.

———

I wait for my friends.

The last rays of the sun vanish behind the hills to the west. I see my friends, crawling up the beach. Crawling on their bellies, moving on their elbows, pushing with their feet. Soldiers crawling into hostile territory. I watch, breathing fast, expecting a shout, a spear, guards to come streaming onto the beach. I'm not given to prayer, but I find myself praying. To Father Sky, to Mother Earth, to God.

Whoever is out there, please please please let things go right. Let justice prevail. Let these men reach me in this disgusting shelter, this valley of evil. Thy rod and thy staff and all that shit. Please please please.

Above me, the bar scrapes across wood. I hear the panels being pushed aside. Footfalls on the wood floor above me sends grit and dust onto my upturned face. Male voices, female voices.

Time to serve dinner.

There's no honour in it.

Fuck honour.

I look down the beach. It's only because I know they are there that I can pick them out easily. They have stopped moving – they are indistinct lumps on the beach. Waiting for the slavers to get the women out of the fish factory. These guys are ninjas when it comes to creeping up on shit. My boys.

There's a gentle tapping from above. I stand and tap three times.

'Charlie.' I can't make out who the voice belongs to. It's not Greta or Salanda. It's the voice of a young girl.

'They've taken mother outside. They've taken the grown-ups outside.'

'Copy that.'

'What?'

'Just stay quiet,' I say. 'Keep acting normal. We will come and get you out soon.'

'I'm so scared Charlie... I...'

I hear the child break into sobs. My heart breaks. But my mind stays clear.

'Stay strong,' I whisper. 'Just a little longer.'

I turn, and almost yelp in fright. Culeg is leading the men in a dash over the last ten yards. They slide under the fish factory.

I motion for Zavik to hand me my clothes. But Tazak lifts me by my waist. Culeg and Zavik slide my trousers over my ankles and legs and belt them around my waist. Others are stuffing my feet into my boots, lacing them firmly. I'm set on my feet and my arms are taken and slid through my shirt. Hands tie the front together. All this takes about thirty seconds. I'm breathing fast, too fast. I'm scared.

Tazak puts his hand on my shoulder. The hand is massive, gentle, and warm.

'Easy, Charlie,' he says. 'Breathe slow.' The hand on my shoulder squeezes gently.

Culeg takes the small knife out of my hand. He produces a holster, with a much bigger knife in it, and proceeds to strap it to my right leg. Nifty.

'I gave the hemlock to Salanda,' I say. 'But she says Greta is being taken away tomorrow morning, taken by someone who has... traded for her.'

Zavik's eyes widen, and I can see the muscles bunch around his jaw. 'And Sara and Raka are going with them,' I say.

Tazak looks at me, nodding slightly. 'We are doing what's right.'

He's talking about killing.

'I know,' I reply.

34

I often think that it was a good thing that the Greeks executed Socrates. He was charged with "impiety" and "corrupting the youth".

Which translates as Socrates pointing out that humans were horribly flawed, morally confused, and generally pretty awful creatures. And when Socrates was told to shut the fuck up about this, he point-blank refused.

This didn't sit well with the established order of political and financial interests in ancient Athens.

Socrates refused to shut up, refused to bend the knee. When he was put on trial, the penalty hanging over him was death. He knew this. And still he wouldn't shut up. He was found guilty. He accepted the cup of hemlock. He drank it, and walked around, as instructed, until his feet and legs became "heavy". Then he lay down and his legs became entirely numb. Then the creeping paralysis spread slowly to his waist and over his torso.

The Greeks believed that hemlock killed by stopping the heart. They were wrong. What actually occurs is that your diaphragm becomes paralysed well before any major cardiac symptoms. You asphyxiate. You die because your lungs stop working.

And the really horrible part is this: your body becomes paralysed, immobile – but the poison has no effect on the brain. So, although you cannot move, you are perfectly conscious, perfectly aware of the fact that you are choking to death.

Nasty.

Socrates' philosophical outlook was pretty awesome, but his greater impact is that he became the world's first martyr for not shutting up about uncomfortable moral issues.

Humanity would have gone down the toilet long before the 21st Century if Socrates had not made such a goddamn spectacle of himself – if he hadn't decided to go out with such style and panache.

If he *had* bent the knee to political correctness, the world would never have had such a shining example of how *immoral and stupid* humans can be: killing a person because his ideas make you uncomfortable and compromise your morally fucked up policies.

The beliefs that Socrates sacrificed himself for have acted as a counterweight for much of humanity's failings.

I crouch, under a reeking fish factory, and ask myself what Socrates would make of what we are about to do, with the very same stuff he'll one day drink.

It's far too messy an emotional and philosophical problem for me to comprehend. And I certainly won't get the answer I want.

Socrates always stuck to his guns, and he was a moral absolutist, so he'd probably say that murdering is wrong no matter what, and therefore we should accept things as they are. That we should bend over and reach for the soap.

Fuck that. Socrates never had his girlfriend stolen.

Time to kill some folks.

Above the dead-fish smell, there is woodsmoke, the scent of fat dripping onto coals. Sounds of laughter. Foreign voices becoming a little louder.

Eat and drink well, my little lambs.

In the darkness, the wolves wait.

———

The slavers bring back whoever they took out to serve them and amuse themselves with. A tapping comes through the floor.

'I did it,' says Salanda, a barely concealed excitement in her hushed squeak. 'A hand ago. They have eaten, mostly all of them I think.'

'Well done,' I say. 'Just stay inside.'

'How long will it take?' asks Tazak. He knows I don't really know. I told him perhaps a hand or two to start working.

'I'll go and look,' I say.

Before anyone can stop me, I step out from under the fish factory. As I did a few days before, I keep to the side of the building and creep to the front. I look out and see their main eating area.

The fire burns high and narrow, flames licking high. Through the haze of smoke, I see men and women. Children.

One man walks around in a circle. He looks a little drunk. He stumbles and almost falls. He calls out. Someone laughs and comes over to help him. I watch as the man demonstrates an uncooperative leg. He tries to walk normally but he stumbles again. The man who was laughing now grabs the man to keep him upright.

They talk. A woman is called over.

I slide back under the building.

'It's happening,' I say. 'Let's wait longer. Better to be sure.'

But after ten minutes, this luxury of waiting is ruptured by the appearance of Raka. Or rather, his voice above us. We listen as he speaks to women and girls above us.

He has been up on the ridge overlooking the settlement, hanging out there with his new buddy, the stranger who has bought Greta. We listen to him talk, waiting for him to go to the feast and eat his fill. Then we freeze as we hear his words, ringing loud. Shouting.

'You've poisoned them!'

Tazak whirls his finger. We lean in towards him.

'We go now,' he whispers.

'To where?' I whisper back.

Tazak is already out from under the fish factory.

'Wherever,' he says, then raises his voice to a war-cry.

'KILL THEM ALL!'

The others stream out and sprint into the hazy smoke, towards the lights of the settlement.

Wolves break cover.

I pelt out, a spear in my right hand, and head straight into the fish factory, meaning to skewer Raka and his new buddy.

A knife swings towards me as I come through the doorway. Raka has hidden in the corner. I manage to get my left arm in front of my face and the knife is buried my forearm. I keep pushing, push him against the side of the building, drop the spear and punch him in the face.

I feel the rubbery tissue of his nose crumple flat in a wet explosion. He screams and I pull my fist back to land another.

A sickening crunch against the back of my head sends me sideways. I see a bright shower of sparks and I think I pass out for half a second because now I'm horizontal but not on the ground. I'm in the arms of the women.

I shake my head. I hear screaming outside. Shouts of rage. Shrieks of pain.

'Help me up,' I say.

I stand, a little woozy. I hold out my left arm to Salanda. The short flint knife protrudes from a spot below the elbow.

'Take this out, and bind it.'

Then I scream 'Now!'

She tugs it free and blood gushes hot over my arm and hand.

'Get out there, all of you! Pick up anything you can, a rock, whatever. Get out there and kill someone!'

I wince as Salanda yanks a knot in a strip of material against the stab wound.

'Charlie, you need to know, I think Raka is leaving now – he was going to go in the boat with the other man tomorrow morning, but I think he's going to leave now!'

I follow the women out.

I plunge straight towards the fire. I need someone with me if I'm going after Raka.

The slavers are in the middle stages of hemlock poisoning. Most are unable to stand. Men, women, and children. They put up little resistance as our guys knock aside their clasping arms and slit their throats. One of them has gone straight into the fire, knocking it apart, sending flaming branches all over the ground. Smoke fills the air like some Hollywood movie.

I slip in a muddy slick of red and almost go down. I grab onto someone who I think is one of our men. It's not. The man turns and leans into me. His hands go around my throat, and he squeezes *hard*. I cough and splutter. The man's face looms out of the smoke, his eyes crazy. He screeches something.

Then he's flung sideways, away from me. Tazak has battering-rammed him with the heavy post from the door to the fish factory. Tazak doesn't stop to check on me. He steps away, raises the post above his head and brings it down on the forehead of a woman who's trying weakly to rise from the ground. Her head disintegrates.

I see a child, maybe ten years old, his legs kicking weakly. His throat is cut. He's bleeding out. The men are butchering the people like animals.

There's a pile of little bodies. Small arms, small legs.

'Zavik!' I scream. 'Help!'

He trots up, his hands red, splashes of blood over the front of his shirt, on his face, on his white-blond hair. Even in his beard.

'Greta?' he shouts at me.

'The boats! Come!'

I turn, wobbling a little, still slightly punch-drunk from the crack on the head. Zavik grabs my arm and rushes forward, propelling me with him. Together we run towards the beach. From around the side of the fish factory a woman comes, screaming, straight at us, a hatchet raised above her head. Her eyes are fucking crazy. This bitch is *mucho loco*.

I would be too – if someone had poisoned my entire crew and started slitting their throats.

Payback's a bitch, bitch.

Zavik just barrels into her. She bounces off him and as he runs over her, he makes sure to stamp on her throat. It makes a cracking sound.

We get to the boats.

Skydaughter is slim but she shows me enough. There is one boat in the surf. The stranger is standing, pushing it forward. As I watch he hops in next to three people-shapes that must be Raka, Greta and Sara. Ropes are pulled, the mast is being raised. The wind has shifted a little. They can make good progress northwest. They'll outpace us even if we paddle with twenty men.

Sara.

Someone waves at me. I hear Raka's voice, and I can imagine the smirk of triumph on his face.

'Goodbye Charlie!'

The twat obviously doesn't know that I can sail. I learned almost before I could walk. Behind us, I can hear excited shouts of victory mixed with a few screams of anger and pain. Tazak, the men, and the ladies must be wrapping up the wet-work.

Zavik, the man-mountain, is already pushing a dugout on rollers along the beach. I grab the slim trunks of birch trees and feed them in front of the moving dugout. We hit the water. We hop in.

Game on, bitch.

We waste two minutes faffing around with the pulley system, but we manage to get the sail up. It's a simple rudder/reef design: pull the rope to move the sail inwards, let it out to move the sail outwards. A child could run this thing.

Their boat is a Tazak-spear throw away, heading out westwards, their sail a black patch on the silvery moonlit horizon. I bet Raka isn't so smug now. In the empty silence of this inland sea, I can hear paddles. He'll be bent to the water, paddling for all he's worth.

Paddling for his life. Because coming hard up his ass are two *real* pirates, Captain Blondebeard and first mate Charlie, aka Seawolf, both of us high on blood. Cracked-up, out of our gourds on a drug that is called *killing fucking slaver-traders*.

The other guy can't sail well. In my previous life as a well-mannered adolescent, I would have politely waved, somewhat abashed I was catching up to him so easily. But if you transport me back in time and make me fall in love with the lady that he's currently abducting, I'll dispense with the pleasantries and proceed to the knife-wielding boarding party.

We pull up alongside them, ten feet between the two boats. I properly see for the first time Greta and Sara. Their arms are behind their backs, no doubt tied. Raka drops his paddle.

The stranger let the sail-rope go, turns, and throws a spear at Zavik. He doesn't flinch as it hits him high up on the hip as he is standing, getting ready to throw himself bodily into their dugout. Zavik plucks it out and drops it in the water. His face is grim. No change there.

We move closer. It's boarding time.

Raka moves, *quickly*. A spear appears in his hands and seems to fly from it in the exact same instant. It hits Zavik in the abdomen. He stumbles and loses his balance. The dugout wobbles, and it pitches Zavik overboard.

Zavik can't swim.

I reach over the side, praying they don't have any more spears to launch at my exposed back. I grab Zavik's arm and lift, so he is able to grab the side of the boat. The stranger grabs the sail-rope and pulls it tight. I hear the sail puff out as it catches the wind.

'Go!' Zavik shouts, spluttering and coughing.

Sara's arms come away from her sides. She's holding a length of cord that was around her wrists. From behind Raka, she loops the cord around his neck and pulls tight.

I launch myself onto the stranger. His arms come up to fend me off, but my weight knocks him hard against the side of the dugout. He grabs my bleeding left arm and twists it. I let him. My right hand pulls the knife from my ankle holster, and I bury the blade in the side of his neck.

Sucker.

I lever it, hoping to sever all the important stuff. I succeed. When I pull the knife out it leaves a gaping wound that froths blood all over me, all over my hands, my body.

The sail sheets out and hangs limp.

Blood sloshes in the bottom of the boat. I pitch the stranger over the side.

I turn to Raka. His hands are grabbing at the slim cord that bites into his neck. In the faint moonlight his eyes are bulging. He heaves backwards against Sara, but Greta, her own hands still tied, leans into Sara's back, supporting her. It's not enough, and he's about to push them both over.

I step forward and bring my foot down on Raka's knee. His leg. . . inverts. He can't scream but he makes a keening, huffing sound. He crumples forward and tries to reach over his shoulder and claw at Sara's face. I grab his wrists and pull them away. I sit on the recently vacated seat and tighten my hold on his wrists. I hold his weakening arms immobile as Sara strangles him.

He stares at me, his face growing dark with congested blood.

'Adios muchachos,' I whisper. His eyes bulge, impossibly wide.

I don't bother to translate.

He understands.

He slumps forward. I move aside, and his face splashes into the bloody water in the bottom of the boat.

Sara breathes raggedly. She blinks several times, looking down at Raka's prostate body. She looks at me, and tears spill from her eyes, they track down her cheeks, shining in the moonlight.

'I promised,' I say.

Sara's arms come around me, crushing me to her.

fter the bloodletting.

After the smoke and pain and sprinkled blood, after the slaughter that is spread out on the ground.

After this, and so much more.

After the blood, Father Sky rises in the east, his eye opening on the bodies piled upon the ground.

Was it worth it?

Father Sky watches us as we carry all the bodies of the tribe into their fish factory. He watches us torch it. We stand in silence as the building burns, the wood so grimed with years of accumulated seal-fat and blubber that it burns as if doused with gasoline. The pall of smoke that rises like a mushroom cloud is oily and black, through whether due to the wood or the bodies, I can't be sure.

Was it worth it, after all?

The smoke rises, a signal. A stain of black on one unknown day in human pre-history.

I suppose you might say it's our flag, our banner. One that says *don't fuck us.*

————

The ground is marshy with blood, so we make a few small fires a minute's walk away from the main settlement. I make Zavik leave the spear embedded in his torso just below his ribcage. It stays in until we got back to the settlement. Zavik holds Greta's hand and stares at her, a happy expression on his normally furious-looking face, as Culeg and I remove the spear.

Now, after the shock and adrenaline has leached away, Zavik lies on his back, his face grim, and pale. I'm not a doctor. Neither is Culeg.

I *think* the spear went in below his lung, but above his kidney. But I don't know. For the moment, Zavik is neither coughing blood nor is he pissing blood. There is nothing we can do except bind the puncture. Culeg says he will survive. I don't know if he's just being positive for Zavik's benefit.

That's not exactly accurate. Culeg is the shaman. I think he *is* positive. He puts a good whack of dried herbs all over it and binds it. Then he begins a spiritual chant. Zavik seems to appreciate this.

Better than nothing.

Greta lies next to him, her head on his shoulder. She cries.

————

Grease has always been a lot less greasy since the walkabout when they found me next to the glacier. His hair is brown and curly, and falls in natural ringlets about his shoulders. Even smeared with blood, he looks good. His beard is lush. His real name is Shezelak. Which is a bit of a mouthful, hence why I've stuck to Grease. But there's a time when a man's due is due.

Shezelak and Tazak carry Raka's body up from the beach. Everyone wants to see it. It matters to them to fix their own eyes on the body, to banish all doubt that the traitor is *definitely* dead. If I hadn't watched the light of consciousness go out – permanently – in his eyes, I would also need to see the body.

My own sense of Raka's betrayal is difficult to absorb. For everyone else, who *lived* with Raka for years, who nurtured him as small kid, who led him into manhood – I cannot even begin to get my head around how deeply he has hurt them.

The men have released their anger through killing. Many of the women didn't get their share, and they take it out on Raka. They stab the body, they spit on it, they kick it. They scream and curse him, using words that I've never heard.

Universal language for *burn in hell.*

Tazak gives them a few minutes of this, sensing perhaps that they *need* this. Then he orders for the body to be thrown into the collapsed but still-burning fish factory.

———

In the bright midday sunshine, the wind combs back the white hair of the waves and blows the sea white and blue. I'm the only one who can swim, but the shallows are wide, extending like a shelf.

Except for Zavik and Culeg, we all strip, all of us. If the water is cold, I don't notice. It cleans me. It cleans all of us. We stand in a group, chest-deep and *scour* ourselves.

The water, up to the hollow of Sara's throat. She's said little, up to now, but she's stayed close to me, ghost-like. Now, in the bright sunlight and clear water, her blonde hair shines, her green eyes are alive. She smiles at me.

Among all the men, all the children, all the women of this tribe, she takes my hand, and gently tugs me close to her. My arm goes around her slim waist, and her legs encircle my waist.

Tazak watches me, his two twins girls cradled in his arms, a smile on his face.

Sara's forehead rests against mine and her eyes are open. Her lips touch mine. My heart stutters, restarts. I close my eyes. I feel her mouth part, and her tongue touches my lips. A shiver runs through her, and her arms tighten around my shoulders, her breasts are soft against my chest.

I kiss her.

It was worth it, after all.

———

Zavik's temperature goes skywards. I make aspirin tea by boiling up some willow bark. I don't think it makes much difference. Infection bloats his side and runs out in gushes of foul yellow pus. I wander the surrounding forest for wild garlic. I find none. Greta lies next to Zavik, who lapses in and out of delirium.

None of us can do anything for him. It is all down to Zavik. All down to what the man has left to give.

Nature is a sneaky thing. Biological life proliferates, grows, flowers, blooms, blossoms, changes, speciates, changes, becomes *things fantastical* when shown beside long-ago ancestors. But it also fights with itself – constantly. Biological life adapts to feed off of *the other*, to maim, to kill – all in the service of survival.

It is billion-year-old bacteria versus the organised cellular material that makes up Zavik. A deathmatch: if you lose, you die.

No contest.

No contest when you take one look at the mad bastard pirate king. I don't know what those bugs thought they were doing, going up against him. After a week-long pitched battle, the gouts of pus slow to a dribble, then stop.

———

We spend another week at the village, mainly so I can give swimming and sailing lessons to the tribe. Apologies: to *my* tribe. We pack all the useful stuff – the spoils of war I suppose – into the large dugouts and set sail upriver.

———

'What does *The Moby* mean?' asks Willow. He's asking about the name of the dugout-sailboat that is now my personal vessel.

I look at the boy as we make our way up the estuary, the Black Sea at our backs, our prows pointed homeward. His hair is long and straight and in the wind it flies about his face like expelled confetti streamers.

'Turn around,' I say. I gather his hair and tie it into a ponytail.

'Moby?' he repeats.

'Well, it was a big fish that I once knew.'

Willow turns around, and looks from my face to Sara's, his eyes wide, looking for any hint of adult bullshit.

'Obviously, I didn't ever *speak* to the fish. But it was famous. Many people knew of it. Some say that it was half human since it had lungs – not gills. Some people wanted to catch it, very badly. But it was too big, too fierce. Its name was Moby.'

Sara waves to the people who watch us go. Tazak leads those who have elected to hike overland – which is most of the group. In these boats we can ferry our booty, as well as make much quicker progress. There is anxiety about staying away from home for too long. Anxiety about those we left behind, who now wait for us. We can't just pop them a text. We have to get back.

Sara, Culeg, Ela, Willow, Salanda, Greta and I share *The Moby*, in which Zavik sits comfortably at the stern on a throne of rolled up seal pelts. I really wanted to find some black fabric and fly it from the top of the mast, but leather is too heavy. I've promoted myself to Captain (Captain Seawolf, obviously), and I have *The Moby* well in hand. The only rough going will be hauling the dugouts overland past some of the small waterfalls we saw on our hike downriver. But after everything, it'll be a walk in the park.

Sara's breath is against my cheek, on which she plants small soft kisses. The sun is warm.

I sail.

Upriver.

Thank you all for reading! If you would like a sneak preview of the next book in the *I, Charlie* series, please visit my website and sign up to my newsletter.

You can either click the link, type it into a browser, or use your phone's camera to scan the QR code below.

www.christopherbarnard.online

Please note: this is a work in progress, and alterations may well be made to the final text upon publication.

DEDICATION

For Ailsa

ACKNOWLEDGMENTS

Gunilla Karlson, Paula Jones. My two constant readers who gave up much of their time to read drafts of this novel. And who offered constant improvements and encouragement. Writing is a lonely business, and you need people who you can ring up and say, 'Hey, read this and tell me if it's utter bullshit.'

Thank you Gunilla, for the coffee and the dog walks.

My warmest gratitude to you both. I couldn't have done it without your support.

COPYRIGHT

ABOUT THE AUTHOR

Christopher Barnard is a Saint Lucian who now lives in London.

 facebook.com/christopherbarnardauthor
twitter.com/barnardchristop

Lightning Source UK Ltd.
Milton Keynes UK
UKHW012041290821
389673UK00001B/51